PRODIGAL AVENGER:

A STORY OF THE SECRET WAR IN AFGHANISTAN

ENDORSEMENTS

Forgive the cliché, but Tim Moynihan has crafted a genuine barn-burning, page-turning story about a few good men (soldiers not Marines) who get together to execute near-impossible missions. I especially enjoy that Moynihan seeks opportunities to insert critical issues of faith into the story making it God honoring in compelling ways. Prodigal Avenger grabbed my attention from the first chapter and kept me on edge until the final pages. Well done!

—**Rich Botkin,** military historian, author and producer of *Ride the Thunder* and former USMC Infantry Officer

Brad Meltzer, Mark Dawson, and the rest had better watch out: Tim Moynihan has arrived with *Prodigal Avenger*, the best military/suspense novel I've read in years. The book is well-written, fast-paced, and fun. It grabs you from the very first scene and drags you along behind a MH-60 on a low-level insert. Moynihan not only knows the jargon, he knows the characters from real life. As a former intelligence officer and a tabbed Ranger, he's been there and done that behind the scenes. His experience all comes through in this excellent novel. I especially liked the faith element which merges seamlessly with the tales of military intrigue!

—**Joseph Courtemanche,** actor, author of *Assault on Saint Agnes,* and former Navy Security Group Direct Support Operator

Every war draws a superabundance of books in its wake. Every GI has a story and an opinion. Some are mere chest beating. Others offer actual wisdom for life beyond combat. *Prodigal Avenger* is the latter in spades. It is well-written, intensely engaging, electrifying in its action; and reflective in its after-action. You will not want to put the book down. And even when you do manage to set it aside temporarily, the story will follow you and will draw you back. The story, while human to the core, potently manages to lift the reader to a higher plain. Enjoy it. And live the better for having read it."

—**Stu Webber,** pastor, former Green Beret Vietnam Veteran and author, *Tender Warrior* and *The Warrior Soul*

Tim Moynihan has written a fantastic novel and story—I highly recommend *Prodigal Avenger* to anyone who likes military genre stories. Although fiction, the book reads more like nonfiction because of the substantial detail and research which the author put into its creation. Moynihan has written a masterful inside account of a breed of soldiers few ever really know. The 'operators' about whom he writes are a close-knit group of individualists who are the 'backbone' of Special Ops and whose missions are never revealed to the public except in extraordinary circumstances like the killing of Osama Bin Laden by Seal Team Six. I know because I worked and flew for the 5th Special Forces and the CIA in Vietnam for nearly three years during the 1960's and then again for the CIA six months in 1971 in the Middle East.

—**Stan Corvin, Jr,** author, *Vietnam Saga: Exploits of a Combat Helicopter Pilot*

This book will keep your focus and grip you with respect for those that fight for the USA and freedom. Everyone should read this book and recognize the real motivation for our freedom—God.

—**Rob Scribner**, senior pastor at Lighthouse Christian Church and former NFL football player with the Los Angeles Rams

A gripping special ops novel featuring a cast of characters focused on rescuing an American missionary kidnapped by the Taliban.

—**Les Stobbe**, author, editor, and award-winning literary agent

PRODIGAL AVENGER:

A STORY OF THE SECRET WAR IN AFGHANISTAN

TIM MOYNIHAN

PUBLISHING THE POSITIVE

ELK LAKE PUBLISHING INC
Plymouth, Massachusetts

Copyright Notice

Prodigal Avenger: A Story of the Secret War in Afghanistan

Cover and Interior Design: Derinda Babcock
Editor(s): Cristel Phelps, Deb Haggerty
Author Represented by the Steve Laube Agency

PUBLISHED BY: Elk Lake Publishing, Inc., 35 Dogwood Dr., Plymouth, MA 02360, 2018

Library Cataloging Data
Names: Moynihan, Tim (Tim Moynihan)
Prodigal Avenger: A Story of the Secret War in Afghanistan / Tim Moynihan
298 p. 23cm × 15cm (9in × 6 in.)

Description: A covert rescue mission no one expects to succeed—who will survive?

Identifiers: ISBN-13: 978-1-948888-78-3 (trade) | 978-1-948888-79-0 (POD) | 978-1-948888-80-6 (e-book.)
Key Words: War, terrorism, special ops, Taliban, PTSD, US Army, Al-Qaeda
LCCN: 2018962826 Fiction

ACKNOWLEDGMENTS

Special thanks to my wife, Sue, and my two sons for their patience, motivation and support. All three of them have served in this great Army of ours and I am so proud of them. To my father, also an Army veteran, who made me watch all those old war and spy movies with him; and to my mother who put up with me during the difficult years before I got right with my Maker.

Thanks to my faithful Pastors, Bob Mammen and Dan Jones, my long-suffering agent, Bob Hostetler, my risk-taking publisher, Deb Haggerty, my ever-patient editor, Cristel Phelps, and my long-term advisor and friend, Les Stobbe, for keeping me on the straight and narrow.

Appreciative thanks to the editors–the 2014 ACFW judges, the Crosshair Press ladies and especially my sister, Sue Keating--for their reviews and tweaks of my initial rough manuscripts. Finally, to LTC (Ret.) Andre Thibeault, who made me into an Army officer, thank you, sir.

I must acknowledge the large number of non-fiction writers who researched and wrote about the war on terror, special operations and clandestine intelligence agencies thus saving me considerable research time. And fiction writers who cover similar ground. Thank you all. Errors and mistakes are my own.

Finally, I thank God for all the men who influenced my life when and where I needed it most. "As iron sharpens iron …"

Tim Moynihan
Oceanside, California
September 11, 2018

AUTHOR'S NOTE

None of the characters, organizations, special programs, events or military operations described in this book are real. Any similarity is purely coincidental. Old friends in the military intelligence and special operations community will surely be amused by my artistic license, fantastic inventions and imaginative depictions of clandestine and covert operations and units.

This is a book about a man coming to grips with his past, present and future. It is also a book about Americans and the American experience during a peculiar phase of the war on terror, circa 2003, when special operators and their tactics dominated the war. The war has changed since then (and so has America). This is Afghanistan before ACUs, OCPs, UCPs, IEDs, MRAPs, ISAF and ISIS-K. Veterans returning from the war after 2003 will report a much different experience than described in this book. I also took some artistic license with certain place names. Outpost Nari resembles FOB Naray (later FOB Bostick) in Kunar except my descriptions and depicted events of 2003 are pure fiction. Due to my interest in Afghanistan, my experience in the military and my continued association with veterans I chose the specific circumstances of the story because they were convenient for the telling.

Tim Moynihan
Oceanside California
September 11, 2018

PART 1

Chaos

CHAPTER 1

Sunday, July 13th, 2003. A village on the Afghanistan-Pakistan frontier

The last thought that passed through Khalid Zahar's mind before his head exploded was *that woman in the burqa has very large feet.*

Until that moment, he was fixated on her eyes. Or, at least, the place where her eyes were supposed to be. They hid behind the screen covering the face. He felt the hair rise on the back of his neck. The woman across the square clad in sky-blue seemed to cast spells.

Zahar tilted back in his chair at the tea stand, took a long drag on his cigarette, and stole another glance at her. Her concealed eyes were still there, he could feel them boring holes into him. In Pashtunistan, women did not wander in a village alone. When seen at all, they were always accompanied by a trusted male relative. Always. But, there she stood. Alone. Facing his direction, like a witch sent to obliterate his peace of mind.

As she ambled across the street, gathering up the long garment from the inside so she wouldn't trip, Zahar noticed something else. The woman in the burqa had very large feet.

He acknowledged his companions at the tea stand with an uncomfortable smile and rubbed his hands together. Blood, he thought, looking down at his hands. And then he suppressed the idea.

He had just missed the end of a witty story, which was fine with him, he was bored. But he also felt out of sorts. The vexing woman only made things worse.

He listened with cultivated contempt as his companions reminisced about mutual friends in Beirut. He had never been to Beirut and hated they all knew it, holding it against him. Or so he felt.

PRODIGAL AVENGER

But I am their leader in Afghanistan, and that is all that matters. It is the divine will of Allah and my destiny. Men like Rahman will always be destined to follow those of pure faith.

Zahar despised the popular Filipino with the easy-going irreverence and endless supply of ribald stories.

He is too much like the pork-eating Indonesians I knew in Sulawesi. Good fighters but inferior Muslims. These barbaric Afghans with their pederasty and their cruel customs are not much better. How true were my father's words—the further one went out from Arabia, the lesser the purity of the faith.

But Zahar, despite his disdain, accepted the companionship of the others. It was the camaraderie of *Jihad* which bonded them. And there was nothing quite like it.

How ironic. The Afghans call all of us foreign fighters Arabs.

Zahar relaxed, sipped his tea and savored the moment nonetheless. Here they were, *mujahedeen* from all over the world, enjoying the traditional hospitality of *Puktanwali*, the Way of the Pathan. At least in this village, the Afghans treated them with deference and respect. *All but one of them.*

He glanced around and saw the indiscreet woman in the burqa again. Still standing and staring. *This Afghan woman is brazen! Where are the religious police? They will teach her respect.*

Khalid Zahar watched the burqa cross the street. He saw movement inside the burqa, as if she were gesturing toward them.

How could she do such a thing in public? Where is her husband? Where are her male relatives?

He tried to penetrate the garment's face screen, but it was impossible. He scanned down to her feet. Ugly, flat footed, open toed sandals exposing painted toes.

Khalid Zahar's mind raced.

Is she a concubine? A Powindah woman? No, the Powindah observe purdah wearing only a headscarf. This one wears a burqa. But she should not approach us in the village like this.

As she gestured again inside the cover of the burqa, he leaned back in his chair and opened his mouth to speak. Such big feet!

Jake Drecker stood on a dusty street and enjoyed the sensation of near invisibility as he counted heads. *It must be him. The large, arrogant bearded*

man in the middle of the group. But in the bright sunshine, the light screen covering his eyes played tricks on Jake's vision. He had to be sure, and he had to get it right. He could not afford a mistake.

The previous evening, Jake had timed everything, even counted steps to each point along his planned path. Now, to really confirm the identities and finish the job, he had to cross the square. He lifted the material between his legs so he would not stumble, a move he had witnessed countless women perform during his operational preparation for this mission. His legs were properly covered down to the ankle and would draw no undue attention. He was focused now. It was time.

The man in the middle glanced around and seemed to momentarily make eye contact with Jake, which sent a shiver down Jake's spine but sealed the deal. *He was Khalid Zahar.*

On Khalid's right, the two Jordanians wore similar mismatched mujahideen uniforms and arrogance. To his left sat a smaller man, brown skinned with sleepy eyes. That was Rahman, the Filipino. Each wore a hodgepodge of local tribal and military clothes. They had side arms but no rifles. These were the "Arab" advisors to the local Taliban commander, sipping tea and eating nuts under a tin awning at the village tea stand.

Jake looked around. They were the only customers, reflecting their unique status as respected but not beloved outsiders. These were the right men, and this was the right time and place.

As he neared the group, Khalid folded his arms and tilted his chair back against a wooden support post, opening his mouth as if to speak, glaring at Jake with contempt and incredulity.

Perhaps Khalid is about to comment on this lady's oversized feet. The strange thought settled his nerves. His bold approach was out of character for it violated *purdah*, the tribal custom of separation and respect between the sexes. There would be other violations.

Jake aimed his suppressed pistol from underneath the burqa. The sky-blue material lifted ever so slightly up from the ankles as the material stretched to accommodate the motion of his right arm.

The pistol jumped in his hand as two squishy snaps, like the breaking of a twig, and near simultaneous clack-clack sounds signaled the silenced bullets erupting from the burqa. Khalid's mouth stayed open as his head flung back and bounced off the post. Jake swept the group with his burqa-clad pistol. Red spots sprouted on each man's temple as six more snaps and clacks put each of Khalid's companions through their own synchronized dance of death. Each man tipped over as if pushed from his chair by his head. Only Khalid remained seated, his head thudding forward on the table to expose a gaping exit wound at the base of his skull. A big mouth makes a convenient target.

Jake didn't stop to verify his hits. *Double-tap, baby!* They were dead. Moving through the tea stand, he counted his steps and aimed down an adjacent alley. He resisted the urge to turn and look at his finished work, to check if anyone noticed the change in the atmosphere or if he were being tailed.

A drama unfolded behind him as the tea stand owner investigated the sudden silence of his foreign customers. Don't look back, feign obliviousness, focus on moving forward and counting steps.

He walked to a pre-selected darkened alcove in a dingy alley and removed the body-covering, sky-blue garment. A woman dressed in black *shalwar kameez* pants and blouse with black *dupatta* scarf wrapped about the head and neck emerged from underneath the burqa. He moved down the alley and emerged back on the street. For a moment, he caught his own reflection in the glass of a war-weathered Toyota pickup truck. Dreamy green eyes, heavy with mascara, stared back at him. He resumed his momentum, stuffing the sack-like burqa into a canvas bag. One calloused hand remained inside the canvas bag clutching the still-hot pistol. He focused on the road intersection ahead.

An old, yellow and rust-spotted Datsun pickup pulled to a sudden stop and blocked his escape route at the end of the street. Jake froze.

"Woman, get into this truck," the driver growled in slurred Pashto. He was a burly, bearlike man in traditional Pathan attire.

Jake skirted the front bumper, grasped the door handle and climbed in. The truck lurched forward as the driver let forth a torrent of curse words in elegant Farsi. As they drove through the center of the village, Jake caught site of a curious crowd gathering at the tea stand.

Jake stared. The tea stand owner was speaking to the Taliban militia men, gesticulating wildly. One Taliban shook his head in shocked disbelief, while the other glanced from person to person around the square, his face a mask of paranoia and fear, as if expecting another shooter to appear among the onlookers. The terrorists lay where they fell, the hard, dry ground already absorbing the crimson halos of their spattered blood. It was a good day.

Ahead of the truck, a middle-aged man with a Kalashnikov appeared in the street, directing traffic away from the crowd. Jake tensed as his driver pulled alongside.

"What is happening?" the driver asked in Pashto.

"Somebody shot the Arabs," answered the traffic guard.

"Who was it, American spies or jealous husbands?"

Both men laughed.

The traffic guard leaned into the driver side window to keep bystanders from hearing. Jake caught the man's eyes, leering at him, undoubtedly attracted to his painted, green eyes. He pulled the dupatta across his face in a customary display of modesty. *If you only knew, old man.*

The traffic guard shifted his gaze back to the driver.

"Jealous woman, we think."

The driver smiled, waved him off, and maneuvered the truck around the crowd.

Jake kept his guard up as the truck bounced along the rutted road through the village. They passed people going about their daily business, not a few of them waving at the familiar face of the driver, the man they knew as Mustafa Khan, village gunsmith. The trip was a short, three-minute drive to a modest mud and stone house on the edge of the village, their safe house, but Jake resisted the urge to drop his guard. He wasn't "safe" yet, not until he was inside with the thick wooden door bolted shut behind him.

Jake scanned the exterior of the one-story, khaki-colored structure with its flat roof and walled-in, refuse-covered yard. No signs of compromise during their absence. The house was just as when he'd left on his clandestine mission of death.

A small table and chairs under a tin awning stood in front of the house. This was where Mustafa Khan, the safe house's native resident, conducted business over tea and cigarettes. It resembled a miniature version of the tea stand where Khalid Zahar and his cronies met their fate. He smiled with satisfaction.

He climbed out of the truck still carrying the canvas bag with his hand inside gripping the pistol. He pushed through the heavy outer door into the house. The front room, a cooking and eating area with a dirt floor, gas stove and paper-covered windows, looked untouched. In a normal village home, the neighborhood women might come here to squat in the dirt and exchange gossip. But this was not a normal home.

Once inside with the door closed behind him, Jake removed the pistol from the canvas bag. Dropping the bag to the ground, he pushed through a second wooden door of surprising strength and thickness which separated the front room from the very private "women's room" toward the rear of the house.

Jake had no intention of getting ambushed in a compromised safe house. He dropped to a crouch and swept the end of the pistol over the entire room from left to right. His heart jumped at the sight of a woman seated on a stool in the middle of the room. He froze with the pistol aimed right at her head.

"Congratulations, Jake. Scratch another one from the Al-Qaeda hit list."

He lowered his pistol.

"Thanks, Jannat. Another day, another $26.00 an hour with no time off for good behavior."

He shut the door behind him and began peeling off layers of clothes. He sighed. In this sanctuary at the back of Mustafa Khan's traditional Pathan home, he enjoyed a small measure of security. He struggled to loosen the breast prosthetic he had been wearing under his female garments. He glanced toward the tall, dark-eyed beauty dressed head to toe in a traditional black *chador*.

"Not exactly what I joined the army to do, but it works." He wiped sweat and mascara off his cheeks.

"I've got nice pictures for our after-action reporting," Jannat said, handing him a digital camera.

He studied the images on the screen.

"Nice work, great Battle Damage Assessment for this mission. Not too often you get great BDA photos after missions like this one. Where did you take them?"

"Oh, I was just hanging around nearby, you know, like we planned." She chuckled.

"You're good, I never even noticed. How did you get back so fast?"

"Ancient Far East secret!" she replied.

Jake grinned and shook his head in feigned disbelief. *Amazing, these two.* "I'm guessing you won't let me in on that little tradecraft secret."

She smiled at the compliment. There was a knock and Jannat let Mustafa in.

"Good work, Jake."

"Thanks, Gino."

Gino, better known in the village as Mustafa, hugged his wife. Then he grabbed the camera from Jake and moved over to the corner where a fifty-five-gallon drum served as a field-expedient vanity, supporting a mirror, basin of water, and various toiletries. Gino removed the loose items and wrestled the drum to one side to reveal a trap door in the ground. He yanked it open, lay down next to the hole, and began manipulating an encrypted satellite communications system concealed below.

"Sending our report and BDA to Bagram now," Gino explained. Then he powered the system down and restored the vanity to its position over the trap door.

Jake fingered the bullet holes in his sky-blue burqa. Jannat smiled as she leaned over to inspect the damage.

"Nice job, cowboy. Didn't your mother teach you not to play with guns inside the burqa?"

He ignored her and looked at Gino.

"So when do we get out of here?"

"We'll load up just as soon as you get back in character. Jannat, get the burlap sacks in the pickup."

"Wilco, sweetie," she replied, slipping out the door.

"You've got a good thing going here, Gino. I can't imagine my wife leaving Fayetteville for a gig like this!"

"It's Mustafa to you, lady. Now move it—we gotta go before they seal off the area."

Jake admired the two CIA operators. Gino Salvetti, the bear-like, six-foot-three Italian-American who looked every inch the warlike Pathan he was not. And Jannat, his wife, an Iranian-American who spoke four languages. A classic deep cover couple who spent the last two years among these tough tribesmen as Mustafa Khan, Afghan gunsmith from Herat. A refugee from the American invasion, living in this Taliban-controlled village near the Afghan-Pakistan border. *Where does the CIA find these people? Crazy!*

Jake refocused on the task at hand, gathering personal items in a burlap bag and getting dressed. Back in costume, he emerged from the house and dumped his small load into the truck bed. Gino-as-Mustafa and Jannat organized the gear as Jake climbed in and made himself comfortable amid the cargo.

"Uh-oh," Gino muttered, "looks like our nosy neighbor is watching."

Jake turned his head and saw a white-bearded, turban-headed tribesman staring at them from a perch by the gate of the neighboring compound, a worn AK-47 nestled across his lap.

"I'll handle this," Gino added as he stopped his organizing and walked toward the old man.

Great, just when I was starting to look forward to a little R and R.

Haji Bahram Khan was no fool. He was a tribal elder, had fought the Russians and been to Mecca. Now he sat upon a stump and stared across the dusty road, his ancient grey eyes narrowing for better focus in the harsh Hindu Kush daylight. His neighbor Mustafa Khan, the gunsmith, and his two wives were loading their truck. They were up to something. He rose on his good leg, steadied himself with a walking stick and tightened the grip on his treasured AK-47. Arthritic joints popping with every movement, he hobbled across the road to meet the approaching giant.

"Mustafa Khan," he shouted. "May you not get tired!"

"Honorable elder, may you not become poor," Mustafa replied.

Haji Bahram Khan sat down on a stool near the entrance to Mustafa's house and pointed the gnarled walking stick at him.

"I have noticed a change in your behavior since your return from Kandahar," he said soberly to the younger man.

"You are an observant man, honorable elder," Mustafa replied. "Since God has blessed me with a second wife, I am greatly prospered."

Haji Bahram Khan replied with an approving smile. He often observed Mustafa's young second wife, the green-eyed Kashmiri girl, as she worked in the yard, cutting wood and sweeping dust from the front step. He had four wives himself and was an expert on the ways of women. This Kashmiri wife appeared to be a strong and devout girl, working tirelessly despite her heavy chador covering—she was even seen to wear the burqa. Such green eyes! And such large, sturdy feet! Mustafa was blessed indeed.

"I am going to Kandahar again today to attend my cousin's wedding," Mustafa added.

"Ah," said the older man, "I suspected such a thing."

"And I would be honored if you would watch my house."

"Of course, and will you be returning with another bride yourself?"

The gunsmith smiled at his question and pulled several rupee notes from his pocket.

Haji Bahram Khan returned the smile, knowing full well what it portended. Mustafa trusted him and he trusted Mustafa, who had repaired his most prized war trophy from the Mujahideen period, his ancient AK-47. Mustafa had also helped him conclude a blood feud with a bitter rival. Mustafa was a good man and his rupees were evidence of the good faith between them.

"If God wills it," Mustafa answered pressing the notes into the older man's right hand.

They embraced, and Haji Bahram Khan gripped the gunsmith's shoulders.

"Since my sons are all dead, I have no other. You are like a son to me."

"And you are as a father to me," Mustafa answered.

"Good luck to you," said the old man.

"May your luck be good," answered Mustafa and they parted.

The old man returned to his perch across the road, turning one more time to watch as his neighbor climbed behind the wheel of the truck's battered cab. One of Mustafa's wives secured the house door with an ancient padlock and climbed into the passenger seat. In the back, the new wife, the one from Kashmir with the beautiful green eyes, sat covered head to toe in a loose fitting, black chador, her back against the cab, surrounded by their things. The truck started with a rattle and lurched forward. Mustafa waved and the Datsun disappeared down the road, leaving nothing but a swirling cloud of dust in its path.

A wife with such green eyes. Khan felt a touch of envy. Then he closed his eyes and went to sleep.

CHAPTER 2

Same Day, Karachi, Pakistan

Isidore Loewenthal winced as he climbed out of the dark Mercedes sedan in front of his apartment building in Karachi. He limped up on the curb and massaged his left thigh. *This thrombophlebitis feels like it's getting worse every day now. If I don't get it fixed soon it will kill me.*

His mind raced.

I've wasted so many years, tore apart my family, lost everything. I know God gave me a second chance. But the results here are so meager compared to what I've wasted in my past. God have mercy on me. And to think my existence now depends on the life or death whims of a rogue blood clot in my leg.

The idea of surgery at a Pakistani hospital, especially at his age, was unsettling.

Maybe it's finally time to go to the American embassy for medical help.

But he couldn't. They would want him to leave, and the work wasn't done yet. *They're already disturbed by my presence here. Former embassy official turned missionary. I am a liability to them. Maybe even better off dead in their opinion. No, I need to believe this is part of a bigger picture, whatever happens. God didn't bring me here just to kill me. But if he does, I know he can build on whatever I leave behind. Besides, I stopped caring what embassy officials think about my work a long time ago. This is none of their business.*

"Brother Isidore, will you be okay?" asked the Mercedes driver, a young Punjabi convert named Asghar.

"Yes, brother, I'm okay. Just pray for me. Thanks for the ride. We had a good study. I'll see you at the prayer meeting tomorrow."

"God bless you," answered the Punjabi.

"You, too, Asghar." The Mercedes pulled away.

Isidore's heart grew heavy as he watched Asghar drive away.

PRODIGAL AVENGER

Such a faithful brother. God, I pray I never let him down. Or the others. They have risked everything to join with our church. Their own families reject them now. All because of Christ. I lost my family because of my reckless sin. The irony.

Isidore fumbled with his keys as he passed the watchman in front of the apartment building. He was lucky to have found this place, an upper-middle class enclave of Western businessmen and secular Pakistani professionals surrounded by ten-foot walls and armed watchman.

Isidore stopped and rubbed his leg. A long-dormant security awareness kicked in. He took measure of the lobby watchman.

Strange. Did every Pakistani security guard look guilty about something? After thirty years here, I should have gotten used to that.

He addressed the man in Urdu.

"Are you the new watchman?"

A long pause before an answer, "Yes."

Isidore noticed something in this man's eyes. Was it arrogance? Contempt? Isidore studied him for a moment. *God, my thigh hurts. Gotta get upstairs.* "Well, God bless you," he said as he unlocked the outer door to the apartment lobby.

"God bless you also," replied the guard.

Inside the lobby, a second guard sat reading a paper. A new employee?

"Where is Samuel?" asked Isidore, referring to the usual security supervisor, Samuel, a Pakistani Roman Catholic trusted by the Western residents.

"He has taken ill. I am Rashid." The man lowered the paper and studied the American.

Something isn't right.

An alarm buzzed deep within his subconscious, but then the pain in his leg overrode his concern. He craved an aspirin and some sleep. He watched Rashid reach over and press the "Down" button on the elevator. Odd. *But I am going up.*

Rashid sat back and glared at him. There was that contempt again.

Isidore opened his mouth to correct the guard's mistake.

Then the elevator door opened, and time slowed down. Two men rushed out, the first sending a terrific blow to his midsection. Isidore doubled over as pain shot up into his solar plexus and the air was forced from his lungs. He could no longer breathe. His Bible and notes tumbled to the floor. Another man shoved him from behind into the elevator car. The men forced him face first onto the elevator floor. A foul-smelling rag was jammed into his mouth, gagging him and preventing him from recovering his breath. His arms were wrenched back, the shoulders forced from their sockets and his hands tied behind him. The strangers shouted instructions and threats back and forth to each other in Urdu.

The elevator sank. The basement! A burlap sack appeared out of nowhere and turned everything black. Its sandpaper roughness scratched Isidore's skin as it was jerked over his head, shoulders, and torso. There was a tearing sound as the men duct-taped his ankles together. Then they jerked a second burlap sack over his legs. Tight cords cut into his thighs.

I knew this day might come. Why wasn't I thinking?

He was lifted and carried, helpless as a child. Doors creaked, voices echoed down a narrow chamber. There was a moment of free fall before he slammed onto hard concrete. Sharp repetitive blows struck his back as he was dragged and repeatedly dropped down a set of stairs. Then the men picked him up, lowered him, and he heard the muffled sound of a car trunk shutting over him. The vehicle's engine revved, and the trunk vibrated. He took a long breath through his nose as his body rolled to the motion of the trunk moving forward.

So, this is it. This is what it's like to be kidnapped.

CHAPTER 3

Same Day. Incident at a classified location in the mountains north of Jalalabad, Afghanistan

Master Sergeant Randy "RJ" Jenkins shifted his weight, leaned toward the eye-piece on his high-powered day and night telescope, and studied the valley floor. The cave entrance was still quiet. Too quiet.

Come out, come out, whoever you are!

"They're down there. I can smell them," he sniffed.

Sergeant First Class Jerry "Frostman" Frost chuckled. "RJ, you would be able to smell them with your eyes."

Jenkins let the jab pass. Focus. The valley floor appeared empty, but eyes could play tricks. The quarry was down there. No doubt.

He leaned back, turned his head, and war-gamed their situation. You could lose a man on a mission like this. Get too focused on your target and a skilled opponent could come from behind, cut a team-member's throat, and be gone before you realized it. Count heads. "Chip" Johnson, the intel guy, secured the back of the triangle perimeter while listening to the bad guys on his high-speed voice intercept gear.

"Got anything, Chip?" he queried into his throat mike.

"I do, but it's weak."

Jenkins put his eye back to his telescope and waited for the rest of the answer. Still nothing on the cave mouth ... except ... *a shadow. Fleeting.*

Chip interrupted his thinking. "Doesn't sound like any of the local languages."

"Three days parked on a ridgeline waiting for hajis to infiltrate through from Pakistan," Frost said under his breath. "And not a single, godda ..."

"Shhhhh!" Jenkins hissed into his throat mike. There was a shadow in the cave. *A motion. For a second. Concentrate.*

Jenkins pulled his eye away from the scope and rubbed it. He blinked toward Frost, also glassing the cave through a dusty pair of civilian hunting binoculars. Jenkins turned back toward his scope as Frost resumed his whispered soliloquy.

"Yeah, parking on my eighty-eight square inches of sovereign American territory and peering at a dry hole in the ground." Frost ended with a few muttered obscenities, the bored soldier's universal lament.

Jenkins chuckled at the old joke. Frost's 'eighty-eight square inches of sovereign territory' were his boots, a pair of well-worn Danners. A navy pilot who'd once briefed them referred to his aircraft carrier as four point five acres of sovereign US territory that can be deployed anywhere in the world. All they had was eighty-eight square inches. *Must be nice being a pilot. Work all day and come home to hot showers, hot chow, and satellite TV.*

There it was again. The shadow.

Frost was on the radio sending in the team situation report. "… Team Echo Sitrep …"

"Hold the sitrep."

Frost stopped mid-sentence.

Jenkins concentrated on the shadow. Maybe it was his eyes. Tired. He pulled away from the scope and eyed Frost. "Eyes playing tricks on me …"

"Another day on this ridgeline, and we'll all be bonkers."

"Yesterday's goat herders, you see them today?"

"Nope. They left in the night."

"Those goat herders could have posed a problem if they'd stumbled across us."

"Roger."

Good riddance. What is with the Muslim fascination with goats, anyway? Everywhere I go, from Egypt to Pakistan—Muslim goats and their herders. Where are the sheep and shepherds of Bible times my father taught me about as a kid? Weird.

He didn't dwell on this too long. He turned his eyes away to rub and rest them.

"Frostman, you ever read that book, *The One Who Got Away,* about a British Special Air Service soldier who escaped from Iraq during the Gulf War, after his team was compromised by a goat-herding Arab?"

"Can't say that I have, RJ," Frostman answered. He put his binoculars to his eyes and scanned the ridgeline above the cave where the goat-herders had tended their flock the day before.

"Guy gets chased, trapped or harassed by goats and their herders about every other chapter. It was silly, like Monty Python. Those goat herders on the ridge made me think about it."

Frostman grunted. Then he pulled his eyes away from his binoculars and locked onto Jenkins. "You thinking ..."

Frostman didn't get to finish the sentence.

"Yeah, goatherds on our ridge, and I'm not laughing now," Jenkins added. *God, how could I have missed it! Dang! In a land of vendettas and blood feuds, where Kalashnikovs are as common as cell phones in America, I overlook the obvious.* "Frostman, I need you to take a walk behind our position. I mean way past Chip, about a hundred meters."

Frostman gathered up his M24 sniper rifle, adjusted his ammo pouches, and raised himself to a crouch before heading up the hill toward Chip.

Jenkins peered back into his eye-piece. Three bearded Taliban fighters in filthy US-style camouflage and dusty Chitrali caps sat smoking cigarettes outside the tunnel entrance. *Dang, I didn't even see them emerge.*

Suddenly, as if at the sound of a silent command, the three Taliban stood to their feet.

Chip Johnson came through on his earpiece. "We got chatter on the local network. Something's up. Visitors."

Jenkins burned within himself. *I knew it. I sensed it before. Why didn't I think?*

Five bearded men came into view, moving along the valley floor from the Pakistan side, heading toward the cave. They wore a mixed bag of civilian and military clothes, carried assault rifles, and were strapped up with ammo pouches and other assorted gear. *The give-away is their combat boots and woodland camouflage. This is no rag-tag Taliban militia. These are Al Qaeda foreign fighters!*

"Chechens!" Chip rasped.

Jenkins wondered at Chip's quick assessment. Impressive and spot-on.

"Okay, send an update back to Bagram complete with signals, frequencies, and grid coordinates."

Jenkins took a deep, controlled breath and slowly let it out.

Chechens, not good. The Taliban and Al-Qaeda Arabs were soft. They relied on villages to sustain them. They lacked proper gear to survive in the bleak mountain coldness where the American commandos thrived. But Chechens were different. They were experienced combat veterans who'd fought Russians from their childhood. They knew how to make the most of their equipment, terrain and opportunities. They even looked different, more like Americans and Europeans than Middle Easterners. And they were dangerous. The hair went up on the back of his neck.

Frostman's controlled voice broke through on the headset. "Bingo, RJ. I see movement to the northeast on the ridge, three hundred meters out and heading this direction."

We are in a world of hurt if they find us.

"Clarify, are those our goat herders?"

"Negative."

"Negative? What are we looking at, Frostman?"

"Squad size patrol element. Small arms plus an RPK and an RPG. Maybe eight men. Heading along the ridgeline. They should pass us to the north by fifty meters. Maybe."

"Ok, Team Echo, go to ground and be still," he whispered into his throat mike. *More Chechens, I bet. A security squad covering the high ground for their buddies on the valley floor. They will probably want to stop near our location and cover their team heading for the cave. God, we are screwed.*

Jenkins froze, a sharp painful knot forming itself in his left calf, one eye glued to his telescope. He took a deep breath and his heart rate slowed. No panicking, no anxiety, no nothing allowed. *Something is up. Gotta stay focused on that cave.*

The Chechen squad in the valley was greeted by one of the guards. The squad leader, a tall dark-haired Chechen with a red beard and a Russian field jacket, was led to the cave entrance. Then he stopped, turned, and placed a hand-held radio to his ear. *Did he just make eye contact with me? No, he can't be looking at me! He must be looking at his buddies on the ridge.*

The Chechen giant became animated. He shouted and gestured at his men. They all turned and looked upward toward Jenkins' ridgeline, then dropped to the ground.

We are busted! The Chechens in the valley know we are here!

"Crows heading our way, a hundred fifty meters. They are moving in a trot toward my position." Frostman broke the silence in his ear-piece.

"We got compromised, Chechens in the valley and Chechens on the ridge. Get ready to respond. Chip, see if Sniper 66 is on station." Jenkins ordered, referring to the call sign for a "close air support asset" like a Specter gunship or F-16 ground attack fighter to come to their aid. They needed friends in high places to get out of this fix.

"Sniper 66 not available, no immediate air support available," Chip replied.

Chip Johnson's lack of panic was commendable, because they were in serious trouble.

Then he heard it. Bells. Christmas bells. Tinkle-bells. No ... goat bells!

Goats! Great! The goat herders are getting in on this!

Chip broke-in on the earpiece. "Goatherds and goats heading up the ridge from the west—heading right for us."

We are trapped. About to experience the big squeeze here.

"Okay, Chip, keep your ears on the communication intercepts and your eyes on the goats. Looks like we are getting compromised from two directions."

"Hey, boss, Chechens on the ridgeline suddenly dropped and took a squat," hissed Frostman. It sounded way too loud in Jenkins' earpiece. "They seem to be focused on the goats and their bells."

Strange. The Chechens were as surprised by the goats as Team Echo.

Then everything at the target went to pieces. The ridgeline shook as a massive explosion in the valley floor swallowed up the Taliban guards and red-bearded Chechen squad leader in a swirling cloud of dust, rubble, and rock.

What the heck is happening?

Jenkins watched as five shooters came charging up the valley from the Pakistan end of the trail, dropped to one knee, and put two expertly aimed rounds into the head of each stunned Chechen near the cave mouth. The newcomers wore hodgepodge military garb with khaki headscarves covering their faces. They had suppressed MP5 assault rifles and their attack was textbook commando—aggressive, audacious, and thorough.

"Who is that?" Jenkins wondered aloud.

Frostman and Johnson, as calm and detached as an afternoon traffic report, continued to describe what they were seeing.

"Receiving small arms fire from Chechen squad assaulting down the ridge," Frostman stated.

"Return fire, Frostman. Chip, get a message back! Someone just neutralized our target."

"Wilco, I've got goatherds moving and shooting up the ridgeline, still heading our way, they appear to be engaging those crows!"

Jenkins was confused. Were they in the middle of a firefight between Chechens and a goat-herding opponent? He heard the reassuring crack of Frost's suppressed M24 sniper rifle. Three more commandos appeared down in the valley. They entered the cave while the first three pulled security. They were searching and stripping the dead Chechens, probably looking for something of intelligence value.

"Johnson, call Saber and ask if we got any shooters in the area. Somebody just put a hit on our target."

"Wilco, RJ, but we need a hand up here."

Jenkins turned just as a burst of green tracers impacted on a boulder near his head. Bits of rock and metal sprayed him in the face. Six Chechens bounded down the incline toward them. Bells tinkled. The goatherds would be on their position before the Chechens. He turned to his left and was startled to see the goatherds, led by a pudgy, bearded man in traditional Pathan Kameez trousers and Shalwar long shirt, darting up a steep embankment, firing AK-47's as they went.

Chip Johnson, further up the hill, was right in their line of fire. He was distracted, focused on his communications equipment and getting another message out.

Jenkins yelled, "Chip, get your head down, they're right behind you!"

Something thudded right at his feet.

Time slowed. Jenkins was nineteen again, trapped in a rat-hole in Mogadishu, Somalia. His battle-buddy, Jimmie, made a break for it, stepped out a doorway. He was supposed to follow. There was a thud. Just like this. Something small but weighty at his feet. *Grenade!* Jimmie disappeared in the explosion. There were screams. Jenkins pulled Jimmie back in as small arms from a hundred different windows peppered their position.

Thud means grenade.

Where is it? Jenkins scrambled to find the Chechen grenade to throw it back. He only had seconds. Some stranger was yelling in perfect American English, "Get Down! Get Down!" Then the explosion picked him up and threw him sideways. A thousand little cuts seared his body.

He came to his senses an eternity later, dazed. Patches of shimmering light swam all around him, like the view from the bottom of a deep pool. A bearded man's round, full face appeared. He wore, weirdly enough, wire rim glasses, like a science teacher from his eighth-grade. The man's lips moved, but all sound was muffled.

Jenkins's right side was on fire. He couldn't turn his head. Then sounds began to come back and there was that voice again, in a perfect Brooklyn accent as foreign to his Midwestern ears as Australian or British. It was the bearded man.

"Geez, I told you to get down. You freaking cowboys never learn, do ya? Don't worry, bud, we'll make sure you make it home to momma, safe and sound."

A second bearded face appeared. This one spoke to the other man in another language, a language Jenkins knew and had heard before in another Middle Eastern country.

It couldn't be!

With that, hard, rough hands grasped him as the gray closed over his eyes and Randy Jenkins slipped into unconsciousness.

PRODIGAL AVENGER

In the mountains of Pashtunistan, the land of blood feuds, vendettas and conspiracies, the hills have eyes. One man keeps tabs on his brother. The two keep watch over the cousin. The three observe their neighbor. The four watch out for the stranger. The five spy on the foreigner. The six plot against the infidel. So, it has always been, and so it shall ever be.

Observation of an unknown European adventurer, 1787

PART 2

The Americans

CHAPTER 4

The Ride

Jake Drecker tolerated the jarring ride to Bagram with a mix of stoic fatalism and bone deep weariness. The return from three months undercover in back country Pashtunistan was taking its toll. Tired almost beyond caring, he nonetheless maintained a subtle, precautionary vigilance, scanning each hill and walled compound as they rumbled past. He took slight comfort in his disguise, but it wasn't bullet proof. He placed more confidence in the deceptive talents of his two CIA colleagues in the truck's cab.

The Salvettis could talk their way through anything in this God-forsaken place.

As they turned a corner, the truck came to a jarring halt in the road. Jake's head thumped against the cab. He cursed under his breath with his best Pashto swear words. He rolled to the left side of the truck bed and covered Gino with his pistol.

Two men stood blocking the road, rifles at the ready aimed directly at Gino and Jannat. They were covered in khaki dust and wore the traditional garb of Pathan tribesmen. They hid their faces behind scarves and dust goggles. Bandits, probably. Nobody moved for a good ten seconds.

Then the larger of the two Afghans rushed Gino, barking commands in guttural Pashto.

Jake looked around toward the back of the vehicle to make sure there was no one else around.

Man, their Pashto sucks!

Gino's head was now leaning partway out the truck window to address the mysterious Pathan spokesperson.

Jake leaned over toward him. "All clear, bro."

Gino smiled and spoke to the Pathan.

"What's up, homie?"

The Pathan stopped in his tracks and yanked the shawl off his face. He wore the full beard of the Pathan warrior underneath, except it was noticeably blonder than any Pathan beard Jake had ever seen.

"Dang, how'd you know it was me?"

"Because," Jake answered. "Master Sergeant Jerry Ritter is famous for being the worst Afghan linguist in the whole theater, that's how. Next time try your language school Korean on us, okay?"

Ritter smiled and walked past Jake toward the back of the pickup.

Jake watched the other "Pathan" walk toward the passenger side to give Jannat a high five. Then they both unceremoniously dumped their Russian style canvas rucksacks into the bed before climbing in.

Jake reached out to help the second man climb aboard.

"Thanks, Jake."

"Glad to help, Freddie. Us small guys gotta stick together."

"You guys okay?" Jake asked. "Anything to report from your overwatch and surveillance mission?"

"Not much," Ritter replied. "Just you trained assassins stirring up a hornet's nest back there. But nothing out of the ordinary."

"They just ran around like chickens with their heads cut off while you guys made your escape," Freddie added. "They have no clue the hit was a US military operation. Just another senseless killing on the backside of 'WhoGivesACrapistan.'"

Jake smiled at Freddie Eason's snarky remark. He'd heard far worse epithets used to describe this place, but Freddie's humor was unique. He banged on the roof of the truck to signal Gino to move out.

They resumed their spine-splitting ride, traveling west then northwest to Qalat. Jake didn't breathe easy until their truck turned into a safehouse compound on the city's east side.

Thirty minutes later, freshly scrubbed and sporting imaginative new disguises, Jake and his team reemerged in a different vehicle, a decrepit tan and rust Russian four-door Lada taxicab. The overloaded vehicle was pressed down on ancient, overstressed shocks. A large wooden box, tied down by a rope running through the cab's open windows, threatened to collapse the vehicle's dilapidated roof. After exiting the compound, the taxicab turned northeast onto a pockmarked portion of the Afghan highway and headed for Ghazni.

Jake, in a black burqa, sat in the back on the passenger side and chuckled at his team's appearance. Gino, now a clean-shaven giant in traditional Uzbek garb, drove. Ritter rode shotgun, a glaring, bearded Pathan man in olive drab security uniform and AK-47. In the back, next to Jake sat Sergeant First Class Freddy Eason as a bearded young Afghan sporting a gray suit and colorful karakul hat. And on the left side, sat Jannat also in a black burqa. Just an Afghan wedding party on a ride through the countryside.

As they sped toward Ghazni, Jake reviewed the hit with the others, carefully memorizing all the significant details that would go into the after-action report. But he was exhausted. They all were—adrenaline let-down time. As he gulped down strong Turkish coffee from a metal thermos in Eason's lap, Jake worked hard to keep them awake. They still needed to maintain some semblance of vigilance—their clandestine mission wasn't over yet. Not until they were inside the wire at Bagram Airfield.

On duty seven miles outside Ghazni, Captain Mehrab Ali of the Afghanistan National Army was bored. His unit was conducting a routine traffic checkpoint and inspecting vehicles before they entered the city. Suddenly, he heard chatter bleeding out of his American counterpart's earpiece.

Americans always have their radio earpieces on too loud.

He watched the American walk away before speaking. He was used to this. The Americans frequently talked out of earshot when they had some big personal business to attend to—a minor indiscretion but tolerable. He liked Americans despite their brash shallowness. Their optimism was contagious. They knew how to fight, but they also knew how to be kind.

Ali's American counterpart, Captain Carter, was instantly animated by the mysterious message. Captain Ali watched Carter direct vehicles to one side as a trio of American Humvees appeared from the direction of Ghazni. They drove at high speed around the traffic obstacles and through the checkpoint before disappearing in the direction of Qalat. There was some lingering chatter and realignment of vehicles and obstacles before the checkpoint returned to its previous tedium.

PRODIGAL AVENGER

Always in a hurry, passing through and unsettling everything before moving on to the next task. That is the American way. What a way to live!

Ali had spent his childhood in the shadow of Russian helicopters and Kabul's old Communist minders.

An hour later, the mysterious convoy of Humvees returned from the other direction. The uncovered back of one vehicle revealed five Afghan prisoners, three men and two burqa-clad females. The men sat hunched over, burlap sacks covering their heads and hiding their identities. The women, though covered from head to toe in black burqa, sat upright and proud. An American soldier was driving their confiscated vehicle, a Russian-made Lada taxicab with a box tied on the roof. Apparently, these were important prisoners, and the Americans were in a hurry to get them somewhere.

Captain Ali watched his energetic American counterpart "make a hole," as the US soldiers called it, so the mysterious convoy could pass through. Then they were gone, en route to the US Provincial Reconstruction Team camp at Ghazni, or maybe beyond that to the Combined Joint Task Force Headquarters at Bagram Airfield. He shrugged his shoulders, watched the swirling dust settle on his checkpoint, and went on with his tedious task.

Jake eyed the perimeter security as they entered Bagram. Insights from a blog he'd read ran through his mind, some journalist's musings on the American attempt to bring civilization to this savage place … with on-the-ground shadow warriors and Tomahawk missiles.

Those who fail to learn the lessons of history are doomed to repeat them.

Tension left Jake's body as the vehicle passed the security checkpoint and entered the fenced perimeter. He allowed his team, still disguised as refugees from a Kabul wedding reception, to be manhandled through a security door where they disappeared inside the Bagram detention center. But when they reached a secure area within, Jake pulled off his burqa and put an end to the games. Team Drecker's latest operation was officially over.

Bagram Airfield, the huge former Soviet air base and home to the Red Army's mighty 108th Motorized Rifle and 105th Airborne Divisions, was now a beehive of frenetic American activity. Military units, special operators, government spooks and civilian contractors scurried to and fro in a frantic effort to stamp Uncle Sam's image over the top of the massive monument to Soviet failure. The American eagle hoped to avoid the Soviet bear's mistakes by operating almost entirely from the shadows. But at Bagram, the shadows merged.

Blog of an unnamed American journalist, 2003

CHAPTER 5

Jannat

Jake Drecker read his mail as he walked to the Bagram mess facility, relaxed and refreshed for the first time in several weeks. His regular desert camouflage uniform sported a Special Operations Command patch on his left sleeve, advertising his "official job" at Bagram as Special Operations Command's "liaison officer" to the Joint Special Operations Task Force.

He sensed the presence of a lurker nearby, poised for an ambush.

"Hey, Chief, on your way to dinner?"

Jake looked up and smiled. At times like this, back from a mission and in the relative safety of the base camp, Jannat reminded him not of a trained CIA interrogator and assassin, but of a zealous undergrad psych major eager to try out her stuff on her unwitting male classmates.

"Well, if it isn't Janet Sylvester, my favorite CIA contractor."

Jannat smiled back. Her black sweater, black jeans, and blue down vest accessorized by a nine-millimeter pistol in a shoulder harness were a pleasant change from the useful burqa she wore whenever she entered or left Bagram. A badge on a lanyard around her neck identified her as "Janet Sylvester, Research Technician with Brown Littleton, Inc." her on-base identity.

He folded up his letters and stuffed them into a cargo pocket

"Are you going to the mess hall?" she asked.

"As a matter of fact, I am."

"Then I'll join you," she said, stepping alongside. "We can finally have that talk."

"And what talk would that be?"

"You know, when we were in the field you said you would tell me a little about yourself after we got back."

Jake chuckled at her "technique" but maintained a faraway look in his eyes. *Ever the psychology major turned interrogator.*

"You probably told me that to get me off your back," she added. She looked vaguely hurt by the idea.

He grinned at her and continued walking. *She is way too nice to be in this line of work.*

"No, not really, join me for chow, and we can talk."

"Thanks, Jake. I was hoping you would ask."

Jake stopped mid-stride and faced her in mock indignation.

"But before we continue, young lady, let me ask you a question. Does your husband know you are running around this airbase hitting up GIs for supper?"

She laughed, and her face visibly relaxed.

"I should have known any soldier who makes his living wearing mascara while hunting down terrorists would have a keen sense of humor," she answered with a pout. "But yes, the poor man is locked in a B-hut trying to grow back a full face of hair. So, what's a girl to do?"

They both laughed.

"So …" she continued. "What can you tell me about one Jake Drecker, Chief Warrant Officer in the US Army?"

"Ahh, a nice Jewish kid from Hawaii. But of course, if I tell you I'll have to kill you," he answered repeating an old, often heard joke.

"Jewish kid from Hawaii? Cut it out!"

He didn't reply but took Jannat's elbow and steered her into the chow line in front of the mess hall.

Jake let Jannat enter first. They both stopped just inside and scanned the interior.

"This place is growing."

"Yea," she said. "Lots of kids here now."

A true statement. Six months ago, Bagram had a much smaller footprint. Just a few spies, special operators, coalition troops, and security force personnel. Now there were more and more regular Army and Air Force conventional personnel, eighteen- and nineteen-year-olds, and civilians—lots of civilians. He wasn't sure Uncle Sam getting comfortable in Afghanistan was a good idea. From such things quagmires grew.

Jake looked for familiar faces. An atmospheric change came over the mess hall as men stole furtive, synchronized glances in Jannat's direction.

There were still very few females here, and most of them wore the same, shapeless, desert pattern uniforms as the men. With her five-foot-eight, exotic good looks, Jannat would have stood out in any crowd. But here, in the middle of a male-dominated war zone, she looked stunning. She stood out, that was for sure. Who could blame them for looking?

Jannat seemed oblivious to the hormonal atmospherics in the mess facility.

"What are they serving?" she asked Jake.

"Something hot and something American," he replied.

"I need one to go for my husband."

As they made their way through the line, a first lieutenant from the Ranger Company made eye contact, waved, and bellowed, "Yo, Chief!"

Jake raised his hand in acknowledgment. The young officer, tall and lean in sanitized desert camouflage and battle rattle, worked his way through the tightly packed rows of dining soldiers and extended a hand.

"Hey, Chief, welcome back to Bagram. How's Tampa?" the lieutenant asked.

Jake smiled, secure in the knowledge that the well-meaning young officer only knew him by his cover identity. *Someday, I'll tell you, Lieutenant Snow. But not yet.*

"Tampa is still the same, although I wasn't *exactly* there on this last trip—long story, I'll explain later. How's Quick Reaction Force duty treating you?"

"Still rescuing SEALs, and we're a little busier than before," the younger man answered

"Now, now, go easy. I've got a lot of friends who are SEALs."

The lieutenant grinned. "I know, Chief. Like you always say, 'Best watermen on the planet!' All you surfer types are the same. Hey, can I join you for chow?"

"Not today, LT. I'm escorting a contractor around the base today. Have you met Janet Sylvester before?" He turned and gestured toward Jannat. "Janet, this is First Lieutenant Randy Snow from our Ranger Company."

"Hi, Randy." Jannat stuck out a hand.

"Hi, ma'am. How are you?" Randy responded, taking her hand in a gentle but firm handshake. "First time at Bagram?"

"No, not really."

"She's on temporary duty, LT. She comes out here pretty regularly."

"Well, nice meeting you, ma'am."

"Nice meeting you, Randy."

Snow reached out and shook Jake's hand before departing, "I'll catch you later, Chief."

"Sounds good, we have a lot to talk about, LT."

The lieutenant moved off and headed back to his table.

"Nice guy."

"One of the best. Let's grab our chow," Jake responded as he handed Jannat a tray.

They moved through the line, then made their way to a remote corner in the mess tent where they could enjoy some privacy. The others didn't need to hear their business.

"Snow's platoon is the rescue unit of last resort when an operation goes sour. He's the last guy you ever want to need but the best guy to have when you need him," he explained.

"Right, I heard about their work during Operation Anaconda."

Jake ran his hand through his close-cropped hair and folded his arms. *She isn't interested in Snow or anybody else in this mess hall. She wants to get inside my head.*

"Yep, different platoon at the time but same Rangers. Snow is a West Pointer and prone to occasional lapses of excessive pride. But he keeps it to himself, and I respect that in a man."

Jake began eating, machine-like. Efficiency, that was the key. Knife in right hand cutting while the fork in left jabbed the cut portions into his mouth.

He poked a piece of meat with his knife and put it right into his mouth. Heavenly after the nuts, raisins, fruit or occasional *naan* with lamb meat while undercover.

"You're gonna cut your tongue off if you keep eating with your knife like that," Jannat warned.

"Hmm …" he grunted, smiling and nodding without taking his eyes off his plate. "My mother used to say that."

"So, tell me again what you started to say outside," she said in an effort to redirect the conversation. "That bit about being a nice Jewish kid from Hawaii. Are you really from Hawaii?"

"Yep, and it's all true. I am Jewish, and I went to the University of Hawaii. Next question."

"Drecker doesn't sound Jewish … or Hawaiian for that matter."

"It's neither. It's sort of German, Norwegian, and Polish. It's not my real name."

"Are you serious? Or is this one of those clandestine-operator-who-never-gives-a-straight-answer-to-a-personal-question kind of deals?"

He ignored her provocative question and chewed some more before continuing.

"It's my stepfather's name," he said. "His grandfather was a Russian Jew named Israel Drecker. No one knows where they picked up a gentile name, if they were converts or changed their name to escape persecution in Russia. By the way, it's always Drecker—never shortened. Never, ever call me Dreck."

"Umm, okay," Jannat responded. "Am I supposed to know the reason why?"

"Yeah, *dreck* is a bad word in Yiddish."

"Yiddish? Okay. And it means … am I supposed to know?"

"It means dung," he explained. "You know, doo-doo …"

"You mean …" Jannat lowered her voice. "Like sh …"

"Don't say it!" Jake rasped.

"Anyway," he continued, straightening up and returning to his businesslike demeanor. "Stepgrandfather gets off the boat at Ellis Island as Israel Drecker, Jewish immigrant from Russia. Mom married Solomon Drecker after my parents split up when I was a kid."

"Oh, I'm sorry Jake, I …"

"Don't apologize, you wanted to know about me, and I'm game. My real dad was an Air Force pilot, Jewish but secular most of his life. He lived the hard-drinking, maverick pilot stereotype to the hilt until he finally drove Mom crazy. They split up, and he ran off and did all kinds of crazy things before joining some religious group out in Arizona. I haven't seen him in years. Mom moved on. When I was a teenager, she married Solomon Drecker, a multi-millionaire business guy from New York. He adopted me and my sister, and that's how I ended up being a Drecker. He's a good guy, good for Mom, but different—really different—from my real father."

She looked stunned. He'd surprised her with his candor. Good, maybe she'd be satisfied.

"Does it ever bother you that you haven't talked? I mean, you said he was in some weird religious group. Is he okay?"

He froze and studied his plate before answering.

"Sorry, Jannat, *kapu*. That's Hawaiian for off limits."

Jake looked up from the plate and locked eyes with her.

"Now I *am* sorry," she said.

"No offense taken. My father is my father, just like yours is yours, we can't change that. They were both pilots, right? You know how pilots can be."

She nodded, but shock spread across her face.

Jake chuckled. "Iranian Air Force, right? 1979?"

"How did you know that?" she gasped.

"Just one of those things. I get paid to know things. And your parents escaped when the Shah fell."

"You are good, Jake. I hardly knew myself that my dad was a pilot until a few years ago. I thought he was just another refugee engineer. Wow. But am I allowed to ask you any more questions?"

"Only if they aren't kapu. Try me."

"Wife and kids? That safe?" she asked, redirecting her aim.

"My wife, Ruth, is at Fort Bragg. We have two boys—I'll show you a picture if we are ever stateside together. Actually, I may have a picture attached to an email somewhere I can show you. I don't bring pictures of my wife and kids on operational deployments."

"Of course, I understand. I guess I didn't think of you as a family man, not with your line of work."

He looked up from his food at her without responding. Then he carefully scraped his plate with his fork and finished. He wiped his mouth and slid his tray to one side.

"Break time's over, Jannat. Have any other questions?"

Jannat looked down at her tray. She had eaten little.

"You can't leave me now, Jake. I'm still eating."

"I won't." He smiled and scanned the room.

"Where did you and Ruth meet?"

"Freshmen theater class at college. We were the only Jewish kids on campus during our first Christmas in Hawaii, so we made a vow to spend Christmas Day hiking together. We've been together since then."

"I'm surprised, Jake. That is really romantic!"

"Surprised?"

They both laughed.

"No, I guess not."

"I was a drama major in college," he continued.

"You *are* kidding me."

"Nope, see? That's why I don't mind opening up to you, Jannat. You don't believe a word I say anyway … and neither would anyone else if you squealed on me."

She shook her head and smiled.

"What other major lets you take a handy course like Theatrical Swordplay? You should see me swing a broadsword. Comes in handy."

She giggled and shook her head again.

"You are too much, Jake."

He paused the conversation while she resumed eating. He quickly scanned the mess tent for other familiar faces. Lieutenant Colonel Sanchez was talking to a group of operators from a newly arrived unit. Jake would need to talk to him soon. Where was the not-so-fearless leader, Saber-Six? After taking a moment longer to peruse the area, he looked back at Jannat.

"Yep, a drama major, and then I enlisted," he continued. "What about you? What does your father think of his daughter being a trained cloak and dagger woman?"

She paused in mid-chew then swallowed hard.

"I guess I don't really talk to my father as much as I should. He thinks I'm a college professor teaching Central Asian culture to CIA recruits at Langley."

"Nice cover."

"Actually, my father sent me to school to be a doctor of medicine, a psychiatrist, but I hated undergraduate psychology. I preferred history, culture, geography. The people I met in psychology class were just—" Her brow wrinkled as she sought the right word. "I don't know—they seemed so *ambiguous*."

Jake smiled. "Too many neurotic females trying to work out their relationships with their fathers?"

"Yes!" Jannat chuckled. "How did you know?"

"I know the type, always trying to figure other people out, and they can't figure themselves out."

"Exactly," she said, smiling. "Although, I do think unresolved issues with our fathers could drive us to do all kinds of crazy things, don't you think?"

Hmm, sounds interesting. But now you're starting to sound like one of those neurotic females you were just complaining about."

She blushed. "God, I hope not. I don't know. Mothers are different—they compete with their daughters and coddle their sons—pretty straight-forward. But fathers are complicated. There's definitely more love-hate going on. Like the prodigal son or something."

She smiled self-consciously and blushed again.

Jake tilted his chair back and smiled. She was uncomfortable now. He hadn't intended to make her feel that way, but he knew he had.

"Well, Jake, I think I'm done," she said placing her utensils on her tray and securing the food box for her husband. "I need to get this over to Gino before he starves to death."

She stood and offered her hand in a businesslike handshake.

"Thanks for opening up with me, Jake, I'm looking forward to our next mission together."

He stood, took her hand, and held it without shaking.

"Same here, Jannat, give my best to your husband."

"I will, Jake."

She turned and maneuvered toward the exit, setting off another silent wave of turned heads and stolen glances from the now dwindling mess hall crowd.

As Jannat left she thought of the Hawaiian word he'd taught her, *kapu.* The word was important to Jake. She didn't understand why, but it defined him somehow and was related to something else she'd seen during that awkward mess hall conversation. Jake's eyes. They flashed and changed color, turning from their usual warm green to a cold, icy gray she had never seen before. They pierced her like a knife and caused her to shudder. *That must be how his eyes look when he kills.*

CHAPTER 6

Pancho

Michael "Pancho" Sanchez sat chewing on the tip of an unlit cigar as he contemplated the next phase of his unusually charmed life. He couldn't stay in this job much longer. When he pinned on full bird colonel, they'd pull him out and send him to some cushy job with a big desk and a secretary. Or maybe back to Latin America to be an attaché or something, rubbing elbows with diplomats and foreign banana republic generals with more medals than a Soviet Field Marshal. Either way, there would be no more hobnobbing with the operators on the ground, that was for sure. How would he adjust to being away from the troops after living as a soldier for over twenty years, and six years as a Marine before that? *At least my wife will be happy.*

He put his feet up on the world-weary folding table, kicked back, and turned on the large screen television at the end of the tent. He stroked the Abraham Lincoln beard that framed his beefy face and wiped the dust from his cargo pants. *She's gonna be thrilled when I tell her.*

He smiled. *How many colonels get to live like this, in an ad hoc recreation tent with folding tables, battered aluminum chairs, satellite television tuned to either football or 24-hour news, and some forlorn computers serving as an internet café? This was the life!*

He thought he'd reached the pinnacle of his career as the Executive and Operations Officer for the Prodigal Avenger project's clandestine special operations task force for operations in Afghanistan and its neighbors.

Colonel Greenlight even named the task force after my nickname: Task Force Pancho.

He missed Colonel Greenlight. His former boss was an old school Special Forces Sergeant Major paratrooper officer, and founding Delta operator who'd conceived of the Prodigal Avenger program in the very ashes of the Pentagon on 9/11. Greenlight based the plan on the Operation Phoenix program he'd been involved in during Vietnam.

Colonel "Pancho" Sanchez. I like the sound of that way too much. Ha, ha, ha! I'll just have to give the Army a few more years of my life to make the most of it, I guess.

Life could not be any sweeter.

"Yo, Pancho!"

Lieutenant Colonel Sanchez's eyes flashed toward the entrance. Recognizing the diminutive commando, he jumped to his feet and clicked down the television volume.

"Jake, the Snake—what's up, my man?"

"Heard the word, Pancho. Congratulations!"

They shook hands, smiling in mutual admiration.

"Thanks, Chief. It was the Lord, no doubt, but I couldn't have done it without guys like you working for me."

"Pancho, you are by far the best officer I ever worked for. Making full colonel is nothing to sneeze at. When guys like you make it, I get back my faith in the system. When do you pin on?"

"Ninety days."

"Sweet! Then what? You leaving us?"

"Hope not, but ... yeah, actually."

"Back to South America? Is another Pablo Escobar in need of termination?"

Pancho ignored his friend's snide provocation and shook his head. "God, I hope not there! No, Kabul, maybe, for a while, then stateside."

"Brenda excited?"

"Heck, yeah, she's already looking at a housing upgrade on our quarters."

"Good girl. Do you have any idea about your replacement?"

"Yeah, it's Mike Moon. He should be arriving any day now."

"Really? Mike Moon? Good, he's a pro. I worked with him in Bosnia."

"And he knows Twister and the agency crowd. He's arriving here straight from the Philippines."

"That sounds like the old Lunatic," Jake said, referring to Moon's *nom de guerre*. "Still, I don't know how we'll get along without you."

Jake sat down and grinned at his boss.

Pancho took quick stock of his subordinate. Although Pancho considered him a friend, Jake remained distant somehow, an enigma, a difficult man to decipher. Nevertheless, he knew Jake's special talents and operational style were perfect for the unit's clandestine mission. Jake hadn't let him down yet.

"I'm glad I recruited you for the Prodigal Avenger program, Jake. When Colonel Greenlight conceived the plan, he probably envisioned men just like you wreaking vengeance all over the globe against America's enemies. Task Force Pancho will be fine as long as we have people like you in the field."

"Well, you've come a long way from the wet-behind-the-ears A-team leader I broke in at Bragg back in the day," Jake said. "But truth be told, I learned a lot from you. Even if you are a former Marine."

Pancho smiled at the back-handed compliment. "Nice work on that last op, Jake. That's the best you're gonna get from me."

"Thanks, boss."

Pancho returned to his seat as Jake adjusted his chair to take in the television. Pancho inched the volume back up but low enough they could still talk.

"Have you heard from Ruth and the kids since you got here?"

"Funny you should mention that, Pancho. My wife seems to be spending a lot of time with yours lately."

"Really?" Pancho arched an eyebrow.

"I guess your wife is giving her a lot of advice lately."

"Does that bother you, Jake?"

"You know my wife and me as well as anyone, Pancho. And you know Ruth will do what she is going to do no matter what I think. So ..." he paused. "I guess I'm not bothered."

Pancho tried to see behind the commando's hard jade irises, but they were cold and opaque. Jake's 'You know me as well as anyone' was true but still wasn't much.

"I'm praying for you, Jake."

The commando nodded but said nothing. He turned toward the television screen and changed the subject. "Anything else I missed around here while I was gone?"

"Did you hear about Randy Jenkins's team?"

"RJ? No, is he okay?"

"Okay as in alive, but the three of them got caught in some kind of crossfire between Al Qaeda and renegade Taliban. We had to medevac them all to Germany."

"Renegade Taliban?"

"That's the official story. Or some kind of Pathan blood feud. But the unofficial story is more complicated. Scott and Barnes can give you more on that."

"Is RJ going to be okay?"

"He absorbed a lot of metal—fragments from a Russian grenade. He has a concussion. But all his parts are intact. His teammates are about the same, except I think Chip Johnson was shot through the shoulder. The weird part of the story is one of the elements fighting up there seems to have carried them off the mountain after they got wounded and left them with some friendlies. That's the mystery."

"So maybe not renegade Taliban but friendly Afghans?" Jake suggested.

"There's more to the story than that. RJ got debriefed in Germany. Read the report. Talk to Scott and Barnes. Officially, it's too hot for speculation. You'll see why later."

"Okay, sir. Copy."

Pancho edged up the volume. "Not much happening in the world except for the defeat of Saddam Hussein and the Iraqi military machine."

"I heard."

"And as you can see, we got more people on Bagram than ever. This place is going to get huge."

"I noticed the chow tastes the same."

Pancho chuckled. "Except there is a lot more. Actually, we had a health scare with a bunch of inspectors walking around the mess facility in protective suits and masks—something about anthrax in the food."

"Good for morale."

Pancho smiled. *Old snake and that dry sense of humor of his! Glad he's back safe.*

"We've got one situation our guys up at Central Command are tracking closely," Pancho said.

"You mean besides the Iraq invasion and our hunt for Osama bin Laden?"

"Yeah, a missionary kidnapping."

Jake shrugged.

"I know you don't care too much about quixotic missionary endeavors, Jake, but this one is interesting to me for a couple reasons."

"Yeah, like your father was a preacher, Pancho. You've told me."

"Well, there's that, but I mean operationally. This missionary was kidnapped in Pakistan, our area of interest. And our assets may be on the hook to rescue him. Maybe even us."

"Doubtful, Pancho. I mean. Prodigal Avenger missions are about assassinating killers before they kill us. Not rescuing hostages."

"I know, but we are clandestine capable. And deep, cross-border operation missions into Pakistan are part of our *modus operandi*."

Jake folded his arms and leaned backward, his crystal greenish-blue pupils alternating color. Not being dismissive, just making a point.

"Besides, Jake," Pancho continued. "We are talking about an innocent bystander here. This is an American citizen."

"CIA agree with that?"

"Far as I can tell."

"Sure, Pancho. And if we get the green light, you know I am all in. I am just a little nervy about risking my men on a mission we aren't set up to do."

"Fair enough, Jake. Anyway, it'll probably be on the news today if we watch long enough." Pancho trolled through the channels, then shot a grin and a wink at Jake. "And you know you can trust the media!"

"I hear the Air Force has over five hundred channels on the satellite TV in their rec center," Jake quipped.

Pancho chuckled. "It'll be on here," he said, setting the remote on the table.

Jake turned toward the video as a talking head droned on about embedded reporters in Iraq and the dearth of "weapons of mass destruction" evidence. A news anchor in New York filled the screen to introduce the next story.

"Coming up, an update on the American missionary kidnapped by Al Qaeda in Pakistan. Was he a spy, or was he simply in the wrong place at the wrong time? We'll have more in five minutes, right here on your global news network!"

Jake turned toward him as a commercial came on. "So, an Al Qaeda op?"

"Media speculation. In thirty minutes, they'll have their counterterrorism expert, some retired general or FBI guy, explaining how it must be Al Qaeda because we stirred the hornet's nest or something. But that's not supported by intel. Not yet."

"Interesting. And no one's assigned to work this yet?"

"Task Force Dagger might get the tag. Who knows? We won't be tagged except maybe in a supporting effort. Or ..." Pancho's voice trailed off. Task Force Dagger was the main special operations task force at Bagram.

"Or what?"

"Or unless it's deep in country, involves a very high-level Al Qaeda target, and requires a clandestine solution. But we don't know if it's really Al Qaeda. Word on the street is this was some bush league Pakistani militant group."

Jake nodded. "Maybe this is their way of joining the big leagues."

Pancho turned the volume up as the commercial break ended. Jake leaned over and adjusted a boot lacing. The New York anchor reappeared with a picture captioned "Missionary or Spy?" beneath a head shot of a lean, middle-aged man with gray hair, two blackened eyes, and a bloodied, swollen face.

Pancho watched Jake. He hadn't yet looked at the face on the screen. He was looking at Pancho instead.

"Is this guy a real missionary? Or is he a CIA asset using that for cover?"

"Far as we've been told, he's a real missionary. The rub is he used to be a defense attaché in Islamabad. That's the tricky part. Technically, that makes him a former spy as far as diplomatic protocol goes. But that's all, no agency connections."

Jake looked up and opened his mouth, but nothing came out. A muscle quivered on the left side of Jake's face.

The anchor droned, "…Isidore Loewenthal, age sixty-five, a missionary with Christian Outreach Ministries International, has been accused by the Pakistan Martyr Brigade of operating a covert CIA recruiting operation and converting Muslims to Christianity."

Jake's eyes were riveted to the image on the screen, but Pancho had had enough. There was a call to make back home. With a yawn he reached for the remote and started to stand.

Jake snatched the device from under Pancho's hand. "Hold on, I want to hear this." Caught off-guard, Pancho studied his friend. Jake looked thoughtful, even intent, as he stared at the screen.

"… Pakistan Martyr Brigade has demanded the release of seventeen extremists held by the Musharref regime in exchange for the American."

Pancho settled back into his seat. "You know the guy?"

Jake didn't answer. The newsman's voice continued, "… a spokesman for Mr. Loewenthal's church in Phoenix, Arizona, has confirmed that he is, indeed, a missionary with their organization but declined to comment further citing privacy issues."

Jake turned, fixing him with a piercing gaze. Pancho shivered but wasn't sure why. He watched Jake's face lose its granite coldness and relax.

"This might be our next mission," Jake finally answered. "I'm just curious about this since it's in our backyard. This guy's captors may even be linked to one of our targets."

"Well, they're not, at least as far as I know." Pancho stroked the chin of his beard. "Intel may have more now, but as of yesterday, Pakistan Martyr Brigade is just one of a dozen small extremist groups on the Pakistani landscape. Might be linked to Al Qaeda, might pretend to be linked or might wish they were, but nothing hard on them yet. This guy Loewenthal seems to be the real deal, missionary-wise. But as a former embassy attaché, he must have known the risks."

"He probably knows a lot more than that. Names. Places. Contacts. CIA station chief cover."

The newsman droned on, "… coming up, Hollywood celebrities on the war in Iraq, and the story of a Texas cheerleader gone bad on this, your global news leader …"

Jake slammed his hand down hard on the table. "God, how stupid!"

Pancho swung his feet down off the table and sat up. This was out of character. Jake was always the cool-headed guy in the room. Or, at least he pretended to be. Pancho didn't know how to respond to his friend's outburst.

Jake stood up, rubbed the top of his head, and spoke.

"I need to talk to our CIA guys about the upcoming operation. I think we ought to check out the links on those kidnappers. They might lead us to a target."

Pancho couldn't see how, but he played along. "Okay, Jake."

Jake leaned over the table, stuck out his hand, and smiled.

"Got to go, boss. Congratulations on the promotion. You've more than earned it."

Pancho stood and grasped Jake's hand.

"Thanks, Jake. You know I could not have done it without guys like you making me look good."

"Got that straight," Jake said, grinning again. He turned on one heel and headed out, leaving Pancho to wonder at his friend's abrupt goodbye.

CHAPTER 7

The Bank

Jake Drecker hurried over to the vault-like Task Force Pancho command post to confer with the intelligence analysts. He navigated the labyrinthine entrance through the perimeter of triple-strand concertina wire and held up his badge to the guard inside the wire, a corporal from the Ranger platoon who knew Jake.

"Welcome back to paradise, Chief." The corporal pulled back the single loose coil used as a gate, kicking up a small cloud of dust as the wire scraped along the ground.

"Thanks, Corporal Griffin. Hope this place has my reservation."

Griffin smiled as Jake passed through and pulled the wire back tight again. "Always a place for you, Chief!"

Jake passed between thick concrete walls. Someone had bolted a sign over the inner door—"Welcome to the Bank." He smiled at the reference to Pancho's insistence the place be given a nickname reflecting its distinguished character. But the musty smell inside betrayed the obvious. Jake called it the Latrine. He entered the spartan briefing room and let his eyes adjust to the weak interior light.

The room looked different. More stuff. A green, wooden field table covered with small maps, photographs, and computer print-outs sat in the middle of the room surrounded by old aluminum folding chairs. A huge Joint Operational Graphic map flanked by two large, wall-mounted video screens dominated one wall. Cables ran from a side room into a router and server parked on a pallet against the opposite corner. Not a bad setup—except for the faint smell of urine and mildew ruining the apocalyptic beauty of the place.

Four briefers stood around the table waiting to pitch the latest update to the commander. Jake focused on the two intelligence analysts, Everett Scott and Robert Barnes. Scott, a CIA analyst, looked combat cool in a short-sleeved safari jacket and khaki cargo pants tucked into Australian Army boots. He looked up and saw Jake.

"Chief, welcome home," Scott said.

"Thanks, Scott, but home for me is on the other side of the planet."

Jake grabbed a metal folding chair from against the wall and set it backward next to the table. He shook hands with each of the men, exchanging pleasantries before sitting down, chin resting on his forearms over the chair's backrest.

Jake had questions to ask before Colonel Biggs, the unit commander, arrived for his afternoon briefing. And the thick-waisted, middle-aged Army civilian analyst, Robert Barnes, held the answers.

"What kind of targets are we developing this afternoon, Mr. Barnes?"

Barnes rearranged some sheets of paper as if to gather his thoughts.

"We've identified the suspected position of a high value, Category Two target named Abbas Bin Azzam ... here." Barnes pointed to the map. He was like some old prophet, which is what a good intelligence officer was supposed to be—prophetic. But Barnes possessed a gravitas lacking in others. The staccato cadence of his voice made Jake think of soldiers marching to the beat of drums. Hypnotic. "He's six kilometers south of the city of Dir in Pakistan's Northwest Frontier Province."

"Abbas Bin Azzam leads an organization calling itself Maktab al-Khidamat Pakistan," Everett Scott added. "He's related to Sheikh Abdullah Yusuf Azzam, the notorious Palestinian founder of Maktab al-Khidamat, better known as the MAK. The MAK is the root organization that morphed into Al Qaeda. We call Maktab al-Khidamat Pakistan MAK-PAK for short. It's a separate group from the old MAK that exists mainly to organize grassroots Pakistani domestic terrorists to support Al Qaeda goals to undermine the Pervaiz regime."

"Okay, but what makes him important enough for Prodigal Avenger?"

"Several things. But we also think we've confirmed a link between the MAK and the kidnapped American missionary that's been in the news lately."

What? Jake froze as the thought processed. *Need to keep my poker face on.* "Really? Incredible. Explain to me ..."

A sudden commotion at the door interrupted them.

Barnes looked up. "Saber-Six?"

A captain across the room nodded. "Sounds like him."

Corporal Griffin, battle-rattle and all, stepped inside and shouted, "Attention!"

Everyone straightened up and turned toward the entrance. Jake sighed and reluctantly stood to his feet. He forced his face into a stoic mask he hoped conveyed utter calm, but thoughts whirled on the inside. The boss, Colonel Lloyd Biggs, had arrived.

Colonel Biggs bent slightly at the waist to accommodate his six-foot, three-inch frame as he came through the door. He swept into the room, responding to Griffin's "attention" with an Air Force informal "Relax, relax," instead of the customary "Carry on!" He sat down in the middle seat at the table, ran his hand through his longish, even by Air Force standards, mostly gray hair and squinted at the map in front of him.

Jake took in the man's tailored flight suit and spit-polished jungle boots. *He looks like a poster child for Air Force Special Operations. A poster child of some kind, anyway.*

Jake had long given up trying to figure out how an Air Force special operations pilot came to command a clandestine ground unit. *He's an accomplished pilot, maybe even one of the best, but a ground commander he is not. Just another ambitious career officer with the right security clearance and a need for a successful "joint" command under his belt to make his next rank. But giving credit where credit is due, the man is not oblivious to his own shortcomings. He delegates almost everything to Pancho. And with a promotion due soon, Pancho might just end up as our new commander. Maybe.*

Saber-Six, as Biggs was nicknamed, leaned back on his chair, both hands behind his head. He greeted Jake with a simple nod.

Jake returned the nod.

Pancho, Major Cutter, and a couple more staff members came in on the heels of Saber-Six. They took their places around the table or against the wall. Pre-meeting banter buzzed about the place. Nothing formal would begin until Pancho said so.

CHAPTER 8

Pancho

Pancho settled into his folding chair and scanned the room. There was Jake. Good, he'd need his expertise today. You never knew where the boss would go with his off-the-wall questions. Jake was good for warming up the staff with hard-hitting questions before the colonel arrived. But the interactions between Jake and Saber-Six were priceless. Like watching a mongoose stare down a cobra. If there was one person in the room Saber-Six could not intimidate, it was Jake Drecker. *But then again, there was always Barnes and Saber-Six. A different show altogether. Practically fireworks!*

"Looks like we have everyone we need here today, Colonel."

"Thank you, Colonel Sanchez." Saber-Six looked to his intelligence analysts. "Okay. Gents, what have you got that's new?"

"New target, sir," Barnes offered. "A Cat Two, the one we mentioned at this morning's brief. We've got some updated details and think we have a link between him and the missing American missionary."

Saber-Six's eye-brows arched. A cunning smirk spread across his face.

"Really … A Cat Two? And a link to our kidnapped American in Pakistan?"

Saber-Six took a sheet of paper from Barnes and meditated on the contents.

He isn't just reading it, he's figuring out how to use the information to make himself look good with his Air Force seniors at Central Command Forward. Good ole Saber-Six, as predictable as a Santa Ana wind and just as full of hot air.

"Listen …" Saber-Six scanned the faces in the room.

A lean, spectral giant dressed in khaki cargo pants, steel-toed boots, and a well-worn leather motorcycle jacket glided into the back and hovered within earshot. Pancho nodded at the gaunt newcomer, who seemed to ignore him behind a pair of mirrored sunglasses. *Too cool.*

"I don't need any extra crap right now, just the facts," Saber-Six went on. "If we can develop this target, I can present it at the meeting in Qatar. This missionary thing is hot—I don't need to tell you that. Let's discuss the target details now, and if it looks good, I'll take it on the C-5 in the morning with Major Cutter."

Pancho suppressed a grin that threatened to betray the enormous pride he had in his men. They'd done well digging up a Cat Two and linking him to the kidnapped missionary. *Poor Cutter. If the boss approves this, he's going to get stuck on a plane with Saber-Six to go brief the J3 in Qatar. We can broadcast it to them from here, but no way Saber-Six is gonna be denied his face time. But if the colonel has anything going for him, it's a nose for what senior staff wants. And if this target is solid, maybe we'll get the double pleasure of taking down a bad guy <u>and</u> rescuing an American hostage.*

Scott and Barnes began filling in the blanks on Abbas Bin Azzam. Barnes led with Scott adding details along the way.

"Azzam made a name for himself recruiting Kashmir separatist combat veterans for the anti-American jihad in Afghanistan. He operates a recruiting and training center in a compound just south of Dir. He is a known associate of an extremely dangerous Category Two high value target named Adnan el-Shukrijumah."

"One of the most wanted men in the United States," Scott chimed in.

"El-Shukrijumah was pursuing materials for the Al Qaeda nuclear device—either a tactical suitcase nuke or a dirty bomb," Barnes added.

Saber-Six nodded.

Good, he likes what he hears.

Major Cutter, the assistant operations officer, cut in. "The Prodigal Avenger program exists for the sole purpose of eliminating such people with a minimum of formalities. A clown like Azzam earned his own Category Two high value target status by mere association with people like Adnan el-Shukrijumah."

Pancho looked at Jake. This one was a real possibility. Jake and Saber-Six were on the same page. You couldn't take down a Category One target without Presidential approval. Except Osama bin Laden, maybe. The ultimate Category One had to be an exception. Had to be. And Cat Three was not worth the risk of a cross-border operation that might cause a major international incident. Category Two was the best—and this was a bona fide Cat Two.

Major Cutter continued. "We have blanket approval for Prodigal Avenger teams to take down Cat Two targets in Pakistan while maintaining plausible deniability. Our teams are the best theater assets available for this hit. So, if our CIA partner concurs, we are cleared for action."

Pancho liked it. Thought Saber-Six did too … so far.

The commander's next question interrupted Pancho's musings.

"Pancho, what have we got on Dir? Looks close enough to the border to consider a Predator strike vis-à-vis risking our teams." Saber-Six didn't turn his head, just rotated his narrowed, squinty eyeballs to the right. "Do we have any operators in the task force who have been on the ground around Dir and can give us an area brief?"

Pancho squeezed Jake's shoulder, silently releasing him to speak.

"As a matter of fact, I do, sir," Jake spoke up. "I personally performed a clandestine reconnaissance of Dir district on a previous mission. I know the terrain and would be happy to answer your questions. I also believe it's doable."

"Great. I'll have some questions later, after I hear what we've got."

Pancho smiled. This mission had potential.

"Okay," Saber-Six said. "Where is the confirmation intel we need for targeting? We need to confirm both our target and our hostage locations—plus their established routine—before we go green on this. Hostage proximity is enough to rule out a Predator."

"Signals intelligence, sir," Barnes offered, referring to intercepted enemy communications, SIGINT for short.

"Do we have an NSA rep here?" asked the commander, referring to the planner for the National Security Agency.

People glanced around the room.

"Sergeant First Class Pickett is supposed to be here, but he got tied up with a special request for support over at Task Force Dagger," Pancho answered.

"Well, is it solid intelligence? What kind of reports are we talking about?" Saber-Six asked the room.

There was a pause before Barnes responded.

"Cell phone intercepts, sir. NSA fixed 'em here and here," he pointed on the map. "All within a two-kilometer bubble around the suspected Azzam safe house."

"That's a pretty good fix considering the terrain," added Jake.

"Okay, what's the Agency assessment? Do we have a CIA report on this target?"

"Negative, but the SIGINT is good," Pancho cut in. "In my mind, almost confirms it."

"CIA has confirmed this is the location of the MAK-PAK compound," Barnes continued. "Cell phone traffic, in the clear, has Azzam discussing the missionary with a contact in Islamabad. Alternately referring to him as the Jew, the package, and the spy. Even one-time as the American."

"The Jew? I thought this guy was a Christian missionary."

"Loewenthal is a Jewish name," Scott interjected. "Maybe he's a convert."

"Interesting. So, we know this is our guy?"

"We believe he is, sir," Barnes answered. "We have a pretty good target folder on the compound as well."

"Believe?" Saber-Six asked. "I am not risking my credibility with CENTCOM and JSOC on just your guess, Mr. Barnes. And what does the target folder have to do with answering my question?"

"Sir, we have imagery on this compound and a trail of historical data on this area," Scott interjected. "Chief Drecker even had eyes on this compound during a previous recon."

"Okay," Saber-Six conceded. "Let's look at the pictures."

Pancho nodded toward Major Cutter, who stepped up to the table with a blurry 8 x 11, black and white image he'd recovered from the laser printer. Jim Cutter, a brawny African-American Green Beret from Dallas, Texas, was an especially valuable asset for mollifying Saber-Six. Cutter had worked with Saber-Six in a previous assignment and knew how to disarm the boss's savage aviator ego with a few words of down home, Southern-spun charm.

"Here we go, sir," Cutter handed the paper to the colonel. "Fresh from the oven."

"Very good, Major, hmmm ..."

Saber-Six leaned over the table and began to arrange the image next to a full-color printout of the Dir map. An image of both appeared on the wall screens for the planners in the room to see.

"Okay, Chief Drecker, show me the money."

Jake leaned over the field table and pointed a straightened paper clip toward a curved line running up the middle of Dir District. Pancho grinned. The effect was not unlike a patient school teacher assisting an oversized pupil with a particularly difficult geometry problem.

"The main route into Dir city is Highway N-45 here," Jake said. "Just south of Dir is the village of Nisar Khan. Our target is in a compound just to the west-southwest of the village. Here—where the highway executes a U-shaped bend as it follows the Panjkora River.

"The main compound is this walled-in area here. I passed by it but never got closer than this bend in the road. From the road, you can't see the enclosure, but you can see these other buildings.

"The walled enclosure is a classic Pathan compound with a forty-foot high, medieval looking tower built into the northwest corner of the wall. From the road, you can see the top of the tower over the trees, but not the enclosure.

"Inside the enclosure is this mud-brick house. Pretty plain. It has an unusually steep peaked roofed, about thirty by thirty, no details on the interior. Around the compound are several other buildings. Two stories but hard to say from this image. One is a mosque with a minaret. Not sure which are high enough to look down into the compound.

"The fastest way in is up this road, but I believe Mr. Barnes and Mr. Scott have identified egress routes along these two ridgelines that lead up to the valley."

"That's correct, sir," Barnes concurred. "We have several routes that connect these ridgelines to trails running right up to the Afghanistan border. It's mostly goatherder stuff, but our guys can manage them."

"So, are you recommending we take down this target, Mr. Barnes?" Saber-Six asked. Pancho sensed danger in the way the question came out.

Pancho panned the other faces in the room to see if anyone else noticed. Most stared blankly or looked into their notebooks. Except for Jake. Jake's face was passive but his eyes turned crystalline. Pancho switched back to Barnes.

Barnes rubbed his chin and looked at the image on the table.

"That's a command decision, Colonel," Barnes replied. "I'm just the analyst."

Saber-Six rolled his eyes to the ceiling.

"Okay. Continue."

Barnes and Scott shared details about the MAK-PAK and the area.

"So, you are sure Azzam is in this compound?" Saber-Six asked.

"Yes, sir," answered Barnes. "We have history, we have SIGINT, and we have a fairly recent CIA analysis."

"Fairly recent. Define fairly recent."

Scott jumped in to defend his agency's product.

"As of two weeks ago, we had an active report on Azzam at that location. Our in-place agents are in villages nearer the border. But our station chief in Islamabad has an agent embedded in an affiliated group who provides semi-regular reporting on Azzam and the MAK. It's been consistent over the last eighteen months. If we seem to have a quality gap on reporting, it's an anomaly."

"Then this is a real, honest-to-goodness target," Saber-Six cut in. "Mr. Barnes, you are the military intelligence expert here, do we have a good target or not?"

"We need to do a recon, sir," Barnes answered. "Get eyes on and go from there. That's like basic Ranger School stuff to me."

"What exactly does that mean, Barnes?"

"I mean, sir, it's a target," Barnes answered matter-of-factly. "I describe what I know, you decide if you need more info or if you have enough to execute the mission—or not execute, as the case may be."

Saber-Six narrowed his eyes. "What do you recommend, Mr. Barnes?"

People in the room shifted their feet. A line had been crossed. *Uh-oh ...*

Pancho looked at Cutter hoping for an intervention, but Cutter just stared at the map. *Dang, here we go, fight fans ...*

Pancho remembered back to the first time Barnes and Saber-Six crossed each other. Six months before, the day after Saber-Six took command, during a cultural briefing on Pathan religious traditions, Saber-Six said that Christian and Islamic fundamentalists were "essentially the same."

Barnes, the main speaker that day and a former Baptist minister, took offense and let the commander know it. Saber-Six made a flip remark, and the contretemps took off from there. Barnes asked Saber-Six about the condition of his soul. Saber-Six told him to go "right to h—." The ever-tolerant Everett Scott tried to get the briefing back on track by jumping in and remarking that technically the two fundamentalisms were quite different. He was ignored. It was too late. The train was off the track.

Barnes informed Saber-Six he couldn't go there because he was already saved, but Saber-Six still had a good chance of ending up there.

Saber-Six ordered Barnes out of the Bank and instructed his executive officer to "put all the religious nuts like Barnes on the next plane back to Tampa."

Pancho had to tell his new boss he was of the same religious fundamentalism as Barnes and "should he also get on the plane?"

A funny memory now, but the rancor between his commander and his senior civilian intelligence analyst never dissipated. Every tension-filled intelligence briefing had explosive potential. This one was about to blow.

"Sir, I suppose …" Barnes chose his words carefully. "I suppose I would recommend getting fresh eyes on the target. Put some surveillance out there to see what we have on the site."

"You mean like a Predator look?" asked the commander.

"If we can get one, but strategic recon would be better to observe the target over time."

"So, you are saying we should send someone in there?"

"I am saying, sir, I think we should develop the target."

"And you can confirm Azzam is operating out of there?"

"Yes, sir. That's his operating base, I …" Barnes paused and corrected himself. "*We* can confirm it."

"You know, Mr. Barnes," Saber-Six pontificated. "If the intelligence community had its act together, we would have found Bin Laden by now. We would have seen 9/11 coming."

Pancho noticed Barnes biting his lower lip. Saber-Six had touched the man's secret.

"Get me some actionable intelligence," Saber-Six continued. "So we can put our guys in place at the right time to terminate this target."

"Sir," Barnes added with a shake of his head. "We do know where Osama bin Laden is. He's in Dir. We've known that for some time."

"We've known that," Saber repeated mockingly. "Sure, we have, sure. Then why haven't we taken him out? Quit acting like you know something the rest of us don't, Barnes. If the intel community really *knew* where Bin Laden was, we could finish this thing and all go home."

Saber-Six paused for effect before continuing, "Tell me, then. If we know *so* much …" he inhaled through his teeth. "Tell me why we haven't taken him out yet!"

The former Baptist minister's narrowed eyes bore down on the commander before answering. When he did reply, his voice was low and controlled, each word carefully measured and enunciated.

"Because, Colonel," Barnes replied. "Our leaders don't want to take responsibility for that decision. It's too politically loaded. We would tick off our false friends in the Muslim world and our dainty, pearl-clutching electorate at home if we took it upon ourselves to cross into Muslim Pakistan to kill him. That's why we didn't chase him into Pakistan when we could at Tora Bora back in '01. Politics. And if we asked for permission first, somebody on the Pak side would tip him off and blow another opportunity. It will happen when someone thinks it's politically expedient to do so. Politically expedient for domestic politics, more than anything."

Barnes was out of bounds now, but his earnestness was tangible. Awkward silence followed. Saber-Six took a deep breath, sighed, and the tension evaporated.

"Okay, Mr. Barnes. What about this Azzam? Can we get him? Is Azzam a good target for a clandestine hit? And is he holding the kidnapped American in this compound?"

Barnes did not have time to respond. From behind the group, a deep, whiskey-scoured North Carolina drawl interrupted the exchange. "Colonel, this Azzam looks like a fine target to me."

Saber-Six turned. Pancho lowered his chin and chuckled. Here was the cavalry, come to rescue the briefing.

The gaunt specter in the motorcycle jacket and mirrored sunglasses was known only by his CIA nom de guerre, Twister. But Twister was a civilian equal to Saber-Six in rank and authority.

"I've seen the traffic on this target, and it looks like a great Cat Two opportunity. I don't need to know if there's an American hostage there or not. A Cat Two like Azzam is a perfect candidate for Prodigal Avenger. I recommend we work this one."

"Then we have Agency concurrence on this?" Saber-Six asked.

"That's what I'm saying."

"Then, gentlemen, that's all I need to hear," Saber-Six rose to his feet. "Let's put the finishing touches on a draft concept plan for Major Cutter. I'll take him with me on the C-5 in the morning, and we'll present it in person on my trip to Qatar. Pancho, I'll leave it to you to coordinate across the street with the CJSOTF."

Man! Poor Cutter ... and Saber-Six is as predictable as ever.

"Then this one is a go, sir?" asked Pancho.

"Azzam is our target. Plan and execute," he replied. "Of course, we need more confirmation on where the American hostage is before we add that aspect to the plan. We don't want to go there until we know his status. Is he with our target or not? We also need to develop the target as Barnes suggested. We need actionable intel, like a detailed human intelligence report, to confirm the missing information. If you get the info, Lieutenant Colonel Sanchez, then you make the call in my absence."

Pancho shook his head. Saber-Six had done it again in brilliant, non-committal bureaucratic fashion. Had he just given a command to execute the mission? Or did he tell them to make the plan tentative until there was actionable intelligence? Pancho suspected Saber-Six had done what he'd always done, left it up to Pancho to decide.

Pancho looked over at Jake Drecker. His friend wore his enigmatic smile. Was he pleased with the mission or amused by its ambiguity?

There was a flurry of activity as Saber-Six departed the operations center. His boss's poor handling of Barnes needed to be addressed, but there was too much to do now. Pancho talked to Major Cutter about the planning sequence for a full five minutes before he realized Jake Drecker had followed Saber-Six out the door.

CHAPTER 9

Colonel Lloyd "Saber-Six" Biggs

Saber-Six moved toward the hangar unaware he was being followed. About fifty yards from the Bank, someone called to him from behind.

"Sir, may I have a word with you?"

He stopped in his tracks, looked down at his feet and sighed.

"Yes," he turned on his heels. He stopped short. The commando, Jake Drecker. The one Pancho called "the Snake." *What now?*

Biggs stood a head taller than Chief Warrant Officer Jake Drecker but always felt intimidated by the smaller man. This was due to Drecker's intense, special operator personality—his confident, shoot from the hip professionalism and aggressive determination to beat all odds. Snake was a typical Tier One commando, the kind who seem to make up their own rules as they go. Even when Drecker was outwardly calm, Saber-Six could see intensity in the man's eyes. Those changeling eyes of Drecker's could be absolutely cold, placid, and devoid of feeling, then suddenly mischievous and mocking. Drecker was always sizing him up, like a chess player who is three moves ahead of an opponent—or a seasoned gambler with an impenetrable poker face.

Plus, Drecker was a warrant officer. Some weird rank above Sergeant Major but not really an officer. Saber-Six was vexed there was no Air Force equivalent to the Army's chief warrant officer rank, a technical expert whose leadership authority derived from superior experience and knowledge. Even in the rank-conscious Army, Saber-Six noticed officers and enlisted ranks both deferred to warrant officers like Drecker, treated them as semi-divine, and accepted their correction and scolding without complaint. Odd.

Biggs knew, deep down inside, that no matter how much size, rank, or flying experience he had shoring up his ego, a man like Jake Drecker would be unimpressed.

"Sir, I need to talk to you about the way you handled Mr. Barnes."

Biggs peered, started to glare, then realized he was wasting the look on Drecker.

"Sir, with all due respect …" Drecker continued.

Biggs knew, like every commissioned officer knew, the next line after a 'with all due respect' would be disrespectful. And there was nothing you could do to stop it.

"… your tone and attitude with our civilian analyst was completely out of line. I think you owe him an apology."

"Hah!" Biggs turned red and leaned forward, both hands on his hips. He cursed before rationalizing further. "And why should I? These overpaid civilians have a job to do, and I have every right to expect an answer to my questions!"

"Sir, operational recommendations are not the purview of the intelligence analyst. You are not going to put the weight for your decisions on a man who is doing everything possible to give you the best intelligence there is."

Drecker sounded mad, but his face was as impassive as a stone. Irksome!

"Chief, I am not going to argue with you about Mr. Barnes's responsibilities. I am sick and tired of civilian experts who can't give me what I need. And why is a washed up, religious nut on this team anyway?" Saber-Six surprised himself with his own anger, but he couldn't stop now. "That man needs to get back on the plane to Tampa! What in blazes is wrong with him?"

"Okay, sir, do you want to know why? Really?" Drecker's face tightened then shifted to a spooky sort of calm. There was danger there.

"Do you know," Drecker continued, "that Mr. Barnes is a former Army officer?"

"Yes, I know …"

"And you know he was a pastor back before 9/11?"

"Yes, what is your point, Chief?"

"Did you know that Mr. Barnes's son passed away?"

"No, I didn't, but okay."

"Mr. Barnes was a pastor back in Florida. Anyway," Drecker's voice was calm, steady, like he was sharing a story over a beer. Saber-Six's guard relaxed against his will. "He had a son who wanted to join the military."

Biggs sighed. "Go on."

"Mr. Barnes—Pastor Barnes—loved the military but discouraged his son from joining. He was afraid, after Somalia and all the crap under Clinton, that if his son joined the military he would die in some senseless, politically stupid little war somewhere. Barnes wanted the kid to be a preacher like him. Now his son, his name was Thomas. Thomas wanted a little more action than Florida so, with his father's blessing, he moved north to the big city and became a fireman."

"Why do I need to know all this?"

"Just listen, sir, I'm not done. Well, Mr. Barnes is happy as can be, still worried about his kid but hoping for the best, and then it happened. Something tragic, something that crushes Barnes, breaks his heart."

"Okay, I get it. His son died—happens all the time."

"Hang on, sir, let me finish. Barnes blames himself, quits the ministry, and volunteers to be a part of this work here in Operation Enduring Freedom."

"Okay, so what happened? Why does he blame himself? Tragedies happen all the time, that's life."

"Do you remember where you were on 9/11?"

"Yeah, I was still at the Pentagon. I was there when it was attacked."

"And I was at Fort Bragg, and Barnes was a pastor in Florida."

"Okay, so what?"

"But Thomas Barnes was in New York. He was a firefighter, and he was at the World Trade Center."

Biggs's eyes narrowed with realization as Jake continued. *Oh, God!*

"He was in Tower Two when it went down."

Biggs stared at Jake Drecker, at a sudden loss for words. But he felt compelled to say something, anything.

"Well, Chief, I didn't know."

"And that's why Mr. Barnes is here. For his son. And for us."

Biggs wanted to turn his face away from those eyes. He turned toward the late afternoon sun and noticed the same hardness in the Afghan hills to their west. He hadn't known this about Barnes. Hadn't cared.

"One more thing, sir."

Biggs looked back at the chief. Drecker's eyes were slate grey and blank in the fading light, his face as impassive as a sphinx.

"Yes, Chief."

"With all due respect, sir," the chief paused for effect, but Saber-Six already knew what was coming. "With all due respect, sir, you're way out of your league here."

With that, the commando turned on his feet, marched through the wire and back into the Bank.

Biggs watched him go then turned back toward the setting sun.

Which is true. He resumed his walk toward the hangar. *But I can't change that.*

Pancho

Back at the Bank, Pancho gave his closing instructions to the planners.

"You heard the Colonel, gents. We plan, we execute.

"Major White, let's get our priority intelligence requests fleshed out and into the system right away. You never know what might pop up. And I need the terrain table built over at the hangar. The rest of you need to crank out a concept of operations for Major Cutter to carry on the aircraft in the morning.

"Tomorrow night, we develop the concept and work out the infiltration plan. We can start team isolation simultaneously while we wait for the final piece of the puzzle."

"And what might that be, sir?" Cutter asked.

"A picture-perfect piece of intelligence that confirms everything else we think is true," Pancho replied. "An honest-to-God, credible, actionable intel report from a reliable warm body who has had eyes on Azzam and the American missionary. One who can confirm or deny that they are together, or not, and who can tell us *exactly* what is going on in that compound at Dir. That's what we need."

"Then we need a miracle," Barnes added.

"Amen, Mr. Barnes. A bona fide miracle."

Part 3

The Pakistani

CHAPTER 10

The Martyr Recruit

Shahid Rahmat Ali was a failed suicide bomber.

As he wiped black, sooty grime from each of the car's windshield wipers, Ali was thinking. He was confused. Doing well, but all was not well. He was alive, that was good. Had money, job security, and—most unexpected of all, a girlfriend. But it was at times like this, when he had information to pass to Colonel Pasha, his handler, he felt confused. It was the confusion of the double life, because in addition to being a driver for the leader of the Movement, Ali was a police informer.

It is the Will of God. Praise be to his name. He has brought me to this place, and I must do my duty even if I am unsure.

Ali had seen something both troubling and significant. Troubling because it could disrupt the complicated life of deceit he had become accustomed to living in the two years since 9/11. Significant because it involved the "special project," a high-profile terrorist kidnapping operation in which he was intimately entwined. If he failed to report it, he knew the Colonel would find out by other means. If the Colonel knew Ali had withheld it from him, Ali would surely die.

This special project was what brought Ali to Mardan. His organization had a package to deliver. Ali's job, as the Imam's most trusted driver, was to help make the delivery.

The package was a kidnapped American missionary. More than just a missionary. A missionary who knew secrets.

Ali did not know all of the man's secrets. But the man knew one vital secret that might cost Ali his life. The man knew about Ali and his double secret life. For Ali had confessed two things to the missionary—his secret life with the Imam and his secret faith in the God of the missionary.

Ali also knew the missionary as a real missionary despite his crimes against Islam.

The special project was the exchange of the missionary for money and prestige for the Movement to which Ali belonged. Prestige due to its perceived association with Al Qaeda.

Ali knew people were looking for the missionary. Dangerous people. Americans. The Colonel also and probably the whole Pakistani government. Even Al Qaeda wanted him. Yes, the missionary was quite a prize. And Ali was in trouble if the missionary confessed what he knew about Ali.

Ali was quite sure if the Colonel knew of his secret faith, he would make Ali's life as a police informer even more intolerable. Or Ali could die. But if the Movement found out anything about any of Ali's secrets, God forbid, there was no need to doubt—Ali would surely die. Painfully. Either way, if the missionary revealed his secrets, Ali was a dead man. Ali wished to change the events of the past two years that had brought him to this place. But it was not to be. This, apparently, was the will of God.

Back before 9/11 and the American invasion of neighboring Afghanistan, Ali was a simple car mechanic in Lahore, a Punjabi living at home supporting his widowed mother with odd jobs. He loved his mother, though she nagged him constantly about finding a wife.

But Ali was going nowhere. He was thirty years old, unemployed, unmarried, and with no sense of purpose or direction.

Then, on one fateful day sometime in late 2000, Ali met the Imam. The Imam led a small *madrassa,* a Koranic school, in the city and spoke to Ali about his duties to Islam. Ali knew he was a bad Muslim. This accounted for his failure to find a wife or secure a respectable job. So, he began to study with the Imam.

The Imam was a jihadist. He led a movement called the Pakistan Martyr Brigade which recruited desperate men like Ali for jihad. He spoke glowingly of paradise and the coming global Caliphate. He told Ali he could be a *mujahid* in Kashmir, leading younger men into battle against the hated Indian Army. He said that there were pious women in Kashmir who pinned their hopes on mujahid like Ali.

"By the will of Allah—merciful and compassionate—might there not be a future wife waiting for you in that place?" the Imam speculated. "Or maybe several wives? And if you are martyred, there are the *houri,* the voluptuous, lovely-eyed virgins of Paradise, awaiting on the other side."

The Imam's words were like so much candy for a man like Ali—sweet words that filled the ears and the heart with an overflowing desire to perform jihad. But although the Imam preached jihad against the Jews, India, and the West, he also plotted against fellow Muslims in Pakistan.

"Pakistan must be purified," he had preached. "Death to the traitor, Musharraf, death to Shi'ite heretics!" Heady stuff. And in Pakistan, it could get a man in trouble with the police ... *or worse.*

After several months, the Imam selected Ali for a secret mission. He would be a suicide martyr here in Lahore instead of a freedom fighter in Kashmir. This was a relief to Ali, a lazy jihadist, physically incapable of being a guerrilla fighter in Kashmir. He didn't want to experience pain or die, but he was sick of his life and his nagging mother. If he succeeded, the Pakistan Martyr Brigade would take care of his mother and the houri would take care of him. So, he complied.

The Movement's veterans took Ali and several other aspiring jihadists to a rundown warehouse in an industrial part of the city to learn the wonders of the suicide suit. The suicide suit was very fashionable among international terrorists. The one-legged instructor was a crazed Kashmiri veteran named Usman. Usman, leaning on a crutch, spoke to the recruits who were seated on the concrete warehouse floor. It was hard to pay attention. Two armed men were behind the group, pointing assault rifles at their backs.

"This suicide suit is a technological marvel." Usman lifted the suit above his head so all could see. "A battery-powered, plastic-explosive charged vest that fits under street clothes."

"The suit was designed by idolaters, a Hindu group in Sri Lanka called the Tamil Tigers. Infidels are clever. But we will use their own weapons against them."

Yes, it is the will of Allah!

Usman brought the vest down to his face, closed his eyes, and placed it affectionately against his left cheek. Then, looking at his eager charges, he held up for their attention a small, push button triggering switch.

"It explodes with the press of a button."

Usman squeezed the unconnected triggering mechanism for effect.

"Boom!" A crazed grin spread across Usman's face. "And if, by the will of Allah, you succeed in achieving martyrdom, the only identifiable part of your physical remains left will be your head. But you will be in paradise, my mujahedeen!"

"You will each don your suicide suit so you can become familiar with its feel under your clothes."

The weight of the explosive vest on Ali's body sent his heart racing. Sweat formed on his palms, his forehead, and ran down his spine.

I am wearing death.

In his training, Ali wore the vest under his clothes and walked around town. He needed to get comfortable with how it felt in case he was questioned by a policeman while on his mission. The batteries were removed for this training so he couldn't accidentally set it off (there would be no martyrdom glory in that), but he thumbed the push button detonator over and over again until he felt confident in its performance.

I can do this! I can succeed and be a martyr!

The training went on for a week, and then the suit was set aside. Now Ali would case his target.

The target was a mosque. This surprised Ali and added to his confusion.

"I thought I was going to kill infidels! Indians, Hindus, Jews, idolaters!

"Ali, this is an important mission." The Imam spoke in confident, reassuring tones. "Pakistan must be purified. It is okay. This is a Shia mosque. Shi'ites are heretics! Besides, most of the people at this mosque are foreign students or Baluchi's."

Ali's Sunni and Punjabi pride accepted everything. *Yes, it is better this way, praise be unto the prophet.*

Every day for a week, he went to the mosque with a mujahid named Abdul to conduct surveillance. Abdul had been to Afghanistan and Kashmir. Ali feared him even though he suspected Abdul was a bit of a liar about his exploits. *If he is such a mujahid why is he still alive? He should have been in paradise by now!*

The Imam told Ali that Abdul would be martyred with him on this mission.

On the day of the mission, a beautiful, pleasantly cool Friday in April 2001, Abdul and Ali rode in a taxicab together wearing their death. A fine day to be a martyr, the mild weather ensuring a good crowd at the target location.

They arrived at the mosque, exited the cab, and immediately separated. Ali expected Abdul to go around to the back of the block. Ali was to dart across the street, enter the crowd at the entrance, yell a slogan, and detonate.

Instead he froze. There were children near the entrance. A lot of them. He hadn't thought before about the children.

Out of the corner of his eye, he saw the taxicab had not left. Something was amiss.

The cab driver wanted his fare. Neither Ali nor Abdul had brought money. They were sanitized for the mission—no wallet, no identification, no money, not even a wristwatch! And Abdul had disappeared into the crowd.

The taxicab driver, a *Muhajir* from India, began cursing in a baffling multilingual babble of ... what? *English and Urdu?* He jumped from the cab and came around the back, shaking his fist and breathing down fiery threats.

Ali wanted to laugh. They hadn't thought about the cab fare. Martyrs don't carry money. Who needs to pay for a cab when one is on one's way to paradise? A mix-up, but nothing would stop this mission. There was only one thing to do. Fulfill martyrdom and consign this ignorant cab driver to the flames with all the rest of the heretics.

Ali ran in the opposite direction. An adrenaline rush erased all his scruples as he leapt over the hood of the taxicab and sprinted into the midst of the Shi'ite worshippers. He angled his body like a knife blade to penetrate the shoving, jostling, now-shouting, now-cursing crowd. He had failed all his life, but he could do this! He was a mujahid, a warrior for True Islam!

He stopped in the entranceway. The crowd pressed against him. He spun about and made eye contact with all who were near. He was in control.

"Look at me, you filthy Shia dogs!" he screeched in Urdu, "Prepare to die! Death to all heretics! Praise be to Allah, the merciful and righteous one!"

He crouched slightly, squeezed his eyes shut, steeled his body for the disintegrating blast and thumbed down on the detonator.

Nothing.

He opened his eyes. Everyone was frozen. He pushed down frantically on the detonator switch.

Nothing.

PRODIGAL AVENGER

Terror swept over him—*he had forgotten the batteries!* Two nine-volt batteries lay back at the safe house waiting to be loaded into the detonator.

The Shi'ite mob realized what had happened and grabbed at him from every direction. Fingers tore at his face, hair, and clothes. Evil oaths, wild punches, and spit covered him from every side. The game was up. He was a dead man but no martyr.

The cab driver's booming voice broke through and parted the enraged Shi'ite mob. Ali forced his head up as someone locked his body into a choke hold from behind.

"You low-life Punjabi scum!" the cab driver roared. The babbling, cursing cabbie struck Ali with a terrific body shot in the upper stomach.

Ali doubled-over, his arms still held from behind. A woman's foot came up and caught him right between the legs. Then everything went black.

CHAPTER 11

The Missionary House

Ali awoke with a start on a bed in an unfamiliar place. He jerked up to protect his face from further blows, but the motion sent paralyzing bolts of pain shooting around his chest and down into his arms. Then, he realized he was no longer in the street under the mob.

A man leaned over the side of the bed and gently placed a hand on Ali's chest, guiding him back into a horizontal position.

"Be still," the man said in Urdu. "You are too injured to move."

Ali looked wide-eyed into the face of a bespectacled Punjabi man with a small mouth and a graying, neatly trimmed moustache. The man was leaning over him with a concerned look. Then he sat down in a chair by the bedside.

"Pastor Loewenthal," the Punjabi man shouted in English, a language Ali recognized but could not speak. "He is awake!"

Ali sensed sincerity. *Why is this total stranger concerned about me?*

Another entered the room. A foreigner, European-looking, with pale skin, blue eyes, and white hair. The man grinned at Ali. Ali looked to his fellow Punjabi for support. This was too strange. The Punjabi only smiled back as if to reassure him. *What is this place? Who are these people, and what do they want?*

The European-looking man sat at the edge of the bed and greeted Ali using the traditional Muslim greeting,

"*As-salaamu Alaikum.*"

Ali was too confused to respond in the traditional way. "Are you a doctor?"

"Not really. But welcome to my home," the Westerner continued. "My name is Isidore Loewenthal, and this is my associate, Dr. Singh."

The man by Ali's bedside nodded. The foreigner's Urdu was very good. Perhaps he spoke Punjabi also.

"We have been waiting for you to awaken," the man went on. "Don't try to move, you are badly hurt. Dr. Singh tells me you probably have some broken ribs and a mild concussion. You are actually quite fortunate to be alive."

"Why am I here? How did you find me?" Ali rasped.

"We found you by the mosque. You seemed to have angered some people. My car was trying to get through an angry mob coming down the mosque steps. When the people saw us, they moved out of the way and there you were, battered and bruised, lying stripped to the waist, and left for dead in the street. Asghar, my driver, reacted quickly, or we would have run you over."

Ali panicked. He ran his hands down the blanket covering his chest. *The suicide vest is gone!*

Ali stared into the face of the foreigner. His blue-grey eyes seemed to draw him in, demanding attention. Yet they projected a tranquil sense of well-being. There was something about the way he spoke. Hypnotic. Magnetic.

"You appeared to be in some kind of danger from the mob. Christian compassion compelled us to take a risk, to take you with us before you became seriously injured … or worse."

Ali blinked. *What in the name of the prophet, praise be unto him, does this mean? I failed again? I failed to martyr myself? Marriage eludes me. Now martyrdom also? Nothing comes for me, not even death!*

The man continued.

"I suppose, being a western foreigner, the mob was too shocked at my sudden appearance to try to stop us. As we drove off, they became enraged and chased after our car."

"It is a miracle of God's grace that you were able to escape with Pastor Loewenthal," Dr. Singh added.

Ali nodded but said nothing.

"May we ask your name, sir?" asked the foreigner.

Ali swallowed. The dryness of his throat hurt, but he wanted to answer. "I am Ali."

"Well, Ali, as I said before, welcome to my home," said the foreigner.

"Are you a Britisher?" Ali asked.

The man smiled at Ali. Friendly. Ali felt himself relax further.

"No," the foreigner answered. "I am American."

Ali blinked back. He had never seen an American before except on television. He knew them to be very rich.

"And," the American added, "you are welcome to stay as long as you need to recover from your wounds. It may take a while."

"Thank you."

"The only condition we have is that we must share some things with you."

The American smiled again. Everything was going to be okay.

For the next several days, Dr. Singh tended to Ali's wounds and talked about his religion. He had converted to Christianity while studying medicine in the United Kingdom. This was an unpardonable sin for a Muslim, especially a jihadist like Ali aspired to be.

The conversation never seemed to vary:

"For God so loved the world, he sent his only begotten Son, Jesus Christ, to die for our sins!"

"But Allah has no son," Ali retorted.

"Exactly!"

"I don't think I understand."

"Our heavenly Father loves us," Dr. Singh explained. "Jesus Christ was like an ambassador, a representative of a great leader. He came to represent our Father in Heaven. His message was about the Father's love. The Father's love is expressed through the Son, Jesus Christ. If you know the Son and his love, you can know the love of the Father. Allah has no son, because Allah is not our heavenly Father."

"You are brainwashed by Christians!" Ali would charge.

"Changed. Yes, I admit it. Changed by Jesus. Ali, don't you believe God can change someone?"

"Allah can change anyone. Dumb question." *But Allah has not changed me.*

The American was busy, coming and going, going and coming. But he would always take a moment to stop, read in Urdu a verse from the Christian book or pray at Ali's bedside.

Ali's own father was not a man of love. The Christian's words about the Father's love were like trapped birds flying round and round inside

Ali's head. He could not get them out. "In my Father's house are many mansions: if it were not so I would have told you."

Infidel talk. Godless. Allah has no son. But this American. I should hate him, desire even to kill him. But I cannot. What is wrong with me?

The American's persistence was remarkable. He prayed by Ali's bed in the morning and read a Christian Scripture to him each evening before another prayer: "If you have known me, you would have known the Father also; and from henceforth you know him and have seen him."

Ali had an epiphany about the American. *The American is a missionary! I have heard terrible things about these people. They heal the sick and feed the poor, but then they take advantage of the people. Is this not true?*

The American told him a story of a prodigal son who ran away from home, wasted his inheritance, and then repented. Ali felt like the prodigal, like the story was about him. When the prodigal returned to his father, the father received him back with love and acceptance.

That cannot be true. What kind of father is like that?

"Why wasn't the father angry?" Ali asked. "He should have beaten the impudent son!"

"Because he loved his son and wanted him back just as God loves you and me and wants us to come home to him," the American explained. "God is your Father. He is a Father who loves you. Jesus is his Son who became your sin and died on a cross as your substitute. Jesus is like the goat the Imams slay on *Bakr-Eid* as a substitute for Ishmael. But Jesus is your substitute. Paying for a punishment you deserved. Jesus took it for you. Jesus is a door to the Father's heart."

Ali barely remembered his own father, an angry drunken man who beat his mother and died when Ali was a boy. *My father did not love anyone but himself. And I feared him, hated him.*

The words of the prophet Jesus, as read to him by the American, were haunting, "As the Father has loved me, so have I loved you."

After several days, Dr. Singh began asking Ali probing questions about his past. Ali was not sure how to answer.

"Dr. Singh, when you found me, what was I wearing?"

"You had only a pair of trousers. Your shirt was torn to shreds. You were barefoot."

The missionary and this doctor don't know about my secret mission!

"And," the doctor continued, "we wondered why you were attacked by the mob."

Ali's eyes raced around the room. *How to explain such a thing...*

"Were you in trouble, Ali?"

Ali clenched his fists and chewed his lower lip. "Something like that."

The American overheard. He slid a chair up to Ali's bedside next to Dr. Singh.

"Ali," the American's blue eyes probed deep. "Confession is good for the soul. Why don't you tell us? You must know your secret is safe with us."

Ali closed his eyes. Tears welled up and ran down his face.

"Maybe it would be easier if you started from the beginning, from your childhood," the American suggested. "Why don't you start from there. And tell us everything."

Yes. Yes. I will start from the beginning. Maybe they will understand then.

And so, he did. While sipping water through a straw, Ali began to tell his story. He soon forgot his fear, and the words poured forth. By the time he came to the part about his mission, the Movement and the Imam, everything was flowing.

The American and Dr. Singh never dropped their look of concern. Nor did they frown, scold, or judge. At the end, they prayed and asked Jesus Christ to forgive Ali. And that very night, Ali, for the first time in many long, lonely years, slept the sleep of the innocent.

Confession is good for the soul.

Ali's confession changed nothing. The American and Dr. Singh maintained their routine while Ali grew stronger. As his second week at the missionary house ended, Ali felt comfortable with the American. Could he entrust him enough for one small favor?

The American was sitting next to him reading from the words of the prophet Jesus, "And whatsoever you shall ask in my name, that will I do, that the Father may be glorified in the Son."

The American paused and took a breath. A propitious moment.

"Pastor Loewenthal, I need to ask then. For a favor."

"What do you need, Ali?"

"It's my mother. I have not seen her in many, many days. She is used to my being gone, but sometimes she relies on me for things. A few rupees here and there, food from the market. She lives alone in a small apartment. I need reassurance she is okay."

"It will be done, Ali. I have two older women in our Bible study your mother's age, I think. I can send them to check on your mother."

"When?"

"Soon. Trust me, Ali. We will make sure she is okay."

Ali closed his eyes. *Does my mother even know about this love of the Father?*

The next day, the American arranged to have two Punjabi Christian women visit Ali's mother. They brought her some food and money and arranged to meet with her again.

On the morning of the sixteenth day with the missionary, Ali spoke with his mother on the phone. At the sound of her voice, he broke. *I am a wretched son.*

That evening, the American missionary knelt to pray. As was his custom, he read a verse of Scripture, " … flesh and blood has not revealed it unto thee, but my Father in Heaven."

The missionary's spirit felt tangible. *Truthfully, these Christians are good people. Not at all what I have been taught.*

Ali interrupted the American's prayers.

"Sir, I believe I am a great sinner."

The American looked up, concern etched across his face.

"We all are, Ali, Dr. Singh, myself also, your mother included."

Ali winced. Despite her bitterness of spirit, Ali did not want to think of his pious mother as a sinner, like some common street woman.

"Allah has abandoned me here to you, I am sure of that."

"Has he, Ali? Your heavenly Father will never leave you nor forsake you."

Ali paused before responding. Disoriented. Conflicted. Convicted. *How to put into words this feeling?*

"I am persuaded that Jesus is more than a prophet," Ali said.

Dr. Singh, who had been dozing in a nearby chair, sat up.

"Is that all, Ali?"

"I am starting to believe that Jesus is God's Son," Ali added.

"But Allah has no son, Ali. What do you believe?"

"Sir, I think I am very confused."

"Ali, would you like to decide the matter right now?"

Ali paused. He looked at Dr. Singh then back at the American.

"No, sir, I cannot decide now. I think I must leave here and see my mother first."

The American missionary and the Punjabi doctor shifted their feet.

"When will you leave?" the doctor asked.

"In the morning. I feel strong enough now. I will be even much stronger by then."

"All right, Ali, we will pray for you to make the right decision. Now get some sleep."

Ali nodded, rolled over on his side but did not go to sleep. *What do I believe? I believe Jesus is very, very real ... and very, very near.*

The next morning, Ali ate breakfast with the two Christians and packed for his departure. The American gave him clean, western style clothes, a cloth jacket, and some rupees before sending him on his way. They offered to drive him, and Ali accepted.

At the elevator doors, the missionary held Ali's hand and prayed over him. Then they said their good-byes, and Ali departed with Dr. Singh and Asghar, the driver. A premonition. *It will be a long time before I will see this man again. God willing.*

This was the first time Ali had been outside of the American's apartment while conscious. So many westerners. So opulent and clean.

They took the elevator to the basement where the car was parked and climbed in. It was safe here in the back seat of the car, peaceful and strangely comfortable. Except for a troubling thought bubbling in the background. *What will I find when I return to my mother's flat?*

The car emerged from the basement into bright sunlight and paused as two security guards tilted the heavy steel security bar that served as the entrance gate. The guards, dressed in old Army khakis, saluted as the car drove past and onto the dusty, crowded thoroughfare. The car meandered through crowded, jostling streets. *I mustn't be seen coming from a car like this in front of my mother's flat.*

"Can you please drop me off in this park?" Ali asked as they drew near his mother's place.

Asghar glanced into the rearview mirror. Doctor Singh, in the passenger seat, turned in his seat. Both eyes bore concern.

"I think it would be better," Ali explained, "if I was not seen in public with Christians near my mother's home."

The two nodded. They understood. Ali's future hung in the balance.

Asghar pulled the car over to the curb, and Ali stepped out. Both Christians also got out and took turns embracing him. Asghar presented Ali with a package.

I know what this is.

He tucked the package into his shirt and kissed Asghar on both cheeks. He watched them reenter the car and pull away in a swirl of dust.

Ali turned and walked the road toward his mother's flat. Loneliness gripped him. The American possessed a father-like benevolence. The Roman Catholics called their priest, "father." But Dr. Singh called the American, simply "pastor." Pastor Loewenthal. Like the word for a shepherd. He reached inside his shirt and removed the package sitting next to his heart. He peeled away the paper wrapper and read the Urdu title in Arabic script, *The Holy Bible*. He opened the cover. Such words. He glanced upward. Mother's gray, lifeless shell of a crumbling public housing estate. How unlike the missionary's home.

He felt sudden lightness and then something new—*joy.*

There was a van parked in front of the building. Ali paid it no mind, his eyes focused on his destination, his thoughts elsewhere.

Across the busy boulevard, a man in a gray Mercedes sedan watched Ali through black aviator lenses. If Ali could have seen through the glaze on the front windshield, he would have seen the driver raise a small, hand-held radio to his mouth and speak a command. Seconds later, the doors of the van parked in front of his mother's flat exploded as four masked gunmen leapt out and knocked Ali to the ground. His face slammed the sidewalk as rough hands patted him down, secured his hands and feet, and picked him up. He was tossed into the back of the van, and two of the gunmen climbed in after him. A third jumped into the driver's seat and started the engine.

The fourth gunman, whose black ski mask and clothes bore no official insignia or rank, swept around the vehicle one time making threatening eye contact with any potential witnesses. People turned away, quickly going about their business. One man turned completely around as if to communicate, "I see nothing." Only some small boys stared from a nearby trash heap, seemingly immune to the man's fearsome gaze. But then they, too, gave way to their fear and ran off. The man jumped into the passenger seat, and the van sped off. As people watched it disappear, the gray Mercedes drove off in the opposite direction. The entire incident took less than a minute.

On the sidewalk where the van had parked, an Urdu-language Bible lay open where it fell, its hand-written, Punjabi dedication facing upward, towards heaven:

To Brother Ali,
May you find peace, trust, and salvation in the arms of your Heavenly Father who proved his love for us by sending Jesus Christ his Son to die for our sins. I am praying for you.
Your Brother in Christ,
Asghar

CHAPTER 12

The Agent Recruit

Ali awoke from a murky grey unconsciousness to find himself on another strange bed.

Where am I now?

Pain revealed itself to him. Head, face, ribs, forearms, legs. Everywhere. He tried to move an arm. Immobilized.

He glanced at his arms and down toward his feet. Strapped in. Like a … prisoner.

He sensed people nearby and turned his head. Pain in the neck muscles. In the gloomy darkness stood a man. Solid looking, in black leather jacket and full mustache. Ali turned the other way. A slight, young woman in headscarf and cloth coat.

Ali looked back at the man. The blue shirt of a policeman underneath that jacket and something with black straps. A shoulder-holster. *Perhaps I am a prisoner of the police.* He turned his attention to the woman. She was so beautiful. She leaned toward him and in the glow of the harsh light he glimpsed cream colored skin and soft, hazel-colored eyes. *Such beauty! Such eyes!*

"Ali, you finally awaken," the man spoke in Urdu.

Ali did not respond but looked at the woman again. *Lovely! Or perhaps I am dead? Is this paradise?*

Then a stab of pain pinched his upper torso. No, still painfully alive.

"Don't try to move," the man said. "You have several broken ribs and a concussion among many other injuries. You have been unconscious for some time now."

Ali tried to speak, but his throat burned. His tongue, dry and swollen, was unwilling to form words.

"Shush," the woman whispered as she pressed two fingers down on his lips.

Ali tasted something sweet against his cracked lips. The woman squeezed his forearm before withdrawing her hand. He had never experienced such a touch of affection from any woman before except his own mother. He tried to raise his arm in response but could not move.

"You are immobilized for your own safety."

Ali glanced toward the man as the woman stepped back. She was in the shadows and out of reach. The man spoke again.

"Allow me to introduce myself. I am Colonel Pasha. I am the policeman assigned to your case. The young lady is my niece, Jassi. You are in a special police hospital. You will remain here as a prisoner pending disposition of your case."

Colonel Pasha paused. Anxiety, frustration and hopelessness welled up inside Ali.

"Shahid Rahmat Ali," he continued. "You are charged with treason, terrorism, blasphemy, attempted murder, inciting a riot, and resisting arrest."

Ali trembled against the straps which held him captive. The brief shock dissipated as reality and fear set in. There were severe penalties in Pakistan for such crimes. The man reached into an inside pocket and removed several documents. He unfolded them and held them up so Ali could see them before continuing.

"Do you know what these are?"

Ali barely shook his head. He was not a good reader, only recognizing Arabic script. The words appeared to be in English letters.

"This is the state decision involving your case. You have already been charged in a special anti-terror court and condemned to death by hanging."

Ali's eyes grew large. Too much happening at once. Can't breathe. *Death by hanging? My God!*

Ali looked at the ceiling, then at the woman. She sobbed, face downward, lifting a tissue to jab at the corner. *Why is she crying? I am the one who should be crying!*

Colonel Pasha threw the papers down on Ali's chest. They felt heavy, too heavy. Ali began hyperventilating. His broken and bruised ribs burned each time he inhaled. He tried to lift his chest so the papers would fall off of him, but he could not move. A jackhammer headache began to pound behind each eye.

Colonel Pasha finished. "I must go now. May Allah have mercy on your soul."

He turned on his heel and withdrew from the circle of light around Ali's bed. The steady martial beat of his footsteps faded in the dark.

Now, Ali began to cry. His eyes sought for the woman and her apparent sympathy. She leaned out of the darkness and wiped his dripping brow with a damp cloth.

"It will be fine," she sobbed in Punjabi. A single wet tear fell from her cheek and dropped onto the papers. The effect was devastating. Ali needed this surrogate mother to comfort him in the darkness of his misfortune.

"I'm here for you, Ali," she whispered.

"Thank you, thank you," he croaked through cracked lips.

She removed the papers from his chest and placed them out of sight somewhere over his right shoulder. When she turned back, she held a needle.

"This will help you relax."

She inserted the tip into his IV and something icy entered his bloodstream.

She is an angel ... an angel sent by God.

Then, the fog rolled in.

The next time Ali awoke, Colonel Pasha was again standing by his bedside. He appeared to be reading a newspaper and took no notice that Ali was awake. It was still dark all around except for the circle of light from the fluorescent tube over his bed.

This is hell. I am in hell.

He considered his situation more clearly. His hands and feet were held down, his forearms strapped to the iron rails of the bed, and his feet pinned to the corners. Tubes ran under the sheets. He strained to see if the woman, Jassi, was close by, but he saw nothing in the dimness.

Colonel Pasha glanced toward him.

"The doctor removed your catheter and many of the other tubes last night. Today, you will be permitted to walk around and eat."

The colonel turned toward the foot of the bed and made a side-to-side gesture with his head. In response, a giant in a blue hospital uniform stepped into the circle of light at the foot of the bed. Colonel Pasha glanced back at Ali.

"Let me introduce to you Sergeant Khan, your hospital orderly."

Ali gasped at the thickly muscled Khan with the closely-cropped hair. *This Pathan giant will kill me.*

Khan nodded toward Ali.

"*As-salaamu Alaikum,*" Ali croaked with a replying nod of his own.

The giant said nothing. Ali's hands trembled and his chest seized. Something terrible was about to happen.

"Today you will sign your confession paperwork," Colonel Pasha informed him. "It is a minor but necessary bureaucratic requirement."

Ali nodded, his eyes locked on the intimidating giant.

Khan's eyes were black and close together. Ali sought for a flicker of humanity in the giant's face but there was nothing. Just an emotionless, dutiful attentiveness. Pasha's attack dog, patiently awaiting a command from his master.

I hate these swaggering monsters. These mountain-dwelling Pathans. I am like an insect in this one's eyes.

Sergeant Khan began to remove the straps which bound Ali's feet. Ali felt suddenly hopeful and smiled.

Maybe I am going to be allowed to get up. I was looking forward to walking again.

But instead of freeing the legs, the giant grabbed the ankles roughly and bound them to each other and then to the iron rail at the foot of the bed.

What now?

"You will sign your confession?" the colonel asked. A rhetorical question.

Ali bit his sore covered lower lip. *What do I say?*

Colonel Pasha glanced toward the giant and nodded. Sergeant Khan stepped back and reached behind him. Suddenly, he slashed a length of bamboo against the flesh of Ali's feet.

Ali screamed as a bolt of pain raced up his legs into his lower back and into the base of his skull. His body arched upward in a vain attempt to lift itself off the bed. Every chest muscle contracted. Broken and bruised ribs sent additional volts of pain into the base of his skull. He strained against his wrist bonds sending additional torturous currents up fractured arms and shoulders. He screamed until he ran out of energy and was reduced to great sobs of self-pity.

Colonel Pasha nodded toward the giant again. The sergeant restored Ali's legs to their original position then stepped backwards into the gloom. Colonel Pasha looked down at Ali.

"Death by hanging requires a detailed interrogation of the convicted beforehand. The Islamic Republic cannot afford to simply execute terrorists without extracting information that might preserve the state and protect Islamic society. Do not think that you will be treated any differently. It is true that there is a possibility for a parole in some special cases."

He paused before continuing. "But there is no parole without confession."

Ali squeezed tears from his eyes. He was unsure how to respond. Too many whirling thoughts raced around his brain.

Why is this happening? Where is the Heavenly Father the American missionary spoke of? Where is the prophet Jesus, praise be unto Him? God, save me ...

Colonel Pasha went on.

"Might I also add there are no possibilities for Paradise for one who betrays the Islamic Republic and its sharia law. You will be tortured, executed, and dispatched to a fiery hell."

With that, Colonel Pasha turned and walked back into the shadows. Ali was left alone, whimpering, despairing of life.

I am lost again. So lost.

He laid still and eventually managed a fitful sleep.

Hours later, Ali awoke to the touch of a damp cloth running along his forehead. *Jassi.*

He tilted his head up to speak, but she silenced him.

"Shhhhh, don't talk, don't move," she commanded as she placed two fingers to his lips. For a moment, he caught the sweetness of her fingers.

His head fell back against the pillow. His body ached, his feet were on fire, and his tongue was thick with dryness. She brought a cup of cold water to his lips. His parched tongue received it graciously. Most dribbled down his chin where it left its cool wetness around the neck of his hospital gown.

She gave him another shot of painkiller and proceeded to feed him chips of ice. He summed up the courage to speak again.

"Why are you helping me?" he asked in a low tone.

She blushed and looked away.

"I must not say," she replied.

"But your uncle, the policeman … I am accused of crimes."

"My uncle does not know how often I visit."

"But how? You are a virtuous woman, people must know …"

"My uncle is a dangerous man. And a smart man. But I am as his daughter. I have many privileges, and I am somewhat indulged by him. It is okay."

"Why are you helping me?"

She looked him in the eye.

"You are a noble man, such a mujahid," she whispered. "I suppose you could call it something like love."

Ali closed his eyes. This was unreal. The whirling fog of confusion filled his head. He opened his eyes again, but she seemed far away.

"You can be paroled, Ali. Please don't let my uncle have you killed."

He nodded. His vision began to narrow. It was the painkiller. He tried to say something more but it slipped away.

For the next three days, Ali was alternately tormented by Sergeant Khan and comforted by Jassi. He slept little, ate little, and only left the ward to relieve himself under the aid of Sergeant Khan and a battered wheelchair. The wheel chair had English letters on the seat, "Donated by the Rotary Club of New Haven, Connecticut, USA."

The sessions with the sergeant were mercifully short but unforgettably painful. They usually followed a visit from the Colonel in which a peculiar point of his legal case needed to be reinforced. He began to associate the Colonel with pain and found himself wanting to stay on his good side.

Jassi's charms were varied and included obtuse words about love and parole. She asked him to never leave her, a concept he could not even comprehend. With her head on his chest, she would lay the palm of her hand flat against his stomach and hum Punjabi lullabies.

When apart, he yearned for her. And impure, sexual thoughts troubled his soul. When together, he felt consumed by frustration that he could never reach out and hold her.

I have never known a woman like this. Only my mother. This is like a television drama but real.

Real. But shared with the Pathan. The pain giant. Khan.

Khan's hands worked their own kind of intimacy. Moments of yearning, desire, and desperate frustration with Jassi interrupted by sheer terror with Khan. Ali's mind twisted with the agonizing, mind-bending, cycle of torture, longing, and shame.

I no longer know who I am. Why I suffer. Or why I live.

How long had this lasted? Three days? Four days? A week? Time ceased to mean anything in this dark place.

Ali broke.

"I will sign. I will confess. Please, please. I will not stray again. Please have mercy on me. Parole, imprisonment. Anything!"

Pasha smiled. And nodded toward the foot of the bed. Khan emerged into the circle of light. *No!*

"One more time." Pasha sniffed. "To reinforce the lesson."

"Noooooo!"

Pasha disappeared, and Khan put his rough hands on Ali again.

He rolled his head. Jassi was nowhere.

He clenched his eyes shut. *The last time! The last time!*

Pain and then indeterminate blackness.

He awoke in blackness. No light. No Khan. No Pasha. *No Jassi.*

Only God knew how much time passed before Pasha returned. Meanwhile, Ali slept fitfully.

Bright lights came on, piercing Ali's eyelids. He woke with a start. Not the spotlight this time but ceiling fluorescents, some dim, some sputtering, but bright after the darkness. He scanned around the room. Dingy, whitewashed walls stared back at him. A large mirror and steel door dominated the wall to his front. A large room and all his. His own private place of perdition.

Pasha entered while another lurked in the doorway. The colonel smiled as he picked up the conversation where he'd left off before.

"Your confession and parole are approved. But there are conditions," Colonel Pasha explained. "You will be appointed a state attorney. You will report your activities to an assigned police case officer. You will sign a statement promising to never become involved in religious extremism or conspiracies. You will receive a small stipend to perform certain reporting activities for the police."

One of the lurkers, a short, fat bearded man, now entered the room. His *sherwani* and red *fez* gave him the formal, scholarly look of a *mufti*.

"Ali, this is Dr. Faisal, your state appointed legal advisor and an expert on Islamic law."

Dr. Faisal smiled and tilted his head toward Ali. "Salaam."

Ali said nothing. *What do I believe? Only that I am lost. I have lost my soul, God help me.*

For the next forty-eight hours, Dr. Faisal led Ali on a marathon lecture through the byzantine world of Pakistan legal history. He started at the beginning, when Pakistan was just a dream. The Muslim leaders of India, he said, dreamed not only of their own separate homeland but also of a purer form of Islam that, "in the words of the great poet Muhammad Iqbal, would rid itself of the stamp of Arabian imperialism." Ali learned of his duties to the Islamic State, its need for secular institutions, and the religious and legal implications of extremism.

Ali grew weary of the repetitious lectures but never complained. He dutifully repeated certain phrases. Swore oaths to ideas he did not understand. Signed documents he could not read. The lessons helped him. His time with the Movement had been a mistake.

The Imam lied. Pakistan does not need to be purified. Pakistan is the Pure Muslim State. Many non-Muslim Pakistanis have assisted Pakistan in the wars against their great enemy, The Republic of India. Therefore, Pakistan Muslims must be patient with nonbelievers for the sake of national unity. I will be a good Pakistani citizen.

From time to time, Ali caught a glimpse of either Sergeant Khan or Jassi orbiting in the shadows just outside the circle of light.

They are there to remind me to heed Dr. Faisal's instruction.

During the course of the lectures, Ali confessed many secrets to his handlers. He told all he knew of the Movement, the Imam, and his own involvement. The Colonel and Dr. Faisal took many notes. He began to feel comfortable telling them things, but he hadn't mentioned the American missionary yet.

One day, the Colonel brought a visitor. A tall, broad man in a white, collared shirt opened at the neck and tan sports jacket. He was round-faced, brown-haired, balding. His eyes hid themselves behind black sunglasses. A westerner.

"Ali, this is my friend Mr. Ajax. He is American. He is here to help us rid Pakistan of the corrupted Islamic extremism you have unwittingly participated in. He will accompany me during some of our meetings."

Ali grinned. *Another American to help me! How strange is the will of God? Perhaps it will all be all right after all!*

Ali couldn't hold back. "I … I know an American … he helped me!"

Mr. Ajax's face was unmoved, but Pasha betrayed his surprise.

"An American? What?" Pasha looked to the American for unspoken guidance. The American folded his arms but said nothing. Pasha seemed to catch hold of himself and continued. "When? Do you mean before your act of terror or after?"

"He … he gave me medical care in his home … he was a … a …" Ali felt unsure how to explain his relationship with the missionary.

"A doctor?" Pasha suggested. Mr. Ajax remained as silent and unmoving as a stone.

"Yes, yes, he was a doctor." Ali was a poor liar.

Pasha moved to Ali's bedside and placed a large hand on his forearm. Mr. Ajax unfolded his arms and put his hands on his hips. The black sunglasses revealing nothing.

"I suggest you tell Mr. Ajax and me all about your relationship with this American doctor."

Ali's eyes widened. *I have made a mistake … Mr. Ajax is not like Pastor Isidore.*

Ali looked around. Sergeant Khan in the doorway.

"Go back to the beginning, Ali. Tell us about your American friend. Everything." Pasha squeezed hard on Ali's forearm. "And keep in mind, to protect your identity as police informant, you must never mention your relationship with either myself or Mr. Ajax to any foreigner either. In the future, avoid your American friend and any others for that matter. Failure to do so means a resumption of your original death sentence, do you understand?"

Wide-eyed and trembling, Ali bit his lip and nodded. *Why couldn't I keep my mouth shut?*

Eager to please, Ali told Colonel Pasha and Mr. Ajax everything he knew about the American.

PRODIGAL AVENGER

Ali was a poor liar, but Colonel Pasha was not. Nor was Jassi. Ali would have been disappointed to discover Jassi and Colonel Pasha had their own secrets. That Jassi recorded everything they shared in their intimate moments on a tape machine back in the shadows. Or that Colonel Pasha was not really a policeman but an intelligence officer with the dreaded Pakistan Inter-Services Intelligence organization—better known as the ISI. Nor could Ali know that his beloved Jassi was not really Colonel Pasha's devout, overindulged niece but an ISI recruiter. Furthermore, he would not want to know that pious Jassi was from a secular establishment family in Islamabad, had attended university in the United States, and was carrying on a love affair with a German businessman named Hans Richter. He could not and would not ever know the truth about these things. Then again, Jassi had no way of knowing that her lover, Hans Richter, was really one Benjamin Cohen, a Mossad agent from Haifa. Deception is a cruel master.

On his final day in the hospital, Colonel Pasha woke Ali early and briefed him on his next moves.

"You will be provided with a set of clothes and a cover story about your whereabouts during the last two weeks."

He showed Ali two newspapers.

"Fortunately for you, we were able to insert these stories in the newspapers," the Colonel continued. "You are being treated as an unnamed suspect who attempted to blow up a Shia Mosque. Your identity is unknown to the authorities. You are believed to be dangerous, and a police search has failed to find you. Such a story may earn you some respect from your former associates. The Imam has a man named Abdul watching your mother's house. He has orders to bring you back to the Movement or, if you refuse, to kill you."

Ali swallowed hard. His fate might be in the hands of the cold-blooded liar, Abdul. Colonel Pasha continued.

"You will be placed in a hospital managed by a Roman Catholic society called the Sisters of Perpetual Mercy. It's the Saint Thomas Children's Hospital in Lahore. Have you heard of it?"

Ali hadn't but nodded nonetheless—anything to please the Colonel.

"The lead nun is a European named Sister Beatrice. We have a special arrangement with her society. To ensure their protection from religious extremists, the nuns perform certain services for the State. In this case, providing cover for the time you disappeared after your criminal, terrorist actions.

"You will be transferred to their hospital this evening and remain until contacted by Abdul. An undercover police agent will pass a message to Abdul that you are in hiding at Saint Thomas and recovering from your wounds. He will find you, and Sister Beatrice will lead him to believe you have been there since your escape.

"You will return to the Movement and reestablish yourself with the Imam. It would be in your best interest to earn back his confidence while refraining from personal involvement in terrorist incidents that jeopardize the delicate religious and ethnic balance of our secular, Islamic Republic. I will be in contact with you again shortly."

Ali understood. He was a police informer now.

"And if I fail?"

"You will be shot."

CHAPTER 13

The War on Terror

The September 11, 2001, attack on the United States changed everything.

On the day of the attacks, Ali was in a Movement safe house in Lahore. He was scheduled to stand before the Imam the next morning to give an account for his failure at the Shia Mosque. He expected to be rebuked and humiliated before the others. And killed. Ali feared for his life.

Then the news reports came in. America had been attacked. Ali, Abdul, and the others at the safe house sat gleefully transfixed by the images on the international news network. Throughout the surrounding slum, there was dancing, shouts of joy, men kissing men, and rifles fired into the air. Al Qaeda had struck into the heart of everything the Muslim world resented about the decadent West—its power, its wealth, its smug grandeur, and its confident love affair with life.

The next day, Ali reported to the Imam still expecting the worst. But things had changed. The Imam was in a celebratory mood and welcomed Ali with a kiss. Ali was regarded as a hero now, a man of cunning who outwitted the secular authorities. His failure was attributed to the inscrutable will of Allah. All was forgiven.

Later, in a room full of aspiring mujahidin, Ali watched the television news reports. American experts blamed Islam. Especially Al Qaeda, the Movement led by the Emir, Osama Bin Laden. But how could that be? The Americans and Osama Bin Laden had worked together to help drive the hated Russians out of Afghanistan! An analyst on the Al Haqiq News Network had a different opinion.

"The Jews did not show up for work at the World Trade Center on September 11. We all know why. The Israeli Mossad spies destroyed the Twin Towers to force America into war with Islam!"

Ali nodded his head. Not that it mattered. September 11 restored Ali's usefulness to the Imam. That was all that mattered.

In six months, Ali was promoted to driver in the Movement. He was a skilled mechanic who, thanks to the covert assistance of his government handler, possessed an uncanny gift for circumventing security checkpoints. The Imam took note of Ali's ability to talk his way out of situations involving the police while avoiding the customary inconvenience of paying bribes. Ali became one of the Imam's personal drivers.

He even enjoyed a reputation as a bit of a lady's man. He was sometimes observed, with a bit of irreverent awe, sitting on a park bench in the company of the beautiful and ever pious Jassi. In the Movement, Ali was a winner among the losers. He had found his jihadist groove.

Ali's secret life, the one the Imam knew nothing about, was also doing well. Ali provided Colonel Pasha with excellent intelligence. Jassi was the intermediary between them, the honey-scented carrot on Colonel Pasha's heavy-handed stick. Ali's sentimental obsession with her made his double agent lifestyle tolerable, as did his salary. As a police informer, Ali was qualified to have his mother taken care of by the state. And he had money now, not much by some standards, but more money than he ever dreamed of as a common mechanic.

American forces invaded neighboring Afghanistan and removed the Taliban supermen from power—a setback that spilled across the border into Pakistan. The Northwest Frontier Province was flooded with refugees, many eager to return to fight the hated Americans. Among them were the Arabs, Al Qaeda fighters from around the world whose allegiance to the mysterious Bedouin, Osama bin Laden, caused them to follow him to a new base of operations in the mountainous tribal areas of Pakistan's Northwest Frontier Province.

Things changed for the Movement as well. The Imam grew ambitious for a piece of the action. He preached more and more on the future, glorious Caliphate that was emerging from the ashes of global jihad. But until it did, the Movement needed the power and resources that came by association with Al Qaeda. From this seed thought, the "special project" sprung—the plot to sacrifice a kidnapped western hostage on the altar of association with the dreaded Al Qaeda network of terror.

That was how, on this hot September afternoon in 2003, Ali ended up in Mardan, washing the Imam's car, preparing for a drive north on Highway 45. A branch of Al Qaeda was waiting for them at the Chukyatan Bridge, about seven kilometers south of the city of Dir. And it was very hot, indeed.

Ali looked toward the back of the gray Mercedes.

The trunk was open, and one of the guards was sitting on the rear bumper.

He wanted to look in and see how the missionary was doing, but he was afraid.

What if he recognizes me and makes some kind of a sign? What if he tells them about my time with him?

The way Ali understood the Imam's special project, they were to kidnap an American, a Britisher, or a Jew and turn him over to Al Qaeda up on the border in the Northwest Frontier Province. Al Qaeda was paying generous rewards to anyone who could get them a good hostage. Just as long as the Pakistani government didn't find out.

Which makes it even more dangerous for me. Where will it all end?

Ali hadn't seen the missionary's face. Heard the name. Saw the picture in the newspaper. Bandied him about like a piece of oversized luggage wherever the Imam wanted to take him. But the guards kept the man blindfolded and bound. Yet, Ali knew it was him.

For two days, they carried their cargo west to Peshawar, where a statement was released that an American CIA agent named Isidore Loewenthal had been kidnapped to stand trial for crimes against Islam. It featured a blurry photograph of the missionary holding a current copy of the *Dawn*, Pakistan's largest English language daily newspaper. The Pakistani government was embarrassed, but people like the Imam and his followers rejoiced.

Ali was torn. The missionary was no CIA agent. He wasn't like the grim-faced Mr. Ajax. Now Colonel Pasha was looking for the missionary. The same missionary he'd been warned to avoid to the point of death. The same missionary who could expose Ali to the Imam if tortured. Yet, the missionary was a just and innocent man. The whole thing was wrong.

So the mighty Imam promised to get a CIA or Mossad agent for this Arab, Abbas Bin Azzam, the leader of Maktab al-Khidamat. But all these fools managed to do was kidnap a kind, harmless American missionary who walked with a limp and helped poor Muslims who were left beaten in the street by other Muslims.

Ali shook his head in disgust.

Oh, how I long to run off with Jassi and escape the pressure of this double-life!

Ali reminded himself of his duty to the State. Of Jassi's veiled promises. Of Colonel Pasha's naked threats. If the Imam only knew. And the missionary. He had performed such good works. Miraculous works. How the love of Christ compelled this foreigner, this infidel, to stop and help him when he should have been left to die like a dog in the street. *Such a love was not human!*

The Imam emerged from the house where he had finalized arrangements with their contacts in Dir. He barked instructions, and his two guards lifted the old American from the trunk of the Mercedes and stood him on the ground.

To Ali's relief, the hostage's face was completely covered. *If he is blindfolded he can't recognize me. My secret will be safe.*

"Place him in the back of the Land Rover," the Imam instructed. "Abdul and I will ride in the Mercedes with Ali. We will take the lead. You four will follow with the American in the Land Rover. If Allah doesn't intervene and we are somehow stopped and the police inspect your vehicle, we will leave you to your own devices. It is the will of Allah, bless his holy name. If we are separated, you will return to this location to await further instructions."

Ali winced as he watched the others roughly manhandle the compassionate man who had once called him "brother." He opened the door for the Imam, but his mind was in a different place. *I need to stop this somehow. What can I do? I am at the mercy of my past.*

He came around the back and shut the trunk, his eyes still following the missionary.

The guards pulled down the hatchback of the Land Rover. The missionary was instructed to sit knees to chest in the small cargo space. One guard opened a bottle of water then, before Ali realized what was about to happen, a second guard pulled the sack off of the man's head.

For the first time since he'd left the missionary's apartment, Ali saw the face of Isidore Loewenthal, the American missionary who had saved his life and taught him about a heavenly Father and his Son, Jesus Christ.

Ali swallowed hard as he watched a guard pour water on the sweating missionary's head then force the end of bottle into his mouth. The missionary's hands were still bound. The poor man was like a child at the hands of the guards.

As Ali stared and the Imam cursed at him to hurry, the missionary turned and looked at him. Time froze.

The missionary's eyes locked onto Ali. Something powerful and intangible passed between them. A burden, a deep sadness and—despite betrayal—an understanding love.

He knows me.

Ali blinked back tears as the guards placed the burlap bag over the man's head. The missionary's compelling gaze disappeared under the coarse, brown material. Ali exhaled as tension left him. Through it all, the missionary had neither smiled nor frowned. He'd spoken not a word. Ali's secret was safe with the man who'd once saved his life. *But I betrayed him.*

Ali turned back toward the car and the Imam's withering glare. He did not care if the Imam was in a hurry. The Imam was never satisfied anyway. He started up the vehicle, pulled out in front, and began the northbound journey through the mountains to their rendezvous with destiny at the Chukyatan Bridge.

For the first time, Ali knew what he would do.

Colonel Pasha sat in a car in Peshawar drinking Coca-Cola from a bottle and trying to keep his eyes open. It was three in the morning, still and dark, and his contact, an opium addict named Armaan, was late. One of his special cell phones buzzed.

"Salaam," he answered.

"Salaam, Colonel, I need to talk."

"Okay, first things first, who is this?"

"Colonel Pasha, it is I, Ali," Ali replied in a hoarse whisper. He spoke a coded recognition signal.

"Yes, Ali, how are you? Jassi tells me you are back in the tribal areas on a job."

"Colonel, I cannot talk very long. I have to tell you what this job is about."

Colonel Pasha said nothing. Ali was a good informer, but his information had grown increasingly mundane. He sometimes wondered if Ali was still worth his informant wages.

"Colonel, are you still there?"

"Yes, Ali, go ahead."

"We have him."

"Have 'him'? Okay, you have who?"

"The American."

"The American?" Colonel Pasha repeated the words, the thought not yet sinking into his head.

"The kidnapped American, Isidore Loewenthal, the one on the television. The one we call the CIA agent. He is here. We have delivered him to Abbas Bin Azzam in Dir Province."

"Wait, Ali, speak slowly." Colonel Pasha shook his sleeping partner in the passenger seat. He put the call on speakerphone and took out a notebook and pen. "Okay, Ali, let's start from the beginning. Tell me everything."

And Ali did.

PART 4

The Concept

CHAPTER 14

Pancho

Pancho didn't expect an answer to prayer so soon.

Saber-Six and Cutter departed with the basic concept plan. The initial excitement had evaporated as they waited for their elusive missing puzzle piece. But nothing met Saber-Six's ambiguous requirement for actionable intelligence. They busied themselves going over the same details again and again.

Pancho stepped outside to get some fresh air and shake off the dankness sunk down into his bones. The sun felt good on his face. He turned around to let the sunshine warm his back.

Oh, that feels good on my back. Thank God, it's only early autumn. Hate even the thought of another winter here.

A gentle breeze carried away the musty stink of the Bank that permeated his clothes and fogged up his brain.

A hot shower, some fresh coffee and a six-month vacation would do it. But then what would I do with myself? I'd be bored in days.

Someone called. He took a deep breath and went back inside.

It was Barnes.

"Sir, we have an answer to one of our priority intelligence requests this morning," he said, pointing at Major White.

White handed him the report.

Pancho skipped the details and scanned it for the highlights. This was good news indeed. He shook his head in disbelief at the providence behind it all. "So we have a Pakistani border-crosser prisoner in friendly hands up at Nari who just happens to be a member of the MAK-PAK terrorist organization. And who may be able to confirm both our target's exact location and the possibility of the American hostage."

"So it seems."

"Unbelievable, good work. This is almost too good to be true. How soon can we pick his brain?"

Barnes answered. "Way I see it, we have two options. We can put some questions into the system and let the on-site team do the interrogation or we could request they transfer him back here as soon as possible so we can do it here."

"Or …" Jake added from across the room. "We can send a team by helicopter and get him ourselves."

"Who would I send?" Pancho tilted his heard toward Jake without taking his eyes off the report.

"I'll go."

Heads swiveled toward Jake Drecker.

"I can't allow that, Jake." Pancho handed the report back to Barnes, folded his arms and looked at Jake. "I need you to prep your team."

"But I speak Pashtun and Punjabi. I could start picking his brain in-flight or find out on the ground if he's worth our time."

"Might not be a bad idea, sir," Barnes interjected. "We can't send any teams anywhere without actionable intel."

Pancho shook his head and exhaled. "That's Indian country, men. That forward outpost gets hit every other day. Too risky."

"So who are you going to risk that's expendable?" Twister, arms crossed, leaning in the doorway.

Pancho winced at the CIA operative's poor choice of words. Didn't even realize he was in the room. *But he's right, I need someone I can risk but who can get the job done. Guess this is why I get paid the big bucks.*

"Sergeant Olmos, get Lieutenant Snow on the horn. Tell him we need two of his most capable Rangers to go out to Nari and pick up that prisoner."

"Okay, sir," one of the staff sergeants picked up the landline to the Quick Reaction Force hanger.

Pancho scanned the giant wall map in search of Nari when Twister interrupted his thoughts. "I need to send one of my guys on the pick-up."

"Because … ?"

"Because if you're gonna send your bluecoats into Injun country, I wanna send along my Apache!"

"You want to send Apache on this prisoner pick-up?"

"Why not? My company has a vested interest in the success of this mission. Apache is one of my best guys."

Apache was a CIA contractor. Or mercenary if you preferred.

"Your 'company,' yeah," Pancho smiled at Twister's euphemism. "Okay, fine."

"And me too." Jake added.

Pancho looked at Jake. Drecker was heavily invested in this operation, that was for sure.

"I don't think it's wise to send a clandestine asset outside the wire like this. Don't want to screw up your cover."

"But no one can even see my face when I'm under cover. What good is my cover if I can't operate in the clear for stuff like this? Besides, in my role as a JSOC liaison officer, I need to see what our assets are doing up north. This is a great opportunity."

"He's got you there, Pancho," Twister chuckled.

The idea had occurred to him. He let it reverberate around the inside of his head for a few seconds. "Ok, you're on. Contact Nari and let them know we are sending some guys to pick up this prisoner. Jake's in charge. Call the JSOTF and see if you can rustle up a DAP bird with room in the back for our team to fly you up there. A little extra firepower might come in handy."

The command post came alive as everyone talked and moved at once. Pancho turned toward the map board again to look at the outpost in Nari, in Taliban-infested Kunar Province.

A prisoner. Wow, unbelievable. It really sounds too good to be true!

CHAPTER 15

Major John Avery

Major John Avery eyed his Pakistani prisoner with a mixture of contempt and curiosity. He was the proverbial fish-that-almost-got-away. Avery hoped he'd be worth the trouble.

Here was a Punjabi Pakistani border-crossing, smuggler-cum-messenger boy, a bit far from his home town in Islamabad. His name, Falah, meant success. He didn't look successful, having been on the losing end of an encounter with one of Avery's A-Teams. Falah was dressed modestly in what Avery's men referred to as a "filthy nightshirt"—a soiled, off-white, straight-cut men's *shalwar kameez* with matching brown pants and waistcoat. He wore a tan *pakol* on his head, the ubiquitous Macedonian hat that was introduced to the country by Alexander the Great's army nearly three thousand years ago. He'd lost his AK-47 and stylish, antique Russian web-gear (which contained exactly three empty magazines for the AK). And his bandaged right arm was in a sling having been broken in two places by 5.56 x 45mm NATO ball ammunition. The poor, miserable sod lay at his feet writhing in pain.

Then there was the other fact they'd discovered. They'd dragged Falah up to Arundhu for Avery's monthly meeting with his counterpart, a major in the Pakistan Border Guards. Falah wasn't just a common smuggler. He was a member of a homegrown Pakistani terror group that was trying to get into the big leagues by trafficking in kidnapped American missionaries. That was what made Falah such a fine catch.

What a shame if we had turned him over to the Paks.

"Hey, Nolan. Get this guy some MRE crackers and water. I'm tired of listening to his simpering. What's he crying about now?" Avery was a competent Arab linguist but spoke no Pashto or Punjabi. Falah spoke little

English and that with a thick accent. Thank God they had an interrogation team on hand with a bonafide Pakistani-American contractor to pull answers from the poor wretch.

Avery's team had snatched Falah coming across the border. Avery assumed he was a low-level Pakistani smuggler. He intended to turn him over to his Pakistani counterpart during their monthly meeting as a gesture of cooperative good will. But their contract linguist, a college student from Saint Louis named Lahda Maan, picked up on something when they arrived at the meeting. Some Pakistani border guard VIP, a colonel, expressed an undue interest in Falah. Avery's Pak counterpart let slip that the prisoner was a courier for an outlawed Pakistani group called the MAK-PAK, and the colonel wanted to personally interrogate him. Nolan remembered there was an outstanding priority intelligence request in the system for information on the MAK-PAK and alerted Avery. Avery agreed to let the colonel interview their prisoner but not take him into custody, which ticked off the Paks, but US interests reigned supreme in Avery's mind.

So, they were back at Outpost Nari, waiting for a team from Bagram to arrive and secure their prisoner. Falah writhed on the ground with his broken arm close to his body all tagged up and ready for transport.

Avery took out a small notebook and scribbled.

Weekly situation report time. Let's see …

Winning hearts and minds continues at a blistering glacial pace due to the fine work of our overextended and under-resourced Civil Affairs weenies and engineers. The medical team reports our platoon of friendly ethnic Tajik Afghan mercenaries are all in good shape except for needing their usual daily dose of VD shots and parasite pills. And Intel reports that despite the best efforts of our allies across the border, our Taliban neighbors still manage to make the daily trek over the mountain with fresh recruits and overzealous Al Qaeda volunteers eager to test fire their new weapons on Outpost Nari. Not a problem as long as airstrikes were available now and again to remind them who was in charge.

Avery held no illusions as to his small task force's ability to really win the locals to their side. After all, some of those jokers coming over the hills were family.

The radio squelched outside the front of his command post.

"Hey, boss. Got comms with our prisoner escort guys. A team of Marine interrogators are coming down the road now for him."

"Sounds good, Nate." Avery turned toward Nolan. "Blindfold him and bring him down to the road. I'm gonna go greet our Marines."

"Ay, ay, Captain," Nolan snagged a camouflage bandana from a hook to wrap around the prisoner's face.

Avery grabbed his M4 and sauntered out the door. He squinted in the late afternoon sunlight and took a deep breath to clear his head from the dampness of his command post. A faint mixed scent rose up from the valley. Pine and sewage.

This terrain ... so much like Big Bear Lake, California. Like Boy Scout camp and winters snowboarding the San Bernardinos. Except for the sewage smell and the killing.

He put on his ballistic sunglasses and trudged down toward the main road coming up from the valley. The Marines' khaki-colored Humvee kicked up dust as it approached. *Strange.* Usually helicopters did the pickup.

"Hey, sir, how's morale?" The Marine driver pulled his goggles off and up over his Kevlar. A captain with about five-days growth of beard. *Odd.* A bearded Marine Corps Captain Humvee driver.

A sullen sergeant slumped in the passenger seat, his M-16A2 resting on the window frame pointing outward. Another Marine in the back seat, and a fourth one sticking up out of the top hatch manning a Mark 19 grenade launcher. Everyone and everything covered with Afghan dust. The headlights and bumpers were covered in dark, olive-drab hundred-mile-an-hour tape.

"Couldn't be better, Captain. You the prisoner escort?"

"Yes, sir," The captain pulled a glove off his right hand and extended it toward Avery. "Epstein. Captain Brian Epstein, US Marine Corps. Operating out of the joint interrogation facility in Bagram. We were just conducting some field interrogations down in Asadabad when we got the call. We were heading back today, so it's good timing for us."

Avery reached in and shook his hand.

"Major Jack Avery, US Special Forces. Welcome to Outpost Nari. Unfortunately, the pool is closed for the season, or I'd invite you all in for a drink in our poolside lounge."

Epstein chuckled. The rest of his men remained silent, the Marine in the turret scanning the hills, the sergeant in the passenger seat staring straight ahead and the Marine in the back seat, a young, black lance corporal with fine, narrow facial features like a Somali or Ethiopian, blank-faced in dust-covered goggles, betraying no emotion whatsoever.

Quietest bunch of Marines I ever saw.

"Hmmm …" Avery continued. "You guys got some guts to be driving around Kunar province in this rig. We were expecting some guys from Bagram to come in by air. Seen anything along the way?"

"Oorah, sir. Not today. The bird got delayed, so we took the call. We figured this was a job for intel. You special operators got better things to do than escort prisoners to the rear."

"That's probably true," Avery said. "Your guys like having an officer drive?"

Epstein laughed. "I'm a mustang. I was staff sergeant in the Gulf War before taking a pay cut and going to OCS to become a second lieutenant. They don't seem to mind."

Avery smiled. Epstein sounded like he was from the East Coast, maybe Philly or New Jersey. He'd met his kind before. They always got along well with their men in the field but were too rough around the edges to go far as officers.

There was a sound from behind, and Avery turned to see Nolan manhandling the prisoner down the trail. Ladha, their Pakistani-American interpreter, trailed behind.

Epstein backhanded the sergeant in the upper arm, and he jumped out of the vehicle. The lance corporal followed. They opened the hatchback and pulled out duct tape and zip ties to truss up their catch just the way they wanted him.

The lance corporal put a medical kit bag on the ground and began to rustle around inside. He soon produced a syringe and checked the contents. Meanwhile, the Marine sergeant grabbed Falah by his broken arm and pulled him toward the vehicle.

"Ahhhhrrrgggghhh!"

"Hey, go easy with this guy. His arm is broken!" Nolan yelled as he stepped over and grabbed the sergeant's shoulder.

Everyone froze. It was as if some obscure breach of protocol had just occurred.

Epstein broke the spell. "Forgive him, sir. These kids are all a little nervy."

They sat the prisoner down and duly injected him.

Avery turned and frowned at Epstein.

"It's a bumpy ride back there, sir," Epstein explained. "That morphine will put him to sleep."

They wrapped duct tape around the prisoner to immobilize his arm, zip tied his ankles together and trundled him into the back of the Humvee.

Avery had more questions to ask Epstein about what must have been a pretty hairy journey by Humvee to their outpost, but an explosion followed by a hissing sound interrupted his train of thought.

"RPG!" yelled the Marine on the Mark 19 just as the B40 rocket passed over his head and exploded up the hill.

Everyone hit the ground as the Marine turned his weapon toward the RPG's firing point. Another explosion erupted followed by a hiss as a second B40 passed over the hood of the Humvee and exploded thirty meters up the hill.

"Ahhh, I'm hit!" Ladha clutched at his shoulder as a red stain began to spread down the front of his desert camouflage top.

"Gotta go, major! See you on the other side!" Epstein gunned the engine and the Humvee lurched forward. Avery jumped up and helped Nolan grab Ladha and his gear and pull him to safety behind a boulder. Up the hill, one of Avery's men was firing the .50 cal out across the river. Small arms fire was coming in and going out. The Humvee executed a tight k-turn and roared back down the road in a cloud of dust, the Mark 19 gunner adjusting and firing all the way through the turn.

Crazy Marines, hope they get that prisoner back in one piece.

Avery checked out his wounded interpreter. A piece of shrapnel had passed through the meaty part of his shoulder—but he would be okay.

"Hear that, Nolan?" he asked the interrogator.

"What, sir?"

"No more RPGS, no bad guy mortars, just small arms. I'm making a run for the command post up the trail. Put a patch on Ladha and stay with him. I'll send a medic down." Avery tapped Ladha on the cheek with his gloved hand and smiled. "You did good, kid. I'll put you in for a bonus when we get back to Bragg."

Ladha managed a pained smile.

Avery took off running. Occasionally, an ineffectual round zinged by him. These Taliban attackers were obviously too far out of range for effective fire. Radio chatter, the confused voice of O'Neil and some pilot blared from the command post. He assumed O'Neil was calling for air support. Avery grabbed his binoculars and scanned the enemy.

There were about a dozen fighters on the hill across the river. They were nearly five hundred meters away. No wonder their fire was so ineffective. A dark cloud blossomed from a stand of trees from which emerged the smoky tail of another hissing B40 rocket.

"RPG!" Several people on their perimeter seemed to yell it at the same time.

This time the B40 hit the sandbags piled along the easternmost part of the outpost.

"That was close," Avery thought out loud.

"Blackhawk coming in!" yelled O'Neil. He had a helicopter lining up for a gun run on the hill.

"Send her in!"

CHAPTER 16

Jake

Jake Drecker was told before leaving Bagram that the Special Forces B-Team on Outpost Nari was expecting them. But fifteen minutes out, he was on the radio with a very confused Green Beret radioman who informed him the Marines had taken custody of the prisoner and were on their way to Bagram.

Jake shook his head.

The radioman broke off the call to request close air support, as they were under attack.

Jake leaned over to speak directly into Apache's ear. It felt too loud and tight in the back of the MH-60L, an assault aircraft that wasn't meant to carry many troops.

"There's no prisoner here. These guys already sent him back to the rear with some Marines."

"Say what?" Apache released a string of profanities as Jake tuned back in to the conversation between the pilot and the team on the ground.

Looks like we are going in.

The co-pilot switched to intercom and explained the situation. They were going to do a couple of gun runs over a hilltop just east of Outpost Nari. And they weren't landing, because there was no prisoner at Nari.

Apache shook his head and swore under his breath.

He glanced at the two Rangers who'd come along for security.

"Sorry, guys," he shouted over the noise of the Blackhawk's powerful twin turbine engines. "Some kind of miscommunication. We don't have a prisoner, just a gun run to watch."

The two gave Jake a thumbs up. They were all smiles.

Rangers.

PRODIGAL AVENGER

The MH-60L followed the Pech River at a dazzling speed. When they reached the Kunar, they turned toward Outpost Nari and did a flyover.

The world rushed past the open door of the Blackhawk in an exhilarating blur. Not quite like the pleasant illusion at high elevation when the helicopter could be flying just as fast but appear to be suspended in the air, seemingly motionless but for the vibrations of the rotors and the breeze blowing past and through.

As they neared the outpost, they had front row seats to the action beneath them. On Outpost Nari, men were scrambling around like ants. A few looked up and waved, but most were focused on their task at hand. The enemy position was toward the east, across the river about five hundred meters away. To the south, Jake glimpsed a Humvee engulfed in dust, racing away from the action toward Asadabad. But, then he focused on a hilltop across the river.

Suddenly the mini-guns opened up and began chewing up the hilltop. Shimmering brass shell casings fell in twisting clumps from the guns to the earth below. A roar and a deep-throated hiss interrupted the zipper-like mini guns as Hydra 70 high-explosive rockets spurted from their pods. The hilltop erupted.

The helicopter moved cautiously over the target, a predator examining the carcass of a once dangerous foe. Scattered, lifeless bodies littered the hilltop while ant-like men scurried for cover. The enemy's position was neutralized. For now.

"Hey, chief," the pilot said to Drecker. "We have to pick-up a wounded man down on the roof of the outpost. We're gonna hover, not even stop long enough to properly land."

"Sounds good," Drecker replied.

Ten minutes later they were on their way back to Bagram—a pleasant flight. Lahda had never flown in a Blackhawk before.

CHAPTER 17

Pancho

"Still no word on what happened to that prisoner?"

Major White shook his head.

Twenty-four hours since the fruitless trip to Outpost Nari, and the prisoner was gone. Poof! Into thin air. Everyone in the Task Force, including elements from every conceivable special operations and intelligence organization, was mystified. A follow-up call to Avery gave them no answers. The joint interrogation center at Bagram had never sent any Marines to Asadabad or anywhere else in Kunar Province. They'd contacted Marine Corps elements all over the theater to see if they had had anyone in the area. Their requests for information came up empty. Avery gave a detailed description of Captain Brian Epstein and his men. There was no Marine Corps officer with that name in all of Afghanistan. The CIA element was frustrated. Apache's raspy, whiskey-tinged voice engaged Twister in a heated discussion just outside the Bank entrance.

Pancho picked out pieces of their conversation. Despite the spirit of cooperation between their organizations, Pancho was often suspicious of Twister's motives. The CIA often used "sheep-dipped" military men as clandestine operators, men who wore a uniform and were on the military payroll but were secretly sponsored by their real employer, the CIA. You never knew if a contractor or a Marine Corps officer like "Captain Epstein" wasn't one of those operators. An old CIA trick to stay on top of their rivals in the rest of the government was to use this kind of deception to stay one step ahead of any intelligence triumph—for the sake of the Agency.

Pancho sat pondering the problem when his thoughts were interrupted by Everett Scott. Scott, the gifted young intelligence analyst was also an Agency man.

"It could be something else, sir."

"What's that, Scott?"

"An ally or a third-party nation, someone else who needed the same intelligence we do about the MAK-PAK."

"And who might that be, Scott?"

"It could be a British intelligence agency like MI6, although we are already sharing most of our intelligence products with them. They may think we are giving them old or sanitized intel and want to get some firsthand information from one of our sources.

"Or it could be someone more hostile who has their own agenda, like the Russians. Avery said it was mostly Epstein who did the talking. Maybe the others didn't know how to talk American English."

"Seems a bit far-fetched to me, Scott." Pancho paused. Everett and some of the Task Force contractors were CIA. "Are you covering for your own agency?"

The young analyst seemed put-off by the comment for a few seconds.

"No, sir. Although, truth be told, I am not privy to everything our Plans people are up to. That's Twister's area of expertise. There is another possibility."

"What's that?"

"Israelis."

"Israelis? In Afghanistan?" Pancho shook his head. "I think I heard that come up before, but it's more far-fetched to me than MI6 or the KGB."

"But it's still possible."

Pancho studied Everett Scott's eyes. Were they sincere? Or duplicitous? Surely, if Twister's crew wanted to keep the military out of their clandestine ops business, then sending a winsome, good natured analyst like Scott along to deliver their "psyop" deception message was the surest way to divert their attention.

"Sure, Scott, sure. But in the meantime, find me that actionable intelligence we've been looking for to take down our target, okay?"

Everett Scott, his eyes meeting Pancho's, paused before answering. "You got it, sir."

Pancho stood and stretched. He needed a good cup of coffee and a quick run to get the blood flowing in his brain.

"I'll be back in an hour, gents. Let's do that updated concept brief when I return."

Heads nodded.

CHAPTER 18

The Plan

"Did you know that Kabul is found in the Bible?"

Everett Scott was talking about the Afghan capital. The Task Force Pancho planners and operators huddled around the field table in the Bank, sipping coffee and studying the mountain routes into Dir. A twenty-four-hour news network played silently from one screen while an overhead image of their target glared down from the other.

"Actually, I did know that," Jake answered.

Pancho glanced at Jake, one eye-brow arched up in surprise and then back at Scott.

"I didn't know that," Pancho interjected. "Where is it?"

"In First Kings, chapter 9, verse 13," Scott continued. "Solomon gives Hiram, King of Tyre, twenty cities in Galilee as a gift for helping to build Solomon's Temple. Hiram visits the place, is disgusted, and calls the area there Cabul, spelled with a 'C' in our translations, which literally means good for nothing."

"No argument there," Pancho added, thinking of the Afghan capital.

"So, let me guess, this is part of the *Bani Israel* theory also?" Barnes asked.

Pancho rolled his eyes and chuckled. Bani Israel, the so-called lost tribes of Israel. One of Scott's on-going obsessions which provided fodder for many a slow night's bull sessions in the Bank. Scott was hung up on Hebrews in Afghanistan, that was sure.

"Only because we know in the Pathan legend a son of Solomon named Afghan founded their race. They were probably from Galilee. When the Assyrians conquered them, they were transported to eastern Afghanistan where they named the first city they found, Cabul, 'good for nothing', which became phonetically spelled Kabul on the first English maps."

"So, the Pathans are Jews?" Pancho asked trying to keep a straight face.

"Technically no, sir," Scott answered. "Jews are descended from the southern kingdom of Judah and include people from the tribe of Judah, the Levites, and those from other tribes who joined with Judah after the Assyrians destroyed Samaria. The Pathan are *Bani Israel*, children of Israel but not of Judah."

"Okay, Scott," Jake interrupted. "Enough with the history lesson, what's this got to do with that point you were making about the *Mossad*?"

Pancho could almost hear the young analyst's brain reverse gear as he got back on point.

"Yeah, well, not necessarily the Mossad. I was thinking of a clandestine Israeli military capability called the *Mista'arvim*. Mista'arvim are special operators from units like the Israeli Defense Force's *Duvduvan* counter-terrorism unit. They perform clandestine reconnaissance, sabotage, and assassination in Islamic countries."

Pancho rubbed his beard like a sage. "Wow, an Israeli Prodigal Avenger program!"

"Right. They work with Mossad, but they are strictly military. The Israeli Defense Force likes using newly immigrated Jews who still have dual citizenship for their Mista'arvim units, because there's better hope of plausible deniability if something goes sour. Plus, they are darn good undercover operators. Mista'arvim teams keep tabs on the heartbeat of the Muslim world while living among Semitic peoples in North Africa, the Middle East, and in Asia."

"That's pretty incredible," Pancho said.

"And true, sir. They are particularly active among Bedouin Arabs and Palestinians but also among other culturally similar people with whom they possess supposed 'crypto-Hebraic' roots like the Pathan, the Ethiopians, the Kurds, etcetera. I think we have evidence of an Israeli Mista'arvim team in our operational area."

"And those are the guys that saved RJ and stole our prisoner?" asked Pancho.

"Yes, sir. That's what I think. When you consider the nest of Islamic extremists hiding along the frontier here that the Israelis would love to monitor, it seems plausible."

"The Israelis have a philosophy like ours concerning the dead, wounded, or missing in combat," Barnes added.

"What's that?" Scott asked.

"No man left behind," Jake interjected looking toward Barnes.

"Right, 'Never shall I fail my comrades,'" Barnes said, quoting from the Ranger Creed.

"According to the team debrief," Jake went on, "RJ was convinced one of the shepherds who rescued his team spoke Hebrew."

"And English with a New York accent," Barnes added.

Jake nodded and continued. "RJ worked for nine months at the US Embassy in Tel Aviv in 2000 and again right after 9/11. He speaks both Arabic and Hebrew. If anyone could recognize Israeli Hebrew, it's RJ."

The room went quiet, each planner deep in thought. Jake added one more tidbit.

"The American missionary has dual citizenship with Israel."

Pancho's eyebrows arched. "Really? Was that on the news? First I've heard about that."

"Hey, sir," interrupted Major White, seated in one of the side rooms where the deployable intelligence support team kept their computers and printers. "This is incredible analysis and all, but I know, as a fact, we have absolutely no operations in this theatre with the Israelis."

Pancho thought he caught Jake letting slip a brief, enigmatic smile. *Wonder what he's thinking?*

"Someday we'll be able to just send drones all over the place to take out people instead of risking special operators," Scott smiled. *Ever the techno-geek. Classic.*

Pancho sighed. Time to get focused on the task at hand. "This Israeli thing is a distraction. Until we hear otherwise, forget about the Mista'arvim."

"Yes, sir, but look at Master Sergeant Jenkins, sir," White persisted. "These Israelis, or whatever they are, nearly killed one of our teams and have possibly compromised our intel on this new op ..."

"Listen, Major," Pancho raised one hand as he interrupted. "Just get your machines cranking, and get me our own actionable intelligence!"

He nodded at Jake, who rearranged the map on the field table to brief him. Pancho leaned into it.

"The plan is simple. The mission—infiltrate Pakistan, neutralize the target, Abbas Bin Azzam, and return undetected. Azzam is code named Black Cat.

"Dir Town is located here. Code name Tombstone. Tombstone is seven kilometers north of the Chukyatan Bridge, code name London. Black Cat resides in this fortified compound just off the highway we call Campus.

"Team Condor is the surveillance team consisting of sniper observers, Eason and Ritter. And Mitchell, for security and communications.

"Team Condor performs covert reconnaissance to develop the target and determine Black Cat's routine at Campus. They'd then pass their intel to Team Owl and bug out of Pakistan undetected. Or, if preferable, Team Condor can execute the hit at Campus.

"Team Owl is Gino, me, and Jannat. Our job is to take down the target either at Campus, on the road, or in Dir. Team Owl enters Pakistan legally, establishes a clandestine operating base at safe house named Maverick here in Dir, and waits for the situation to develop. They also perform local reconnaissance for a hit on the road or in Dir. Team Owl infiltrates via Highway 45 north, observes the target location from the east, and then proceeds to Maverick at Tombstone. After the hit, Owl hides out in Maverick until it's safe to return.

"Maverick nominally belongs to a Pakistani agricultural concern known to lease the house to employees. A contract authorizing Mustafa Khan, aka Gino, to visit area fruit orchards as a representative of the concern is waiting at Maverick. That, along with a backpack of rupees for the occasional *baksheesh* to grease palms along the way, gives Owl cover and access to the numerous farms south of Tombstone.

"Mustafa Khan will take a particular interest in the poorly harvested orchards surrounding a fortified compound at the last curve in the highway just before the bridge at London.

"We got lucky due to an unusual feature of the Koh-e-Hindu Kush mountain range here. We have a place where the Pak-Afghan border points several miles into Pakistan directly at Dir."

Jake had no notes and briefed entirely from memory. Pancho always found this remarkable.

"Like a dagger," Scott interjected.

"Right," Jake continued. "Like a dagger. Anyway, this gives us additional range for our operations and means flying less than twenty kilometers through Pakistan airspace."

"Give or take," added Scott.

"Right," Jake went on. "Give or take. We'll insert our sniper-surveillance element, Team Condor, via helicopter using one MH-47 escorted by a DAP. We can enter Pakistan airspace up over this mountain vicinity, Natay Kelay, on the Afghan side. The landing zone for the insertion is only about fifteen kilometers inside—a pretty quick ride through masked terrain."

"What's the altitude constraint on our MH-47s?" Pancho looked around. CW4 Rick Parker, a tall grey-haired pilot from the elite Nightstalker Regiment, stood near the front of the crowd. He wore a woodland camouflage flight suit with a huge, black Kimber .45 ACP with customized rubber grips holstered in his chest harness. He was looking down at a hand-held GPS displaying the same map area as the FALCON VIEW map on the wall display. "Given the size of our team, will that twelve-thousand-foot range pose a problem?"

"It shouldn't," the reticent Parker answered. "We've done it before."

"It will be a hairy ride," Barnes added.

"But doable," countered Parker.

Jake continued, "Team Condor traverses overland and conducts a three-day surveillance from the western ridge overlooking the compound. Eventually, the target leaves the fortified compound, and Team Owl makes the hit. Or Team Condor's sniper-observer team might take down the target from its hilltop site."

Jake also went over some contingency options.

"Team Owl can laser-guide a Hellfire missile from a Predator onto the target. But if the missile disfigures Azzam, confirmation will be difficult and would also kill innocent bystanders, like the American hostage, if he is in there."

Jake frowned. Pancho detected frustration.

"Although the contingency is doable and easy, I don't like it," Jake explained. "It violates the spirit of our clandestine modus operandi. Prodigal Avenger operations are meant to terrorize non-state actors like Al Qaeda with a simultaneous display of American omnipotence and plausible deniability. That means a surreptitious hit, one attributable to anyone or anything—a blood feud, a jealous husband, criminal elements, or the mythological, omnipresent CIA or Mossad agents, even credit to the Pakistani Army—anything other than American military operators. The terrorizing chaos of the unknown."

Pancho scanned the room. Everyone had nodded at Jake's last comment. *Good plan. Like the covert sniper-surveillance piece, like the clandestine hit piece, the flexibility, the mystery. Still needs polish. And some miracle intelligence. Because no one knows for sure what or who is inside that compound.*

"Okay, team," Pancho snapped to his feet and faced his planners. "I'm with you on this, but we need more actionable intelligence on the target, so let's get those information requests into the system."

Pancho felt inspired, his infectious smile spreading across his broad, bearded face. A thought popped.

"We're gonna call this puppy Operation Screech Owl. From the Mexican proverb, *Cuando el tecolote canta, el indio muere.*"

"What's that mean, sir?" White asked.

"'When the owl screeches, the Indian dies.' But for us, it's '*Cuando nuestro tecolote canta, el terroristo muer*', because when our Team Owl screeches, the terrorist dies.

"Okay, gents, grab some quick chow, and let's meet back here in ninety minutes."

The crowd in the room immediately broke into smaller, loudly murmuring groups discussing different details of the plan.

Pancho excused himself and stepped out into the gathering darkness. The sun had dropped behind the western hills, and a late summer chill swept across Bagram. He looked toward those western hills as he walked past a guard and through the coils of concertina wire surrounding the Bank.

This place is beautiful.

Something nagged at him. Felt wrong. A missing ingredient. Not just the intelligence. Some invisible force, like the current in the middle of a river, was pushing him along.

This bad-boy is coming together fast. And not a glitch in sight—except for the most critical intel piece. Why in God's name are the CIA, Saber-Six, and Jake Drecker all in such a hurry to execute this puppy when we are missing such a vital piece of the puzzle as the whereabouts of a kidnapped American who might be with our target? What's the hidden agenda I'm not seeing?

Am I paranoid? Or cynical? Better watch myself. Besides, there were always hidden agendas.

"Hey, Pancho, got time to talk?"

Pancho turned at the sound of Twister's familiar voice. Gino Salvetti was with him. Both wore cargo pants, motorcycle jackets and side arms.

"Sure, Twister," Pancho replied. "Anything for my friends at the Agency. Let's take a walk to my B-hut, I've got a coffee pot waiting inside."

No one spoke as they strolled along the runway.

Like a trio of miscast bikers in a spaghetti western.

The thought make him chuckle inside.

CHAPTER 19

The Ranger LT

Lieutenant Randy Snow caught Jake Drecker at a table in the mess tent staring like a Delphic oracle at a vision on the surface of his soup.

"Hey, Chief! How're things going?" asked the younger man.

Drecker looked up.

"Oh, sorry, Lieutenant. Just thinking. What's going on with you?"

Snow set his tray down and took a seat.

He watched Drecker continue to stir and blow across the top of the murky liquid, his eyes downcast. He caught a glimpse of something in the chief's face. The look of a man plotting the next move? He knew Chief Warrant Officer Drecker was a key planner for some of the deepest, darkest stuff in the war. Snow also knew that was none of his business. He kept his discussions with the chief on the professional level, without probing too dark or too deep.

"Nothing much, Chief, same old stuff, different day," he said. "Thought I might pick your brain for a spell."

Snow spoke a blessing over his food. Then he began to lazily chop at a piece of meatloaf with the side of his fork. Drecker looked at him, put his spoon down, and tilted his chair back. Class was in session.

"Go ahead, Lieutenant. You got something specific on your mind?"

We both do. He stopped eating and made eye contact.

"Yeah, I do. It's my wife."

"Sounds like you need a chaplain, not me."

Snow smiled. "No, I mean, she sent me a couple of interesting articles about Iraq. I wanted to get your take."

"Ah, yes. Our president's muddled, mission-accomplished operation. Quite an operation, but hardly accomplished. Go on."

"So, I was wondering, Chief. With all your experience, do you think we are going to win this war, or are we looking at Vietnam all over again?"

"You sound like some twenty-four-hour news pundit interviewing a Pentagon spokesperson. You mean in Afghanistan or the whole enchilada?"

"The war on terror. Here and in Iraq."

Drecker stared at a distant point in the mess tent just beyond the lieutenant's shoulder.

"Well, Lieutenant. I think we can."

He paused before continuing.

"Let me ask you this, Lieutenant Snow. Did we win in Vietnam?"

"No, Chief. I mean, we lost the war, but we won most of the engagements."

"What about Somalia or Bosnia?"

"Somalia—no, I guess, for the same reason. We beat them in every battle. We're still in Bosnia too, and I guess we are still here."

"Well, we can never win a war we don't fight to win."

"Okay …"

"And why do you say we won most of the engagements in Vietnam and Somalia?"

"Well, I mean, kill ratios and all that, we came out a winner at the tactical level in both."

"But we didn't win, so we must have lost."

Snow greeted the idea with a stunned-mullet-in-the-bottom-of-the-boat expression.

Drecker continued. "The Israelis have been fighting a war on terror for over fifty years. Most of us know about their battlefield operations, their technological edge, and if you can accept it, their sense of national destiny and purpose. But they also have a very aggressive clandestine strategy of hunting down key terrorists wherever they live—including in supposedly neutral European nations that turn a blind eye to anti-Israel terrorists living in their midst. That's the kind of aggressive counter-terrorism we need to win this war."

Drecker slurped soup.

"What about respecting their religion?" Snow asked.

Drecker shook his head. "You're a Christian, right?"

"Yeah, Chief. Baptist."

"Okay, and I am a Jew, non-practicing. We believe in freedom of conscience, that you can believe what you want to believe and I can believe what I want to believe. Our society is compartmented. We can look at things both secularly and religiously. We are conditioned by democracy into thinking everyone understands that. Like it's an innate, even God-given mindset. We think everyone wants to be that way. We even think that's why Muslims immigrate to our country, to enjoy our liberty."

"OK." Snow nodded his head.

"But we are wrong in that sense. Islam is a system. It lays out laws for every area of life, religious, political, and even secular. *Sharia* law is supposed to be global and it's incompatible with democratic principles. In democracy we believe in change, progressing from broad principles and open-mindedness. In Islam, which means 'submission,' you have to just accept the unchangeable will of Allah even when it crushes the human spirit. Because the will of Allah is monolithic and destined to advance against all obstacles and arguments. It's like communism. It has an end state, a world-conquering destiny that smashes everything in its way. It's an organism that grows until it completely consumes its host. After Islam takes over everything, there will be world peace."

"How's that?"

"Because people like you and me will be dead."

Snow ate in silence while Chief Drecker slurped down the rest of his soup. Snow felt that what he just heard was truth but discouraging. It wasn't the key.

The chief took a final slurp of the now lukewarm soup before concluding.

"As far as the home front is concerned, you can't expect a nation to win a war when nine-tenths of the population is shielded from any direct cost."

Snow nodded. Junior officers and non-coms in his unit sometimes talked like this. He'd hoped for something more encouraging and concrete from a seasoned special operator like Drecker.

The chief's intensity seemed to deflate a bit. He sighed.

"You know, Randy, we are an uncommitted people at so many levels. It begins in the home … in our dysfunctional families … with our personal convictions…"

Snow was not sure where the chief was going now, but he nodded.

"Our country doesn't want to finish off an opponent—even if it means we end up losing. I don't think we believe there are negative consequences to losing this war. That's scary. I hope I am wrong."

Snow resumed eating in silence. Chief Drecker's jaded words resonated. He wondered if something else was bothering the chief and reducing his usual observant wit and wisdom to an ugly, pointed cynicism.

The chief licked his lips, wiped them with a napkin, and fixed his eyes on Snow.

"Lieutenant Snow."

"Yeah, Chief?"

"Did I answer your question?"

"Yeah, I think so."

"One more thing."

"Yes, Chief?"

"Take it from a nice Jewish kid from Hawaii ... this is one lousy chicken soup."

With that, he stood up and grasped his tray.

"I'll be leaving again this week, Lieutenant."

"Back to Tampa, Chief?"

Chief Drecker smiled.

"Something like that. Keep your head down, Ranger."

"Hooah, Chief."

"Hooah, airborne."

CHAPTER 20

Pancho: The Coffee Klatch

"Did you ever meet Felix Rodriguez?"

They were in the plywood B-hut shared by Pancho and Jake. It was spartan and not very roomy, but comfortable enough for these men who were inured to field conditions that would break lesser mortals. Two sets of bunk beds lining opposite walls, a couple of folding chairs, and a card table completed the furnishings. The hut was meant to accommodate eight enlisted men or four officers or civilians. A stainless-steel coffee maker bubbled along on the table. An orange extension cord ran to a humming "silent" generator just outside. A single fluorescent lightbulb, similarly connected, illuminated the center of the room.

Twister leaned forward out of the shadow cast by the top bunk.

"Yeah, I met him at a ceremony at Langley back in '88," he drawled. "Heck of an operator. Met a lot of old timers from the Studies and Observations Group too. Great guys. They pioneered the kinds of missions your guys do."

Pancho tilted back on his folding chair and propped his feet on the card table. Gino sat the same way in the other chair. Twister looked folded in on one of the lower bunks, his body bent and head tilted to accommodate his height. Pancho stole a glance at the bubbling canister before continuing. Hoping for the orange light. *Dang, she's brewing slow tonight ...*

"Yeah, well, Felix Rodriguez was an idol of mine when I was going through operator training," Pancho explained. "I wanted to be like him, you know, and capture my own bad guy like the way he got Che Guevara."

"You mean a bad guy like a Pablo Escobar?" Twister asked.

Pancho feigned obliviousness at the mention of the legendary Colombian narco-terrorist. Twister grinned and winked at Gino. *Nice try, Twister.*

"Yeah, someone like that."

"Well, Pancho, we may be the ones to find Bin Laden—it's only a matter of time. Someone's gonna get him."

"I hope so, but I'm gonna be getting pulled out any day, now that I'm promotable to colonel. I was hoping for one more field op, one more chance, but I think I'm desk bound for good."

Twister shifted his lengthy frame on the bunk. The bunk was Drecker's with a small pile of personal items at one end. Something flopped off the pile and hit the floor spilling its contents.

"Dang," Twister glanced at the pile.

"That's okay," Pancho said. "It's just Drecker's shaving kit."

Twister leaned over the end of the bed and began to pick up the items. There were the usual razors, shaving cream, soap, and toothpaste and the unusual, like mascara and theatrical makeup.

"Man," Twister exclaimed. "This dude deploys with some interesting stuff!"

"Don't ask, don't tell," Pancho replied. "Jake is a master of disguises, my friend, and his female disguise is his deadliest."

"Hey, give the guy a break," Gino added with a chuckle. "He's under deep cover."

Twister finished putting the shaving kit articles back in the bag.

"Seriously," Pancho added. "Jake's a pro. He lives by a creed from his Ranger Battalion days—'leave no man behind,'—and I suppose you could also say 'he always gets his man.'"

"That's cool," Twister zipped the shaving bag shut.

He was still leaning over the end of the bunk, "What's this?"

A small, white rectangle lay on the floor, from out of the shaving kit. He picked up the white rectangle. Gino stood up to fill his cup. The orange light came on.

"Coffee's up," Pancho announced while eyeing the object in Twister's hand.

Twister returned to his tortured position on the bunk and turned the rectangle over in his hand.

"What is that?" Pancho asked.

"A picture of someone Drecker knows, I guess."

Twister stared down. He turned the object over like he was looking for a notation before passing it to Gino.

Pancho grew more curious as he watched Gino handle the paper. He sensed a secret communication passing between Gino and Twister as their eyes met. Then Gino handed the picture to him. He took it, his interest piqued.

The photograph was an old, black and white picture of a man in a flight suit standing in front of a jet holding a boy's hand. The boy looked about three years old—the man, younger than thirty. The man was stooping in order to reach the boy's hand, and his other hand was directing the boy's attention toward the camera. They were both smiling. The man's smile, broad and encouraging, and the boy's, beaming. His eyes almost closed as if he wasn't quite ready when the picture was snapped. A scene both comforting and sentimental, one that spoke of life's goodness, brightness, and light—a picture of hope, happiness and security—the father strong and straight, and his son, trusting and innocent. *I bet I know who that is! Wow.*

"I wonder if that's Jake's father …"

"Jake's?" Gino asked.

"Yeah," Pancho answered. He held the picture for another moment, and then handed it back to Twister. "Yeah, his dad was in the Air Force. Jake doesn't like to talk too much about his past. I guess they had a falling out when his parents were divorced. This is the first time I ever saw that picture."

Gino and Twister exchanged another secret communication with their eyes, and then Twister returned the photo to the shaving kit. *What are they thinking?*

"Did you ever think about going on this mission?" Twister asked, changing the subject. "I mean, maybe this could be your last op as a shooter."

"Intriguing thought," Pancho replied. "But the Army takes a dim view of sending out the big picture planners on a covert mission. I'd blow our operational cover if I got caught and spilled my guts."

"I was wondering about that," Twister said. "Seems to me that Jake Drecker is a little overly invested in the planning for this one. He's essentially an undercover hit man on a clandestine field team. Should he be this immersed in the planning details?"

"I admit he seems a little deep on this, but he's the best operator and the best planner in this task force," Pancho answered. "I got no problem letting him run with it. In the end, I'm gonna make a lot of changes. It's already a bit over the top. We need a smaller footprint and a quiet hit. A get-in, get-out hit. Or maybe drop a hellfire and keep our risks down."

"Sounds good, Pancho," Gino replied. "We were hoping you would see things that way."

"No problem," Pancho said. "I still need actionable intel to proceed with our planning."

"Look, Pancho, I'm expecting an updated intelligence dump tonight," Twister offered. "Maybe there'll be a magic message in there for you."

"Miracle, Twister, I'm looking for a miracle—none of those Agency magic tricks on this one," Pancho grinned.

"Understood."

Twister unfolded himself from the bunk, stood, and stretched. Gino took his cue and also stood, his bulky frame scraping the metal folding chair back along the plywood floor.

"Then I better get back to the Bank," Twister added, "And see what I can scare up, my friend."

"I'll meet you over there shortly." Pancho blew across the surface of his coffee. "A man's got to enjoy the privileges of rank once in a while. You guys take yours to go, and I'll meet you at the Bank in about thirty mikes."

"Nighty-night," Twister said.

The two CIA operatives stepped out of the B-hut, careful to favor the coffee cups nestled in their hands so they wouldn't lose a drop as they went.

Pancho was left alone. So, he thought … and he prayed.

CHAPTER 21

Pancho: The Puzzle Piece

Pancho felt a tangible buzz of activity as he entered the Bank. Twister, Gino, and Major White were examining a document. Jake was at the map board with an analyst looking at the terrain around Dir. The other planners and operators were either on a computer or talking into a satellite phone. Major White looked up and grinned as Pancho approached the field table.

"We got it, sir," he said.

"What have you got, major?"

The major looked in deference at the taller of the two CIA operatives.

"We've got you your miracle, Pancho," Twister handed the paper to Pancho—an intelligence report from the Agency sent via secure email to Twister.

Pancho didn't expect much. The Agency never shared its juiciest reporting without severe control measures designed to protect its super-sensitive sources. Which made their information nearly impossible to validate using other sources.

Pancho read the message. A CIA source inside Pakistan had firsthand knowledge of their target, Abbas Bin Azzam, and his routine at the Maktab al-Khidamat compound south of Dir. The source described Azzam's personal vehicle, security protocols, buildings in the compound, vehicle routes in and out of the area, and other details. There were blurry images made with a cell phone of Azzam with other suspected Pakistani extremist leaders, including a shady, bearded CAT 3 referred to cryptically as 'the Imam'. The report included a discussion of the Maktab al-Khidamat network of groups, including a little-known entity called the Pakistan Martyr Brigade. The Pakistan source was graded as reliable. He was the driver for a high-level extremist leader. According to the CIA, recent cell phone intercepts confirmed details in the message, such as locations and network associations. If it was all true, it was an intelligence gold mine. Pancho was impressed.

"Twister, Major White, I think you guys are right. This thing is dynamite. Okay, let's get the updated intelligence brief and concept of operations. I'm ready to move this baby forward."

For the next ninety minutes, Pancho led the planners as they meticulously picked apart the new intelligence and updated their plan. Several supporting players joined them. One, an intelligence analyst from the National Security Agency, questioned the accuracy of the CIA's "cell phone intercepts" and their overall conclusions. Twister stood by his agency's report. The Prodigal Avenger crew, ever loyal to their operational partner, accepted the report as gospel.

The grand finale was Jake's ground operations order for Teams Condor and Owl. Jake presented the plan in several phases, starting from their departure point at Bagram through their objective in Dir and back again. He then added back-up plans for each phase. His design was thorough and detailed. Pancho wondered if his warrant officer hadn't been planning the op in his sleep. In the end, Pancho found the plan sound and approved.

"Gentlemen, check the time. It's 2200 hours local time. In seventy-two hours, we launch Team Owl. Seventy-two hours later, we launch Team Condor. Team Owl and Team Condor are to go into immediate isolation mode for planning and rehearsals. Major White, get on the horn and pass the word to Saber-Six at CENTCOM Forward and the guys at JSOTF that we are going live on his CAT 2. I appreciate all your efforts. If there are no more questions, we are now running 24/7 in the operations center for situational awareness. Operation Screech Owl is on."

CHAPTER 22

Pancho: The Departure

A battered two-seat Suzuki pickup idled under a green camouflage net in the middle of the Task Force Pancho hangar. Replete with dents, dust, and rust, it looked like a thousand other mechanical "mules" in the tribal areas of northwest Pakistan. However, this one boasted unique upgrades like a keyless, push-button ignition, an aluminum rack and cargo carrier in the bed, all-wheel drive, and an independent suspension with puncture-resistant, self-sealing tires. The tan exterior paint had a semi-flat finish to prevent reflection, but patterned glint tape on the roof identified the truck to US aircraft. The grimy, stripped-down interior hid an oversized glove compartment with a hand-held, commercial global positioning device, and a Russian made Makarov PM 9mm pistol. Behind the bench seat was a desert-tan camouflage net for quick concealment and an AK-74M assault rifle fitted with a GP-39 40-mm grenade launcher for hasty defensive fires. Night vision goggles, batteries, and spare ammunition completed the list of stores. Finally, Kevlar plates were inserted at strategic points around the cab to improve passenger survivability in the event of an ambush. Although it was a unique version of Pakistan's ubiquitous Suzuki "mule," an identical model, the team's backup vehicle, awaited them at the CIA safe house in Dir.

Gino eased the vehicle out of its cover and out onto the runway as a pair of soldiers pushed up the camouflage net with fiberglass poles. Outside the hangar, ground crewmen from the Army's elite Night Stalkers aviation unit prepared the truck for sling load. Gino got out and headed for a nearby MH-47E Chinook, still dressed for all-the-world like a biker from a Mad

Max movie. Jake and Jannat were already on-board. So were their disguises. They would change en route to Asadabad. Under cover of darkness, they would fly to the US outpost there, unload, and proceed to the border crossing near Zor Barawul. Gino carried with him a very special knapsack with their "Afghan passports," several thousand dollars in Pakistani rupees, and traceable US hundred-dollar bills for use as baksheesh to smooth their journey and open the doors to where they needed to go in Pakistan.

Pancho and his staff stood on the edge of the runway and watched the departure through the green phosphorescent haze of night vision goggles. As the aircraft lifted into the night, he waved. With a dust-swirling whine and the accelerating thump-thumps of tandem rotor blades, Team Owl's aircraft floated over the airfield, picked up speed as it turned east and was gone.

"I've got a new critical intel update for you from Islamabad."

Pancho looked up from the field desk. Thirty-six hours had dragged by since Team Owl departed. He'd spent the entire time at the Bank drinking coffee, forgoing sleep, and monitoring their progress. Feeling grubby and washed out but strangely satisfied, he reached for another cup.

"Things are smooth, the team has just crossed into Pakistan. Only two more checkpoints and they'll be in Dir. Don't ruin my day, Twister, with any bad news!"

Pancho grinned, but Twister's face didn't crack. Instead, looking stylishly apocalyptic, he leaned against the doorframe by the communication room and removed a single sheet of paper from a double-wrapped envelope.

Uh-oh.

Pancho felt something funny in his gut. Twister stepped toward him and silently handed him the classified message. Before he even set his eyes on the words, he knew that somehow, someway, Twister's "critical intelligence update" was going to complicate things.

PART 5

The Operation

CHAPTER 23

The Replacement

An American soldier, head tilted to avoid the decelerating rotor wash, exited down the ramp of a CH-47 and moved to the edge of the runway. He was of average height and medium build with brown hair, brown eyes, and the lightly burned skin of an Irishman who made his living working outdoors. In a crowded room, only his crew cut and ramrod military bearing betrayed his vocation. He was a soldier but low-key and nondescript in every other way.

As he stepped off the ramp at Bagram airfield, however, he looked startlingly out of place—because of his outfit.

Instead of the brown and tan desert camouflage uniform, this man wore the green and brown woodland camouflage Battle Dress Uniform (BDU)—pressed and starched to a cardboard stiffness. His BDU top was unsanitized, sporting both his name tape over the right pocket flap and a host of impressive qualification badges—jumpmaster, pathfinder, scuba, Combat Infantryman Badge, 7th Infantry Division combat patch on the right shoulder (Panama invasion, 1989), and a Joint Special Operations unit patch with Special Forces, Ranger, and Airborne tabs on the left. He sported a cold warrior "retro" look complete with wire-framed aviator sunglasses, black jump boots spit polished to a high shine, and a beret—a green beret—perched on his closely cropped head. His oversized olive-drab rucksack with green jungle boots hanging outside to dry and M-4 assault rifle, lovingly embellished with homemade, green camouflage paint, only added to the effect. He looked like someone out of a Vietnam War movie instead of belonging here—in America's mostly Middle Eastern War on Terror. But he was, in fact, a War on Terror combat veteran. He was arriving directly from the war's unheralded, but successful, third front in the southern jungle islands of the Philippines.

He'd had one wild trip. From remote Basilan Island in the south, he'd traveled to Luzon by vintage Philippine Air Force UH-1 Bell helicopter, which had probably seen service in the Vietnam War, then by C-141 to Okinawa via Guam, joined there by a Marine Corps infantry battalion and a gaggle of oversized Navy SEALs for a chartered commercial jet flight to Qatar with real civilian stewardesses. Then he boarded a C-5A with another mixed group for the final long leg from Qatar to Kabul International in beautiful, war-torn Afghanistan. The last helicopter ride provided him with an introduction—in-country familiarization was the military term—to the bleak, desert vastness that was Afghanistan. In the Philippines, he had grappled with the dangers of heatstroke, malaria, and the Abu Sayef. Here, he faced the contrasting challenges of hypothermia, altitude sickness, and the Taliban. He'd joined the Army to challenge himself and to see the world, and the Army had not let him down. He loved each and every bit of the life.

If he'd expected a welcoming committee when he got to Bagram, he was soon disappointed. A couple of Army and Air Force ground personnel came out to secure the aircraft and help the newcomers with their gear, but the man declined their favors. He was used to working alone, and nobody ever carried his bags.

"Hey, airman," he shouted to the first person he met upon exiting the aircraft, "Which way to Task Force Pancho?"

The young man pointed toward the decrepit cement building and rusting hangar complex that served as operations center and isolation facility for Task Force Pancho.

"Thanks, buddy," he said, moving out.

CHAPTER 24

Pancho: The Revelation

At the Bank, Pancho sat at his field table and digested Twister's intelligence report—raw intelligence from the CIA Station Chief in Pakistan regarding the kidnapped American missionary held by the Pakistan Martyr Brigade. A reliable inside source stated that the American, Isidore Loewenthal, had been transferred to their target, Abbas Bin Azzam. Azzam's group, Maktab al-Khidamat, was holding him at their compound south of Dir.

So, the American hostage was with their target. Great, now we have a rescue operation on our hands. That complicates things a bit.

Even more devastating was the second half of the report about the hostage himself, his past work in Pakistan, known associations, and family members. The missionary hostage had a prior relationship with an unnamed CIA asset, an insider source whose anonymity was jeopardized if the hostage revealed his secrets.

But that wasn't the biggest bombshell about the missionary.

Pancho bit his lip as he read the hostage's brief bio and family information.

"God help us. And this is reliable?"

Twister nodded. "Afraid so, my friend."

"And you expect us to turn our assassination mission into a hostage rescue mission this late in the game? I'm gonna need a platoon of Delta Commandos to make that work."

"True. Or you could skip the rescue."

"Skip it?"

"Yeah, you know. And silence the potential compromiser."

"You mean ensure that the hostage doesn't spill his guts."

Twister removed his sunglasses and looked straight into Pancho's eyes. "I think you knew this was a possibility."

Pancho shook his head and rubbed the front of his forehead with his palm. "Killing Americans? I mean … you can't expect Drecker to silence your source for you, do you?"

"Look, Pancho, we knew Jake would find him. And if Jake Drecker finds him, I am pretty-sure Jake Drecker can figure out how to rescue him. Failing that, we have a Predator drone on-call. We just need to coordinate."

"What do you mean you *knew* Jake would find him? Did you know ?"

Pancho stopped and read on. Something about the message was odd. Unlike many CIA reports in memorandum format, this one had no date.

"Where's the date on this?" Pancho continued.

Twister's face revealed nothing, but he hesitated before answering. "There's no date, but it's current."

Pancho stood. His chair scraped loudly as it slid back.

"Current? How 'current'? How long have you known about this?"

Twister put his sunglasses back on and folded his arms.

"You knew all along, didn't you?" Pancho added. "You knew!"

Twister tilted his face toward the ground and ground the toe of his boot into the soft dirt floor. Then he looked up at Pancho.

"Maybe we did, maybe we didn't," he answered. "The Agency isn't all-knowing, nor are we all-powerful, Pancho. But this is the cost of war. Americans are dying. We need to protect and maintain our sources so we can get the bad guys—the same bad guys you're after, Pancho."

Pancho saw the operation in a new light. *These self-serving, knuckle-dragging agency clowns set us up. They knew about Jake, knew about this Loewenthal character, and they had their own agenda all along. We were manipulated, and one of my men, a man with a very human weakness, has been exploited.*

Pancho recovered his composure.

"I don't see how we can pull back the team now."

"Why would you want to even consider that, Pancho?" Twister asked. "I think you should proceed with the hit as planned."

"And what about the hostage?" Pancho asked. "Isn't he part of your team? Don't you guys protect your own?"

"As far as the Agency can tell, Loewenthal is a real missionary. He's not one of ours."

"But he used to be one of us. He was a defense attaché, for God's sakes! And now he knows your insider source. Great. He's still an American. If he dies, *then* what happens? No one at the Agency cares, because your source is protected, right? And we can't complain or say squat because of plausible deniability, right?"

Twister didn't need to answer.

"God have mercy on my soul," Pancho said.

Then Pancho thought about Jake, Jake's planning and all of Jake's contingencies, just in case the hostage was there. How much Jake Drecker must have been burdened to put all of that together.

You knew, Jake, didn't you? You somehow knew all along that you would be rescuing this American. You planned it all along, because you know who he is and what he knows. This was your plan, and I couldn't even see it.

"Okay, Twister, I got it," Pancho conceded. "I can agree to disagree later, but we'll proceed like you recommended."

He turned and leaned with both hands on the field desk. "But, I think I need to go forward with the team. This could get dicey—Jake Drecker and the guys in Condor. These are my men, men I command, men who trust me."

"Then I think maybe you should go," Twister said.

"I can be added to Team Condor."

"Sounds good."

"But not now. I can't just leave here now," Pancho said. "Not with Biggs and Cutter gone. This is a Prodigal Avenger operation. If the op goes sour, someone has to be here to manage the fallout."

A soldier leaned his head out of the communication room, interrupting them.

"Excuse me, sir, CJSOTF on the line for you."

"Okay, Collins, I'll be right there."

He handed the report back to Twister, walked over to the phone, and took the receiver.

"Lieutenant Colonel Sanchez speaking."

He looked at Twister as he talked.

"Yeah, no problem, sir. Great. Yes, sir. This is good news, timely. Tell them to just send him over. Yes, sir. Thanks."

He hung up the phone.

"Well, Twister, sounds like our contingency plan just arrived in Bagram."

The CIA agent cocked his head quizzically.

"Lieutenant Colonel Mike Moon, my replacement, just checked in," Pancho continued. "Two weeks early, I might add. Anyway, if he's still as good as he's been in the past, I may just be cleared to go forward now on this one."

Twister smiled.

"Funny how that works."

"Yeah," Pancho answered. "Real funny."

CHAPTER 25

Colonel Lloyd Biggs: CENTCOM Forward

Colonel Lloyd "Saber-Six" Biggs, United States Air Force and Task Force Pancho Commander, felt fantastic as he sat at the table in the forward operating headquarters for US Central Command in Qatar. He was getting good face time with his Air Force superior on the staff, the Deputy J3. And Major Cutter's updated Operation Screech Owl presentation to the various staff and special operations leaders in the room had hit one out of the park. The only downside was the disapproving scowl on the senior State Department diplomat's face. But she didn't look like the type to ever smile during a military briefing anyway. The main thing was the Deputy J3, a man who could influence Saber-Six's next officer evaluation report, seemed pleased. So, mission accomplished!

Then two stubborn questions popped up.

"What about the political risks associated with mission compromise?"

Saber-Six strained to see who asked. Someone from State, probably. They always let some junior backbencher ask the stupid questions so the senior diplomat in the room could remain coolly detached from contentious issues.

Saber-Six just sighed. That always came up at Prodigal Avenger briefings. But then Saber-Six bit his lip as a CIA representative answered it for him.

"Pakistan," he insisted, "is turning a blind eye to our mild operational incursions across their frontier. Chief of Station will ensure they won't interfere with this one."

"And besides," Saber-Six reminded the others. "Clandestine operations are designed for maximum plausible deniability. Prodigal Avenger teams are considered expendable."

No one who was read-in to the program would disagree.

The diplomat, a grim underfed careerist, nodded her head in solemn concurrence. Still no smile. But no pushback either.

"What about your contingency plan to take out the target if our human assets fail?" asked a Marine Corps Officer, who looked like a lieutenant colonel, maybe a JSOC guy.

Saber-Six looked at Cutter. He'd only briefed the two human options—termination by Team Owl well outside the compound or termination by Team Condor in or around the compound.

Saber-Six watched as Cutter started to rise and open his mouth. He was interrupted by the CIA liaison officer.

"We have a Predator unmanned aerial vehicle with Hellfire missiles on station along the frontier here." He indicated the map display with a laser pointer.

Saber-Six smiled. A Predator on stand-by—a remotely piloted aircraft armed with sensors and cameras for collecting intelligence. Except the CIA's version was also armed with Hellfire missiles. Of course, they had already considered that in their list of options. Wonderful that the CIA was thinking ahead on that. Twister must have coordinated the deployment—that was the only explanation. A Predator could solve almost any problem arising on Screech Owl.

"Let me get with you afterwards, Colonel Biggs," the CIA man added. "I can give you our preplanned time windows and targets in case we need to go ballistic on this one."

Saber-Six smiled at the CIA officer's odd choice of words. But he preferred employing the Hellfire to risking his men. Or his career.

"We will coordinate the hit with our guy in Peshawar, who is responsible for our operations in the Northwest Frontier Province," the CIA officer added. "We will make sure everyone knows the plan."

"Very good," Saber-Six answered. *They can coordinate through CIA channels to Twister and Pancho at Bagram. No sense in wasting the Deputy J3's time with trivial details.*

Still, Saber-Six felt bothered. The location and identity of the kidnapped American missionary never came up. During the lead-in to Major Cutter's briefing, a young Navy officer presented an intelligence update in which he reported the kidnapped American was "still held by the Pakistan Martyr Brigade, a little-known organization dedicated to Kashmiri separatism."

The CIA representative sat stone-faced at the remark, never volunteering a word of new information about the missing American.

Seems like our CIA partners are keeping their cards close to their vests on this hostage thing. No worries. I am sure everyone knows. No sense making a fool of myself bringing it up.

CHAPTER 26

Pancho: Bagram

Pancho felt the stirrings of the old excitement. The quickening heart and pace. The clarity of mind as a million bits of new information and pre-preparation thinking streamed through his consciousness. Those anticipatory gut flutters the night before the big game. He was back in his element and on a team again.

There was no change in the plan—Pancho simply added himself in. Team Condor would be a four-person team now, led by Master Sergeant Ritter. Pancho, as the only officer on board, could override his NCO if he chose to. But the NCOs were the most experienced operators on the ground in the Unit. Pancho knew how to stay out of their way and let them do their job. The sniper/observer team of Eason and Ritter would perform the strategic reconnaissance as planned. Pancho and Mitchell, the "door kicker," would provide security and extra eyes on target.

Pancho would intervene only if there were a major change of mission or Ritter became incapacitated.

In the isolation facility, they completed their pre-mission checks and conducted virtual rehearsals of every phase of their operation. In one corner of the rusting hangar, they walked through every conceivable eventuality on a sand table map made to scale from dirt, stones, and craft supplies designed to replicate the terrain around their target. In their B-huts, they studied annotated overhead images from Falcon View—the military's classified version of Google Earth—of Dir city, the Maktab al-Khidamat compound, and the hills leading down from the mountainous Afghan-Pak border to the Panjkora River. They also looked at every blurry photo they could find of the target, Abbas Bin Azzam. They read his classified biography, learned his habits and memorized a diagram of the compound where he lived. Behind the hangar, they fired their weapons and tested their communications gear. Team Condor's departure time was approaching.

In the meantime, Team Owl checked in at Dir. They were in place.

Near midnight, four bearded men in loose-fitting, khaki-colored Pathan tribal garb topped off with round *Chitrali* hats threw overloaded rucksacks over their shoulders, adjusted their grip on their weapons, and walked out to a waiting MH-47E Special Operations Chinook helicopter. From a far distance, the men might pass for a group of Pathan warriors. But, despite their traditional clothing and the local headgear, a closer inspection would reveal state-of-the-art night vision devices, Nomex-covered fingers, expensive civilian "tactical" hiking boots, G-shock watches, and a variety of weapons of US and Russian design. That was okay, they had no intention of getting close enough to anyone for a personal inspection.

They took their places on fold-down nylon seats, arranged their loads between their feet, and snapped in. Above them, outside the aircraft's insulated aluminum skin, twin rotor blades beat the thin, high altitude air in an effort to produce the miracle of mechanical lift. The accelerating engines whined and strained. Then, with a frenzied burst of wind and dust, the MH-47E was airborne.

As the helo rose above Bagram, the aircraft resembled a hovering, drunken insect that steadied itself, rotated toward the southeast, and floated away.

Lieutenant Colonel Mike Moon stood on the edge of the field with his night vision goggles and watched Team Condor depart just as Lieutenant Colonel Sanchez had done for Team Owl. He felt a twinge of envy but also a sense of goodwill, content with the knowledge he'd done Pancho a favor by freeing him to go with the team. *They promote you off the team and tell you you're better off in some command post for the rest of your life. Dang! The only thing great about rank is the pay. And it's not that great!*

"Who knows," Moon had joked to Pancho after they discussed the idea. "Maybe on this last operation you will get a chance to take out High Value Target Number One."

"Osama bin Laden? God, that *would* be awesome," Pancho laughed.

Moon smiled at the memory of their discussion. After not much longer, he might end up like Pancho, selected for a promotion above the pay grade of a field operator, destined to a desk job in the hope of one or two more final shots at a command to keep things interesting.

"Gotta love this work," Moon said to himself as he turned and headed back toward the Bank.

CHAPTER 27

Meditations

At ten thousand feet, flying over the Koh-e-Hindu Kush range in a pitch-black sky, the Night Stalker Special Operations helicopter pilots know darkness—both tangible and terrifying. Standard flight instruments and night vision goggles can't compete with the thick cloud cover, shifting turbulence, and the wind shear of these mountains. And no helicopter stands a chance against granite. Fortunately, the MH-47E was equipped with special terrain following/terrain avoidance technology including multimode radar that cued the pilot to climb, descend, or turn to avoid obstacles. The chopper was also equipped with oxygen because at ten thousand feet, oxygen is mandatory for pilots, passengers, and crew to avoid blackouts and death from hypoxia, a lack of oxygen in the blood.

Only idiots worry about things beyond their control. So, as the jackhammer turbulence threatened to shake the craft apart at the seams, the passengers sat calmly in the back like businessmen on a commuter flight. Not that some weren't afraid or even airsick, but each seasoned operator had long since embraced a personal fatalism about helicopter rides. Just part of the job. When your number came up, that was it. In the meantime, wipe your sweaty palms on your pant leg and think about something else.

In the final minutes of the flight, Pancho leaned heavily against the lurching skin of the aircraft to steady an infrared penlight on a photo-map in his lap. He resisted the pointless urge to turn and look out the circular window just over his shoulder. Nothing but darkness out there. Just as pointless as his last-minute attempt to memorize the trails on the photo-map under the reddish beam of his bouncing, shaking penlight. But it was habit.

Pancho cradled the stock of his refurbished M25 "White Feather" sniper team security rifle with his left arm. The reassuring coolness of the rifle's black graphite pressed against the sweaty dampness of his left cheek—a welcome comfort.

The M25 was Pancho's weapon of choice, an eleven-pound, 44.3 inch, .308 caliber, semi-automatic sniper team support rifle designed by Special Forces in the 1980s for the sniper team observer. The rifle was dubbed the "White Feather" in honor of legendary Vietnam Marine Corps sniper Carlos Hathcock, who decorated his helmet with a feather while in combat.

Pancho, who had met and once trained under Hathcock, had carried the M25 as an A-team leader in the Gulf War. The one he held now was refurbished and especially modified for his personal use, a perk for those assigned to elite special operations units. A trusted old friend, good to have around when things got hot. He pulled the rifle close against his shoulder, firmly but lovingly, to keep it from jostling around in the turbulence.

Pancho thought of a book he'd read in college called *Lost Horizon* by James Hilton, about a group of evacuees from a war in Afghanistan, on a night flight like this, who have their plane hijacked and flown to a mysterious valley called Shangri-la. They find a monastery where the monks enjoy the benefits of longevity and indoor plumbing. But the secret of the monastery was no one could ever leave. One, a world-weary British operative, tries and gets back to civilization. But by the end of the book, he has a change of heart, disappears, and presumably returns to Shangri-la.

As they neared their destination, the memory of that novel gave Pancho a peculiar sense of déjà vu. Here he was, flying through those same mountains to another mysterious place called Dir. And Everett Scott had told him that *Dir* was an old Sanskrit word meaning monastery.

"Two minutes!" the crew chief yelled over the noise of the aircraft.

Pancho and the team unhooked from their seats and secured their gear.

Everyone was keyed up at the possibility of a hot LZ, a compromised landing zone covered with enemy fire. But there was little to worry about. High above them, an unmanned aerial vehicle sent thermal images of the site back to Bagram. Hot spots around the landing zone would signal danger, and they would be redirected to land at another one nearby. So far, this spot was deemed safe.

Five minutes later, the last bits of swirling stones and dust settled over the team as the Chinook, having successfully deposited them on a high ridgeline in Pakistan, lifted away and made for Bagram. Pancho lay still, waiting for his ears to adjust to the night sounds on the landing zone. They were in alien territory, and his night vision goggles added to the eeriness by making the landscape phosphorescent green. He lifted the goggles from his face to read the luminescent dial of his watch. There was a twenty-minute security halt before moving out. Just long enough to adjust to the sights, smells, and sounds of their new environment. Twenty minutes that seemed like hours.

Finally, the entire team rose at the same time and moved out toward the northwest in file formation. Master Sergeant Ritter led off, then Eason and Pancho, and finally, Mitchell, pulling security in the rear. They had several kilometers to cover, much of it downhill, to get to their hide site.

Pancho looked to the left where an inky blackness hid a village encampment at the bottom of the valley. Right on track. Which meant the Maktab al-Khidamat compound and their target, Abbas Bin Azzam, was due north. Straight ahead.

They moved fast. They had about five hours of darkness to cover them. If they failed to get to their hide site in time, they would need to go to ground. A delay might cost them an entire day.

Pancho felt his lungs struggling and his heart rate increasing as he pushed over the uphill sections. This was harder than expected. *Dang, too many mess-hall rib eyes over the last year.*

The 23rd Psalm ran through his head, a comforting habit acquired at Army Ranger School when he humped the squad radio over the torturous Tennessee Valley Divide. He wasn't much of a believer then. But the Psalmist had strengthened him with words he knew were true. As a soldier, he had lived them.

The LORD is my shepherd; I shall not want.

He maketh me to lie down in green pastures: he leadeth me beside the still waters.

PRODIGAL AVENGER

He restoreth my soul: he leadeth me in the paths of righteousness for his name's sake.

Yea, though I walk through the valley of the shadow of death, I will fear no evil: for thou art with me; thy rod and thy staff they comfort me.

Thou preparest a table before me in the presence of mine enemies: thou anointest my head with oil; my cup runneth over.

Surely goodness and mercy shall follow me all the days of my life: and I will dwell in the house of the LORD forever.

He thought about his friend. *Wonder if Jake Drecker ever read the Psalms? God, help and save Jake. Wherever he is tonight.*

CHAPTER 28

First Encounter: Track Suit

"What the blue blazes is that?" Eason muttered into his throat mike.

Team Condor froze. Pancho strained his ears. Something pounding. Moving.

They had made the ridgeline just south of their objective, but there was a problem. A wide mountain trail appeared leading up from Kotkay village, obviously well-traversed. The spot was deemed too exposed for their purposes.

They detoured, moving just off the trail and following it to the west to avoid contact with others. They would use an alternate hide site just northwest of the target. This meant crossing the narrow valley and climbing to the top of the next ridge, adding time and distance to their hike. They had to hurry to avoid daylight.

They went two kilometers, turned north, and descended the steep, rocky slope. There was an intermittent stream bed at the bottom with a jeep trail running through it. They were getting ready to sprint across the narrow valley floor when an apparition appeared.

A runner.

More specifically, a jogger. In a track suit and carrying a small flashlight.

Despite their caution and night vision goggles, they almost missed the bouncing flashlight beam moving parallel to them along the base of the ridge.

"Dang it!" Eason added.

Pancho suddenly wished he was in front. Leading.

They stayed rigid, straining their ears, assessing the threat. The early morning darkness amplified the rhythmic crunch of the jogger's feet.

Pancho intuitively measured the Doppler Effect of the sound of the jogger's feet pounding on the sand. It rose at his approach, peaked as he passed, and then descended as he jogged away from them.

Pancho grinned like an adolescent sneaking out of his bedroom in the dead of night.

He can't see us. But we can see him! Who or what is he? Eason was closest to the trail. *What does he see?*

Then his earpiece crackled. Eason.

"One dismount. A tall, fit, European-looking man with neatly trimmed beard. Dressed in a track suit and running shoes."

Pancho immediately dubbed him Track Suit.

The man continued to their left. When he was out of sight, they crossed the trail one at a time in file, stepping carefully on rocks and hard patches to avoid leaving footprints. Mitchell brought up the rear, scrutinizing their trail for incriminating evidence and lagging once across to make sure they weren't followed.

Then, they moved up the top of the ridge and back to the east toward their target.

Pancho was vexed by the encounter.

We must be getting sloppy. Another incident like that and we will be dead men.

CHAPTER 29

Pakistan: Rendezvous

Bob didn't like the setup. The CIA case officer knew the move was risky, trying to pass raw intelligence from an in-country contact to a clandestine US military asset—both of whom were outside his direct span of control. But orders were orders. The Company had an asset to protect, the military had a target to kill, and both interests were converging. What a mess.

He looked at his watch. The clandestine asset, a US SOF commando he knew to be working with the Company on a Prodigal Avenger hit, was running late.

Colonel Pasha was chatting amiably about his upcoming trip to Sri Lanka. The dissipated Pasha assumed the American was impressed by his prowess with Sinhalese prostitutes. But Bob only half-listened. He was glancing outside the windows waiting for a sign from their contact.

Pasha was a good source. They'd worked together to cultivate several fruitful agents inside Pakistan's potent mix of home-grown terrorists and disenfranchised ethnic groups. Now Bob's prize asset, a Punjabi car mechanic turned terrorist driver to whom Bob was known as Mr. Ajax, was threatened by the very intelligence bombshell he'd uncovered himself. A cluster, if ever there was one. Pasha had come clean about the possible compromise.

Bob sipped sweet tea and practiced his rehearsed chattiness with Pasha. In the front seat, his driver, Rashid, kept the tea flowing from a thermos on the middle console. Behind them, Pasha had posted his bodyguard goons and a pair of Pakistani Border Scouts by a Land Rover. From the glow of their cigarettes, Bob figured them to be about fifty meters back. They better be. The instructions from the Prodigal Avenger team were quite specific.

And if the Paks botch this, there will be a price to pay.

PRODIGAL AVENGER

Jake caught his breath before moving too close. He'd run almost the full distance from Dir, about six kilometers to the north, dodging vehicles, hiding alongside the road, and avoiding people with a mix of stealth and audacity. Besides, what does your average Pakistani do if they see a strange, small man dressed head to toe in a black ninja outfit sprinting down the street? Call the police?

Jake gauged the distance to the vehicle—about a two-meter dash from his murky hiding place to the front door handle on the passenger side. Pop the door open, and he would be alongside the driver. In a single motion, he would turn to face the two men in the back seat.

He watched carefully, making sure he confirmed the identity of the two men. The bald-headed, blue-eyed American, wearing a brown bomber jacket—*check.* The man next to him, thick mustache and black leather coat, must be his Pakistani counterpart, Colonel Pasha—*check.* He looked at the rest of the group back up the road, drivers and guards. They were in no position to interfere.

He moved, grabbing the passenger door handle and jumping inside.

The speed and shock of his movement startled the driver. He jumped, spilled tea into his lap, and uttered an oath in guttural Urdu.

"Aw, jeez!" cursed the American fiercely. "What are you trying to do?"

Jake said nothing. Just kneeled in the passenger seat and faced the two men in back as they regained their composure. Only Colonel Pasha seemed unfazed. He had gone momentarily wide-eyed with fear, but he brought his emotions under control before his American host took notice. Now he sat with a bemused smile on his face.

"What was that for, Night Angel?" Bob continued, "You trying to give us all a heart attack?"

Jake smiled inside his black mask at the Night Angel nickname—silly and theatrical. And funny too. Like his black ninja outfit. But he made no comment. He was under strict orders not to utter a word in the presence of Colonel Pasha. Bob knew that and probably shouldn't have engaged him. Except that was funny too.

"Can you excuse us, Rashid?" Bob asked, looking at his driver. "We need to talk alone. Why don't you go coordinate with the other driver and our friends from the Border Scouts?"

"Yes, sir," the driver answered. He got out, wiped at the tea on his pant leg, and took up a position outside the vehicle.

Bob knew he didn't need to do that. Pakistan-born Rashid was a US citizen, State Department employee, and possessor of a high-level security clearance with a wife and two daughters back in Virginia. Bob needed Rashid to keep an eye on Colonel Pasha's men. And he wanted both Night Angel and Colonel Pasha to feel at ease.

Bob continued with the formalities.

"Colonel Pasha, let me introduce to you Night Angel."

Jake nodded on cue. Only his snake-like, steel-grey eyes were visible with the costume.

Bob smiled. He had made up the name Night Angel for the clandestine American operator just for this occasion.

"Pleased and honored to meet you, Mister Night Angel," Colonel Pasha said, returning the nod.

"Per our arrangement, Colonel Pasha," Bob spoke with a honey-tinged, Florida Pan-handle drawl. "Night Angel is not allowed to speak nor to remove his disguise nor to otherwise reveal any part of his operational cover in the presence of a Pakistani government official."

"I fully understand—as we have agreed," Colonel Pasha responded.

Bob knew Colonel Pasha would try to put a tail on Night Angel when the meeting was over so they could ferret out the US safe house. He expected nothing less from his ruthless and experienced counterpart.

Bob reached to turn off the car's interior lamp. Darkness. Night Angel further frustrated the good Colonel by turning in the seat to face forward, away from the men in the back. Colonel Pasha would feel mildly insulted by the gesture but respect its usefulness. Besides, there was little to see now. Pasha would be even more insulted if he knew the other reason the American operator wanted to see him was to memorize his face in case he ever had to kill him.

"So now we can talk," Bob said. "I will be asking all of the intelligence and operational questions on Night Angel's behalf. He is only here to get answers from the horse's mouth, as we say in the States, no offense."

Colonel Pasha nodded.

"Just to remind you, sir," Bob went on, "there are no US forces operating in your country without the expressed consent of your government. Per agreement, Night Angel is an agent of both the US and Pakistani governments. Per agreement, he is considered expendable and operates at the pleasure of both our governments for the intent of neutralizing our common, anti-democratic, terrorist enemies."

"Yes, and you may skip the formalities, Mr. Bob, we have covered all of this before."

"Yes, but you know, Colonel Pasha, I never skip the formalities." Bob continued, despite Colonel Pasha's little-disguised contempt for the American's feigned preoccupation with international law.

CHAPTER 30

Pakistan: Targets

"Target location in sight."

Except for the altitude, which forced him to stop often to catch his breath, and the surprise brush with Track Suit, the Movement was easier than Pancho expected. *Not bad for an old staffer. Hope these guys can't tell how tired I am.*

He examined his global positioning system. *Right on target. Amazing. Not like the old days of shooting compass points to triangulate a location.*

Quickly and quietly, they set-up the hide site. Just in time, it was almost the pre-dawn hour the military called BMNT or *begin morning nautical twilight*, when people would begin moving around the compound.

Pancho aimed his thermal night scope at a looming tower toward their front. It was too dark to see much detail, but he noted a narrow thermal glow near the top of the tall structure. There was a man inside, standing guard no doubt, and maybe even watching them settle into their position. Hopefully, the man wasn't equipped as they were, with state of the art night vision devices. Surely these people weren't expecting them, *were they?*

Thus far, Colonel Pasha shared little new intelligence. But, Bob knew they hadn't yet gotten to the key issue for which this entire clandestine rendezvous had been arranged.

"So," Bob said, trying to clarify a point. "We confirm that the American hostage is inside the compound, inside the same building that serves as the MAK headquarters and Azzam's home away from home."

"Correct," Colonel Pasha answered.

"And you confirm that Azzam is inside the compound and has become increasingly reclusive."

"Correct."

"But you can't give us any more details on Azzam's routine, and you can't get the layout of the building for us."

"It is very difficult, Bob, very difficult indeed." Colonel Pasha sipped his tea. "We have our man inside the Pakistan Martyrs Brigade, no problem, but the MAK has many foreign elements living in Pakistan under false pretenses."

"Look, both American and Pakistani interests are involved here, Colonel. We are sponsoring your informer inside the PMB. We expect more details. Hasn't he been inside the compound?"

"I am not aware of it," Colonel Pasha said.

Sure.

"Well, we need that layout. We need to get the American when we take out the target."

"I fully understand, and we intend to get you that information soon." Colonel Pasha smiled weakly.

Bob considered Pasha's tough position. Pasha wanted the Americans to do him and his organization the favor of terminating an irritant alien element that had rooted itself in Pakistan. The MAK had served the ISI's purpose in the wars against India and the old Soviet Union. Now they were upsetting the special US-Pakistani relationship, radicalizing the tribal groups, and, worse of all, jeopardizing Colonel Pasha's prospects of promotion into the elite class to which he aspired. *Tough for us too.*

Bob looked at his watch and tapped on his window.

Outside, Rashid disappeared behind the vehicle.

"Let's get to the new issue, the one I invited Night Angel here for. What about the compromise?" Bob asked.

"Yes, it is very difficult. The hostage and our informant know each other. Our agent was once the recipient of medical care at the hands of this man we believe may have been an American missionary. Fate brought them together beyond our control. This will cause problems for us. If the hostage is tortured, he may expose the name of our informant." Pasha knew the information was serious.

The black-masked shadow in the front seat remained rock still.

"This is the updated information we needed to share with your team, Night Angel," Bob sipped his tea and continued. "Our entire clandestine network could be jeopardized if this Pakistani agent gets rolled up."

Jake, behind the Night Angel guise, nodded slowly to indicate understanding.

"We know your primary mission is to take out Azzam. But we can't afford to have the hostage crack. Or we lose everything. If you can't simultaneously rescue the hostage and take out your target, then you need to have a backup option."

The shadow in the front seat turned slowly around. The eyes above the face mask flashed cat-like from some ambient light source behind them then disappeared again in the darkness. Bob knew the American commando was looking right at him. Knew it, *felt it.*

"… to neutralize the American hostage."

The shadow twisted further to look at Pasha.

"Yes, if the hostage were silenced," Pasha added, as if to reinforce the CIA man's words, "it would solve all of our problems."

Night Angel turned slowly back to face forward again. He nodded. Understood.

"Right. And our military liaison team at your command will be passing the same guidance along so your chain of command is informed. Good luck."

Another slow nod.

"Well, Colonel Pasha," Bob said, bringing the meeting to a close. "I think that concludes our little gathering. Time we let our Night Angel return to his mission while we prepare things on our end."

"Of course," Colonel Pasha replied looking at the back of the rock-still, spooky-silent masked head.

Bob reached over the driver's seat and switched on the vehicle headlights. Rashid had collected the other men, Colonel Pasha's goons and the Border Scouts, and herded them to the front of the vehicle. They were all shielding their eyes against the bright headlights, which were essentially shutting down their natural night vision.

Without warning, the front seat passenger side door flung open, and the Night Angel disappeared.

Bob looked back in time to see Pasha furtively hit the send text command on his cell phone.

PRODIGAL AVENGER

Well, well, Pasha. Releasing your dogs of war, aye? I sincerely hope none of them catch that Night Angel character. It will be their last hunt, I am sure.

Jake pulled NVG goggles over his masked face as he scurried through the pine and scrub. He was heading east of the rendezvous spot, close to where the Kaas Road doubled back on itself and headed up the ridgeline to the west. He plunged, slipping and sliding down a steep embankment with a stream at the bottom. His feet found purchase at the bottom, his flat black running shoes making only a faint swishing and crunching noise on the pine needles and stones. By taking the most unlikely route back to Dir, looping due east over a couple ridgelines and then following the Panjkora River down toward the heart of the city, he hoped to avoid Pasha's surveillance teams.

He hopped boulders, crossed the stream, and headed up the steep ridgeline on the opposite side. He didn't go far before seeing a green ghost about fifty meters ahead.

Blast! A local out for a walk or a surveillance goon?

He dropped to the ground and watched.

The person carried a storm lantern and a weapon.

The NVGs adjusted to the new light source to prevent bleaching out. Jake readied his knife for a quick kill. The weapon was unclear. A rifle?

The approaching footsteps crunched softly among the pine needles.

Jake tensed, a human snake coiling for a strike.

CHAPTER 31

The Recce

Jake scanned the distant area behind the approaching specter.

No hotspots. No specter cordons. A structure up the ridgeline and the smell of wood smoke. There was a road on top of the ridge but no idling vehicles or dismounted goons.

Jake hoped for the best as he lay against a pine trunk and tried to blend in with the bark.

Five more steps and then ...

The man with the lantern walked past. He was wearing a *salwar kameez* and a light-colored *topi* cap. As he passed, Jake noticed something in his ears. Ear buds. With Pakistani dance music bleeding out.

Sucker's gonna go deaf if he keeps listening at that volume.

The man was young, probably twenty-five years old. The lantern swung slightly in time with the music, and the "weapon" in his other hand was a woodsman's axe.

Woodcutter. Dang, kid. That music is killing your ears, but it probably saved your life.

Jake took off up the ridgeline. The woodcutter never broke his stride as he headed in the opposite direction in search of suitable fuel for his fire.

Two hours later, having evaded Colonel Pasha's small army of informants, goons, and special police, Jake slipped over a wall and dropped cat-like to the ground inside the sanctuary of the CIA's Dir safe house compound. He sat down, gained control of his breathing, and listened.

Silence. *No tail.*

Jake moved to a nearby shed, entered through a side door, and closed it against the creeping pre-dawn gray that was now settling across the city.

Secure in his hiding place, he removed his mask.

PRODIGAL AVENGER

From their vantage point, Team Condor enjoyed a magnificent view of the target area, a small valley dropping down eastward, perpendicular to the much larger Panjkora Valley. Kotkay village and the main north-south highway stood less than a kilometer to the east.

With their observation telescopes and binoculars, they could see past the highway to the milky-gray waters of the Panjkora River churning through green fields bordered by orchards and mud tracks. Beyond that rose a set of imposing ridgelines—verdant, tree-covered slopes rising up from the valley floor before finally petering out and conceding to the khaki-colored stone at higher elevation. A one lane dirt road, hard-packed and following a winding, rock strewn intermittent stream bed, led up from the highway to the target complex. Pancho named it the Campus. Their hide site was perfectly suited for monitoring traffic in and out of the area.

Pancho took inventory of the scene, drawing a small map in his notebook for the post-operation debrief.

The Campus consisted of five total structures—the walled Maktab al-Khidamat compound, a mosque with minaret located among a grove of trees on a slightly elevated plateau just to the east of the compound, a two-story warehouse of some kind that resembled a third world parking garage on the south side opposite the compound's gate, and a row of low houses with small sheds that ran along the north side of the little valley.

The road up from Kotkay looped around the compound on the north side, and expanded on the south side to form a hard-packed dirt parking area populated by two formerly white but now mud and rust splattered Subaru pickup trucks. The road then followed the intermittent stream bed into the hills where they had encountered Track Suit. The road, he knew from imagery, dead-ended about three kilometers further amidst a complex of shooting ranges, obstacle courses, and tin-roofed structures most likely used to train budding jihadists. The whole setup was a school for terrorism. He nicknamed it Terror U.

Just below their hide site, less than five hundred meters away, stood the fortress-like compound, a rectangular-shaped, medieval-looking affair in brown mud and brick of the type common to the tribal areas. The area was slightly larger than the average family compound, about the size of a football field. The walls were eight feet high and two feet thick with cut glass, spikes, and other sharp objects protruding along the top. The single entrance consisted of a sliding steel vehicle gate as high as the wall on the compound's south side.

A good-sized, single-story structure of whitewashed brick, topped off with an unusual red-tile peak roof, looked squat in the middle of the compound. High, rectangular windows ran around and under the lee of the roof for light and ventilation. Its entrance faced toward the vehicle gate. The quaintness and architecture gave the house the appearance of a rustic country cottage. But this was no summer bungalow. This was the headquarters of the Maktab al-Khidamat. Pancho nicknamed it the Cabin.

The most dominating feature of the complex was a thirty-foot tower built into the compound's western wall, the looming structure that had menaced them when they first arrived in the dark. The tower was an anachronism, looking like something from the eighteenth century with its narrow rifle ports and sloping, tiled rooftop, and probably held a watchman to give early warning against uninvited visitors. Like them. But it accomplished an unintended effect, partially blocking their view of the cottage's front entrance. This posed a problem. The team needed to monitor traffic in and out of the Cabin.

Team Condor spent the next three grueling days observing and recording the routine in and around the complex. They took digital photographs, wrote text reports, and transmitted everything to Bagram. At night, they circled the complex and observed with their night vision gear. They discovered trails on the ridge behind them, just over the military crest, and took turns pulling a security watch to prevent a surprise from that direction. Their hide site, among a clump of boulders and thick bushy vegetation, was well suited for their purposes. Complacency and boredom were their chief foes.

Pancho decided Track Suit was an advisor or trainer. He'd observed him leading a group of eleven in early morning calisthenics and then on a hike with weapons and gear up into the valley. Distant gunfire suggested firearms training on the rifle range.

There were at least fifteen men sleeping on the second floor of the large structure Pancho called the Parking Garage. Indeed, several pickup trucks were parked on the ground level. Access to the second floor was via a sturdy, handmade ladder long enough to reach to the third level as well—the structure's flat, earthen roof. Such a roof was the traditional sleeping area in warm weather, but this one was bare, perhaps to avoid the unwanted attention of overhead electronic eyes.

A more privileged group lived inside the Cabin, including Track Suit. Pancho and the team were unable to get a handle on the situation in the Cabin, who was inside or what they did. The structure was large enough to accommodate a big group and probably had several rooms. Pancho needed more details, especially if the American was inside, to properly develop their target for termination. Eason submitted intelligence requests to Bagram hoping to find out more, but there was nothing.

During their days of observation, a motley assortment of visitors came and went.

Three goat-herders with white turbans and ancient AK-47s led their flock up the southern ridge on the well-traveled trail out of Kotkay.

Pancho meditated on a flaw in their hide site.

Good thing we didn't stay on that ridge. But the view into the Cabin entrance was much better there. Hmmm.

One of the goat herders down in the Car Park bargained with an armed man over two goats. The armed man took the goats, and the goat herder left with a wad of rupees.

There were other vendors. One arrived driving a battered tractor towing a trailer piled high with what appeared to be baskets of dates, apricots, peaches, and people. A woman dressed in a bright colored chador hoisted a basket of fruit onto her head and climbed off the trailer. She dusted off her garment with her free hand and walked casually toward the compound's south entrance.

That was odd. Women were rarely seen in public in the tribal areas of Pakistan. Couldn't see exactly where she went or what she did, but she disappeared for almost forty-five minutes. And she came back without her basket.

One day an Imam arrived with a small caravan of Land Rovers filled with armed men. Azzam made an uncharacteristic visit outside the compound to greet the man at the Car Park with a traditional embrace and a kiss. Then they strolled together, hand-in-hand to the little mosque where the Imam led Friday prayers.

Five times daily, a loudspeaker mounted in the mosque's minaret issued forth the haunting melodies of the *adhan*, the Islamic call for prayer. The sound rattled the team but also provided a perfect opportunity to count up everyone in the compound as they responded to its call. There were eighteen faithful who prostrated themselves on prayer rugs each time, but on Friday, during the congregational prayers at the mosque, there were at least twenty-six, including Azzam and the Imam with his thugs. Some preferred to pray indoors during the rest of the week.

The minaret was of simple design, about twenty-five feet high and attached to the mosque on the north side. The minaret was always empty, except for several black crows and the loudspeaker. The *muezzin* issued the call to prayer electronically from a microphone inside the open-air mosque. The minaret, situated on a slight rise in the southeast corner of the Campus, enjoyed a direct line of sight to the front entrance of the Cabin.

That gives me an idea.

CHAPTER 32

FRAGO

"So, it's confirmed? The American hostage is somewhere in this complex?"

Pancho took measure of each man's face before answering. "That's what intelligence tells us. So, it's not confirmed until we confirm it."

Ritter took off his Chitrali hat and rubbed his head. They were lying side by side in the hide site with Eason on the telescope and Mitchell pulling rear security. It was Ritter's turn to sleep, but he never seemed to need much.

"Why didn't we adjust the mission before we left?" Ritter asked. "You had some of the intel then, right?"

"We had a lot of information on the identity of the hostage, Isidore Loewenthal, and why he was so valuable to the CIA. Apparently, Loewenthal is a former intelligence guy, an Air Force attaché in Islamabad. But he is currently an American missionary who just happens to know the identity of an inside source in some jihadi group. They think he's going to talk. We couldn't be certain he was here. We think so now." He took a deep breath. "The CIA is prepared to neutralize the hostage to protect their intelligence asset."

"What? You mean kill an American?"

"Not in so many words, but they probably wouldn't mind if he became collateral damage. I told them we wouldn't. Our target is Azzam. We go after him. If we can confirm Loewenthal's location while we are surveilling the target, all the better."

"Well, the way I see it, that doesn't make much difference to us," Ritter said. "We still keep eyes on, keep reporting, and then get out of here and let Owl do their thing."

"But what if we need to do the hit here at the compound?"

"Well, Pancho, I think we just need to cross that bridge when we get there."

Moon had transmitted the new CIA intelligence to them early that morning with a FRAGO, the military acronym for a fragmentary order adjusting their mission to the new information. The FRAGO was very simple. *Collect information to either confirm or deny this updated intelligence report.* Team Condor was still in reconnaissance mode, and Team Owl was still waiting for an opportune moment to make the hit. Pancho, Jake, and the other Task Force Pancho planners always assumed the hit would take place in Dir or along the road to and from Dir. Nothing needed to be changed yet. Except there were complications they hadn't foreseen. Like the fact that neither the target nor the hostage ever left the compound. Pancho's mind spun trying to figure out a new plan.

Azzam is like some jihadist monk, holed up in an unholy monastery of terror, content to let the world come to him. No one resembling an American, let alone Isidore Lowethal, has been seen yet. We need to either get inside and take a look or wait for one of the two to emerge. And we can't wait much longer. Time to consider setting a deadline to scrub this sucker.

The Cabin itself was still a mystery. What exactly was inside? What was the layout? Who was in there? How many? How armed? How dangerous?

Pancho was troubled but nodded his assent. He outranked the Master Sergeant, but that wouldn't make any difference. The non-commissioned officers, with their experience and hands-on expertise, could lead the mission. Master Sergeant Ritter was a consummate operator.

But Twister's intelligence report lay heavy on his conscience. There was one too explosive detail he hadn't shared with Ritter and the team.

Trust the final outcome to Ritter's objective decision-making.

He prayed and kept silent.

Eason watched the Campus through a high-powered spotter's scope.

Two Mercedes SUVs, escorted by border scouts in a third vehicle, rolled up to the Car Park and unloaded some guests. One caught their tired eyes.

"Check out the chick."

Pancho looked through the scope on his rifle. "Wow! Wonder who she is."

They were unusual-looking visitors—the woman and two men, relatively young and well-dressed, carrying clipboards, cell phones, and laptops. They resembled urban professionals of the kind one met on the streets of Hyderabad or in Dubai. The woman was tall, taller even than her two male companions. She possessed super-model good looks and carried herself with confidence, as one who was accustomed to attention. She wore the fashionable head scarf and modern *shalwar kameez* favored by the educated classes in Pakistan's larger cities but which were less common in tribal areas. One of the men wore a silk shirt and dark business suit without a tie. The other, a younger man, sported tan cargo pants, running shoes, and a loose fitting, light blue hooded sweatshirt.

Their official escort was the Imam and his usual retinue. The Maktab al-Khidamat welcoming committee of Azzam and two bodyguards greeted them. They all chatted like old friends. Everyone wore sunglasses, everyone looked cool, even the Imam.

"Wish we could hear their conversation," Eason muttered.

"Who do you think they are?" Pancho asked.

"My guess would be journalists," Eason replied.

"You mean like CNN?"

"No, sir. CNN is too cumbersome and obnoxious to travel in a small group like that," Eason explained. "These are leaner and meaner than CNN."

"You mean …"

"Exactly, our friends from *Al Haqiqa*."

The Continental Hotel was an old trekkers' hangout and the only place in Dir offering western-style accommodations. It had all the modern amenities one could ask for—hot food, warm beds, indoor plumbing, satellite television, English-language newspapers, and even a lack-luster disco on the weekends. In more peaceful days, the hotel had been a magnet for tourists craving a break from the rustic appeal of the tribal areas, an exotic home away from home.

The Continental was also one of the few places where a tourist or a non-Muslim could drink alcohol, mostly domestically produced Murree beer and liquor. This was a boon for several varieties of people with otherwise divergent interests—climbers, hikers, eco-tourists, business people, pilgrims, agents of all kinds, terrorists, spies, and the omnipresent Pakistan security apparatus.

Gino, who in his current incarnation managed to combine several of those interests, established a temporary place of business at a table in one corner of the bar. He sipped fruit juice like a good Muslim, read the papers, met the occasional faux business contact, and observed the foot traffic.

The appearance at the hotel of a television news team didn't surprise Gino. Nobody craves western-style comforts more than the darlings and dandies of the international news media, especially the crews from the anti-western, Islamic news network called *Al Haqiqa*—The Truth. But news reporters chase after news stories. Something was up.

CHAPTER 33

Pancho's Misgivings

Pancho and Ritter crawled down the mountain in the darkness, paralleling the road south away from Kotkay village, and crossed the Chukyatan Bridge to their rendezvous point. They waited in a grove of trees off the road. The nearby river, churning dirty white on its downhill run through the rocky valley floor, provided a comforting roar to muffle voices as they discussed options—a good meeting place.

As they peered across the road, a blinking red pinpoint began transmitting in their direction. Three short blinks, three long, three more short. Morse code for SOS. The blinks would have gone unnoticed except for their light-enhancing night vision goggles. Ritter blinked back the response, and a black figure crossed over to join them—Jake Drecker in shadow mode with night vision goggles.

They all huddled under a camouflage poncho amidst the trees to consider the next move.

"I'm going in," Jake announced.

Drecker's words caught Pancho off guard, and yet was the kind of audacious proposal he expected from Jake.

"No, Jake, I think it's too hot for that," Pancho said. He was violating his own rule of letting Ritter run the show because of Twister's information about the hostage, information he felt he couldn't share with Ritter. Not now. So, he took the initiative to squash Jake's startling offer at its inception.

"Jake, I agree with Pancho," Ritter added. "We don't even know who or what is inside."

"Well, how long do you think it will take for us to realize this guy isn't playing by our rules?" Jake asked. "We need to either pry out what we need or upset his expectations. I am willing to risk it."

"Intel does indeed suck," Ritter sighed.

"Then maybe we just need to pull out and scrub the mission," Pancho suggested. He wondered if he sounded too strong. He listened for the tone in their replies.

Jake wasted no time.

"Pancho, the CIA is gonna wipe out the target and kill the hostage if we let them. We can't do that. We don't kill Americans. We rescue them and kill the bad guys. Like Azzam," Jake said. "I say we do whatever it takes."

Ritter nodded agreement. Pancho was stymied.

Jake, you knew all along.

"And let me do my own risk assessment on this one," Jake continued. "I know the risks."

Ritter stroked his chin, his eyes hidden behind his night vision goggles. Pancho examined his companions in the dark. With their unconventional garb and goggles, they resembled colorless Power Rangers.

"Okay," Ritter finally interjected. "I have an idea. It's crazy, it's dangerous, and it will probably get us all killed, but I think it will play."

"Okay," Pancho said. "Let's hear it."

Ritter laid out his plan as Pancho nodded, and Jake Drecker sat as still and stony as a sphinx.

In the end, and after making a few changes, they all agreed to Ritter's plan.

Pancho warned the two lower-ranking men the new plan would never get approved by their chain of command—it was just too risky. Ritter and Drecker listened but didn't care, and so Pancho didn't override them. He still couldn't bring himself to tell Ritter all he knew. The information was too touchy. How could Jake be so cool headed given the circumstances? But he was, so Pancho decided to resign himself to letting things take their course. He would continue to rely on Ritter's unemotional and objective decision-making.

"Well, Jake the Snake, I guess this is it. Make your own luck." Pancho resisted an urge to hug Jake. Ritter wouldn't understand the gesture, because Ritter didn't know what Pancho knew.

"You know it, boss. You too." Jake grasped Pancho's hand, and then gave Ritter an affectionate slap on the shoulder.

Pancho and Ritter watched the shadow disappear across the road. They had all agreed not just with the plan but also Ritter's assessment.

It was crazy, it was dangerous.
It would play.
And it would probably get them all killed.

CHAPTER 34

Colonel Pasha

Colonel Pasha was enjoying a stellar day when the phone call came and ruined everything.

He was in Marden at a special office he maintained, because he couldn't bring himself to keep one in dreary Dir. He sat alone, cigarette dangling from his mouth, in a darkened room under a rotating ceiling fan. His feet were propped up on the desk, and a bottle of Scotch and a pistol sat within easy reach.

He was thinking, ironically, he would reflect later about his "niece," the venturesome Jassi, when Ali's call came. Jassi was away on holiday with her German lover in Sri Lanka. Pasha rather liked Sri Lanka and had pleasurable memories of the place from a government arms sale junket there. Jassi was probably frolicking near naked on a beach, cavorting with the infidels at some hedonistic get-away favored by decadent Europeans. He knew their ways.

His fantasy was interrupted by buzzing from his cell phone. He answered, "Salaam."

On the phone was Ali, his favorite informer.

"Yes, of course, Ali, this is Colonel Pasha."

They exchanged a verification code, and Colonel Pasha listened before responding.

"Yes, Ali. Jassi is still at the academic seminar in Colombo. There are many good Muslims there to keep an eye on her. Yes, tell me about it."

Ali's success as an informer was both a boon and a burden. He had provided a steady flow of information on the Pakistan Martyr Brigade and its myriad extremist associations. This suited Colonel Pasha's ambitions well. He had staged a real coup in having a paid informer inside the group that had kidnapped an American missionary. It raised his stock considerably, especially among the Americans.

But having an inside informant also raised expectations. This was a problem. The Americans and Pasha's superiors at ISI possessed voracious appetites for intelligence. They now demanded more than he was willing or able to give. Colonel Pasha was one to milk the information flow. Like a card player hanging on to his best cards, he preferred to save his informational nuggets for those times when he needed to advance his own agenda. Now he was under increased pressure to pursue even greater intelligence scoops with little remuneration for his troubles. By ingratiating himself with the Americans and impressing his ISI superiors with his ability to make them look good, he had lost the very thing he feared losing the most—control. And now Ali was going to drop something on him that would force his hand with the Americans.

"You are sure about this? On Thursday? This Thursday morning?"

Pasha broke a pencil. He had only managed a few illegible scribbles before he bent it beyond the breaking point.

"*Al Haqiqa* has already visited the compound and made all the arrangements? This is terrible," Pasha said, thinking of his own inconvenience and professional situation. "Okay. Get me more specific details, I need more information. Can you call me back later today?"

Pasha listened to Ali's assent.

"Okay, Ali, salaam," Pasha finally said, concluding the call.

He leaned back, inhaled long and hard on his cigarette, and exhaled in the direction of the ceiling fan.

"God!" he exclaimed, dropping his feet to the ground and leaning toward the Scotch.

He poured a shot glass full and leaned back as he took a long, slow sip of the hot liquid. He had learned the evil habit while at Staff College in Quetta and never regretted it. A reminder of those old colonial masters, the English, who'd left a few vices behind when they vacated the sub-continent. A poison which evoked class and culture. The Colonel possessed neither.

With a sigh of resignation, he picked up his phone, connecting at once to the switchboard operator in an outer room.

"Get me the American embassy, their cultural secretary, right away. Thank you."

As he waited, he drew another cigarette cloud deep inside and let it out with a second loud sigh.

The cultural secretary picked up on the other end. Pasha did not wait to speak.

"Bob, this is Colonel Pasha, we need to meet first thing in the morning."

The other party responded.

"Yes, Bob, I know. I am sorry to contact you this way, but it's urgent. It involves the American hostage and *Al Haqiqa*."

He paused as the caller reacted.

"Yes, that is correct, the Islamic news network, *Al Haqiqa*. They have something in the works involving your missionary, and it's going down on Thursday morning. Right, we don't have much time to react. Of course, I will inform my superiors immediately, but I wanted you to know."

With that, he hung up the phone.

Colonel Pasha was not looking forward to passing this latest bit of information on to his superiors. They would wonder why it took him so long to find out, though some of them probably knew before he did. The Americans took pretty good care of him, even promised him a future trip to a special security school in Hawaii. He was glad he contacted Bob right away.

Even as Colonel Pasha's phone call with Bob ended, the transcript of his conversation with Ali was being analyzed on the other side of the planet by a language specialist at Fort Meade, Maryland. Bob, before leaving the office for their early morning meeting the next day, read the complete text on his classified computer. As far as the Americans were concerned, there were many things Colonel Pasha didn't need to know.

CHAPTER 35

Sniper

The sniper's tactical disciplines have remained virtually unchanged since 1800, when the British Army, wincing from its demoralizing defeat in the American Revolutionary War, formed the first modern sniper organization—the Corps of Riflemen. The Corps of Riflemen embraced the unconventional sharpshooting tactics of the backwoods American revolutionary as their own. They even exchanged the famous British redcoat for uniforms of forest green.

Eight years later, when the unit took to the field as the 95th Regiment of Foot during the Peninsular War, these tactics wrought devastation among Napoleon's officer corps. The regiment's most famous member, Rifleman Thomas Plunket, was said to have shot and killed Napoleon's cavalry commander, General Auguste Colbert, from a distance of eight hundred meters—a near miracle range for the then modern Baker rifle. To prove it was not a chance shot, Plunket is said to have reloaded and fired again, taking the life of a trumpet major coming to Colbert's aid—a good day in the history of the long gun.

The same tactics guided the sniper well into the twentieth century when the Marine Corps wrote its first sniper manual during World War One. The guide would not be updated until after the Vietnam War, when the legendary Carlos Hathcock was an instructor at the USMC scout/sniper course at Quantico.

Sniper manual updates reflected mostly changes in technology, not technique. The basic rules still applied well into the 21st century, and Pancho had committed them to memory:

Engage the enemy at great distance—one shot, one kill. Never fire a second shot from the same position. Always stay alert. Never return to the same hide spot. Be one with your environment, and rely on cover and concealment for your defense. Never take a life casually. Record everything in a logbook. Know your enemy.

But these rules, like all others in the human record, were often broken. If Ritter's plan had any hope of succeeding, Pancho would need to break several this day. Pancho prayed while working out the complicated details of his task.

When you break these kinds of rules, somebody is going to get hurt.

Pancho considered the ground, about four hundred feet of exposed rock and scrub brush to crawl through to get within sprinting distance to the Campus mosque.

Once there, with a mix of dumb luck, pluck, and grace, I can make it to the top of the minaret without being seen. Security is lax. Just got to avoid being seen by the watchman in that thirty-foot, Middle Ages tower. But I am guessing he's probably focused on the road up from Kotkay.

Pancho was working alone. No problem. Nothing new for a Tier One operator. A definite advantage to remain unnoticed. A disadvantage if compromised. Team Condor would be too busy to render aid. They have their own part to play in the unraveling saga of Ritter's audacious plan. Besides, plausible deniability was in effect. Even Uncle Sam wouldn't come to the rescue out here.

Pancho went over Ritter's instructions. Cover and observe Jake Drecker from the minaret as Jake attempted to enter the front of the Compound and then the Cabin. If the target walked out any time after Jake went in, Pancho was to shoot. If any disturbance took place inside and Jake left in a hurry, Pancho would shoot to prevent anyone inside from following him out. If shooting started inside and fighters from the Parking Garage evaded Team Condor's lead screen and got inside the compound, Pancho was to take them out. If nothing happened, Pancho would sit. It was Sunday evening. The mosque went unused until the arrival of the Imam on Thursday evening in preparation for Friday's religious show. If nothing happened, Pancho would stay until either something did or until Wednesday evening, 2300 hours, arrived—at which time he would return to Team Condor.

The time factor was critical. He had all night to get into position in the minaret, but he had to be there before daylight. The next phase would begin the following evening with the insertion of the recon/direct action element, AKA Jake Drecker, inside the compound.

Pancho crawled on, elbows and knees grinding painfully over the stony ground.

CHAPTER 36

Perspectives

Gino downshifted as the Subaru turned the corner and moved up toward the compound. In the front seat alongside, sat Jannat. She wore the full, sky-blue *burqa*, the Afghan kind called a *chadri* that covered even the eyes behind an eye screen—the perfect outfit for concealing the 9mm MP5 assault gun resting on her lap. Another chadri-clad person squatted in the truck bed, surrounded by baskets of fruit, nuts, and *naan*—the local flat bread made from white flour and sprinkled with sesame seeds. The truck-bed burqa concealed more than just a gun.

Gino hadn't liked the plan, but he obeyed orders. Play the part of just another practicing pilgrim with food for the jihadi fighters of Maktab al-Khidamat. Haji, delivery boy to a house full of terrorists.

Gino had a bad feeling. Exposing his hand to the target or allowing a team member to go inside alone, even disguised, to gather more intelligence or … execute the hit solo. Bad idea. And there were about twenty fighters around this compound. Not good odds.

Gino and his wife only needed to drop off their charge, move back down the road, and wait at a rendezvous point just to the north. If there was shooting, they would return to the Dir safe house and wait things out while Jake extracted with Condor. If there was no shooting, they were to wait two hours for Jake to return down the road on foot. After two hours, they were to assume a problem and move back to Dir.

If they miscalculated …

Someone, as my good Italian grandmother used to say, was gonna lose an eye.

Ritter stacked ammunition and upgraded his position for the next move. He took turns with Eason maintaining vigilance and noting changes in the target area—tedious, exhausting work. Nothing appeared to be happening down there.

He was hopeful, thinking about the odds. Sure, they were a small team, but surprise and superior marksmanship would win the day if it came down to a firefight. And this nasty group of terrorists lived in their own little world. Even the Pakistani government wanted them gone. There was no one for them to call when things got desperate. Team Owl could melt into the mountains before any of the jokers in the Cabin even knew what hit them.

That was the plan. *Hopefully.*

But hope is not a method.

Ritter bit his lip.

Why did I have to think that now?

Ritter got back to the business at hand and tried to forget his lingering, nagging doubts. He reflected on the day's enemy activities.

The fighters in the Parking Garage performed their morning calisthenics and then went to the range. There were eleven today, led, as always, by Track Suit. There were twenty total identified fighters on the Campus, including Azzam's body guards. Ritter wasn't sure where everyone was, but those odds felt good.

Ritter nicknamed one of the bodyguards—a tall, bullish-looking man with a black mustache, green uniform, and Arab headdress—Sergeant Major. He was the one giving orders to people like Track Suit.

The eleven were a pool of young, scrawny-looking recruits dressed in a motley assortment of mostly black clothes and black turbans. Pakistani Taliban-types. With worn AK-47's, Russian-style ammo pouches, and Adidas on their feet, all probably heading to an early grave in either Afghanistan or Kashmir. Or he hoped, if things went down now, right here.

The fighters returned from the range early and everyone assembled for an afternoon class in the compound yard. Ritter could almost feel the Sergeant Major from a distance as he berated them and led them through some Arabic cheers in preparation for a ninety-minute speech by an angry, bearded, Taliban elder. Then class ended, and they broke up. The recruits went back to their austere quarters in the Parking Garage, the others to the hidden comforts of the Cabin.

Ritter eyed the Minaret. Pancho was there by now, no doubt. The spotting scope showed only shadows. It was dark in there. Eason said he'd detected some movement there during his late morning shift. A shadow had moved that wasn't a bird. The Minaret wasn't very large, its top part no more than eight feet across at its widest point. It was more symbolic than practical as the call for prayer was performed by loudspeaker. If Pancho couldn't get there in time, he would have returned. Had he been discovered, they would have seen a disturbance.

No. Pancho must be up there by now ... had to be.

CHAPTER 37

The Infiltration

The early evening sun had found comfort behind the western range of mountains, and long shadows extended over the valley. Ritter shook off a slight chill and watched.

Small fires were lit on the second floor of the Parking Garage as the fighters brewed tea and broke bread. Smoke trailed up from two small chimneys in the roof of the Cabin. Track Suit emerged from the compound in his running outfit and began to stretch in the Car Park area.

A Subaru came up the road, piled high in the back with baskets of fruit and bread.

A skinny, bushy-haired man with a hand-held radio came out from the Compound. Bearded like the others, he was one of Azzam's boys. Ritter nicknamed him Hostess, because he greeted all the incoming vehicles. He had a patterned scarf around his neck and an AKS-74U carbine with paratrooper stock slung over his left shoulder. Like many protocol types back in the world, he wore the best uniform—pressed and starched olive-drab green—with polished black boots and exuded a nervy earnestness and self-importance that probably drove his fellow terrorists crazy. Ritter disliked him at first sight.

Hostess spoke to the driver, who never got out of the truck. Two burqas accompanied the man. The one in the front seat, presumably his wife. The second, in the back, a relative perhaps, one for whom the driver acted as a *mahram* or familial chaperone. The burqa in the back climbed gingerly out and unloaded several shallow baskets. Hostess seemed annoyed. He was arguing with the driver, who finally got out and walked to the back of the truck to show him his wares. His wife never left her seat on the passenger side.

Hostess, caught up in a heated discussion with the bearish, jovial driver, took no notice as the other passenger, the Burqa, placed a basket of bread on her head and carried her load over to the compound wall. In this way, several baskets were unloaded.

The driver called to the Burqa with the baskets and gave several commands, presumably in either Dari or Persian, for the driver was a refugee from Herat in western Afghanistan. Hostess, finally convinced of the driver's good intentions, spoke into his radio. The compound gate opened from inside, and several men came into the Car Park and smoked cigarettes. Burqa made two trips to the Car Park side by the gate. On the third trip, the Burqa didn't stop outside the opened gate but continued right in.

Jannat, still seated in the truck's passenger seat, watched the drama unfold through the grilled eye covering of her own sky-blue burqa. The covering gave her a strange sense of security and invisibility. She felt detached, like a child who thinks no one can see them when they cover their own eyes. Viewing things through the truck's mud splattered windshield only added to the effect. It was like watching everything on television. Only the comforting weight of the MP5 machine gun in her lap reminded her of the deadly task at hand. She knew she should be more afraid.

Her husband spoke to the thin, bearded man with the intense eyes and hand-held radio in a mix of Dari and Persian. The man spoke back in Dari. He was Taliban and probably preferred Pashto. Gino let the man know he was a merchant, an agent for a Pakistani agricultural concern but originally a refugee from western Afghanistan. She listened to the scripted discussion filled with tribal honorifics and poetic clichés which her husband had mastered years before at language school. She was proud. He had been her best student.

Gino was bargaining with the bearded man. There was a negotiation going on involving sheep or goat meat to feed the collection of mujahid in the compound. An agreement was reached. Gino said something about returning with the gift of a goat in the evening.

Jannat was disinterested in the ruse. Her eyes remained on their burqa-covered passenger who kept unloading the baskets of fruit. Jannat wanted to get out and help, but it would be too dangerous. So, she watched, secure in her invisibility.

With the conclusion of the deal, Gino exchanged honorifics and restarted the truck.

The bearded man, distracted by the promise of meat, forgot about the third passenger with the baskets, the Burqa, who was about to be left behind.

As the truck turned, Jannat thought she saw the Burqa take one last look in her direction. She lifted her hand in a silent goodbye gesture. Burqa didn't gesture back.

Jannat had a revelation.

He's not going in there to recon the inside. If he was, we'd be staying and waiting for him. He's going in there to finish the mission. To kill Azzam and rescue the American.

Or die trying.

Jannat shook under the burqa as her husband steered the truck back down the hill, as something horrific knotted deep in the pit of her stomach. Fear.

In his perch in the Minaret, Pancho saw everything. The Subaru, the driver, Hostess, and then, finally, Burqa's last trip to the compound gate as the Subaru moved back down the road toward Kotkay.

He could observe those things which were hidden from Ritter and Eason. He could see the Cabin's front door and several feet inside. He could see the yard between the compound's western wall and the Cabin. He saw the thirty-foot tower's east and south faces including gun ports that were less narrow than the one facing Team Condor on the hill. Finally, he could see the compound gate, the little sub-dramas there among Azzam's people, and the place where Burqa left the baskets.

He watched Burqa take the third trip toward the gate. Over the last four days, they had seen others deliver their goods to the compound. Many had made the same trip as Burqa. But this was different. Pancho hadn't known those others, didn't know what they encountered. Now he wanted to know more than anything else what Burqa would be facing inside that squalid little Cabin. Because this time, the Burqa was Jake Drecker.

PRODIGAL AVENGER

As the sky-blue material disappeared inside the dimly lit entranceway to the Cabin, Pancho felt something horrible churning inside, nauseating him.

He had known fear before but never this extreme. He prayed.

God, I am a fool. Lord, please, please, please, forgive me for allowing this to go on. I could have stopped it. I knew he shouldn't go, but I let him go anyway. I went along with his self-confidence and didn't want to offend him. Now, whatever happens to Jake Drecker, it's my fault. God, please have mercy on my soul. And God, please, save Jake Drecker.

PART 6

The Return of the Prodigal

CHAPTER 38

Jake

Jake, in his female disguise and carrying a basket of naan with both hands, worked his way toward the Cabin door. The door swung open. Someone beckoning from inside. The strong stench of onions and sweat mixed with something else. Blood?

The door closed hard behind him with a muffled thud. A dingy hall filled with tables, debris, and deadly men—mujahidin. Count the doorways. Count the people. *Where does that bolted doorway lead?*

The hallway ran to the left and right of the entranceway. There were two small tables lining the wall on the opposite side. Two young, but tough looking, mujahidin at a table littered with tea cups, cigarettes, and newspapers. More formidable, no doubt, than the recruits out in the Parking Garage.

I can take them.

The rectangular windows high on the Cabin's outer wall provided faint ambient lighting. The weak light didn't reach low enough to dispel the dimness hovering over the filthy concrete floor.

The men at the tables stopped talking and eyed him.

They have no idea who is underneath this burqa.

The men glanced toward the ground.

Ogling my feet. It's the sandals with the painted toenails poking out, no doubt. One of my better touches. The kind of detail that might just save my life.

Jake smiled under the burqa.

The mujahidin who'd opened the door for him gestured to the right. Take the bread that way.

Jake was wound tight. Ready. Speed, surprise, and shock would incapacitate everyone in the Cabin before they could react. Two or three basket-laden trips would confirm their numbers and identify the priority targets. Then, game on.

As he turned right, he glanced to the left and saw another door, almost directly opposite the entrance. It was bolted shut on the hall side with a small slide at eye-level. The prisoner holding cell door. The American.

As he passed the tables, one of the seated men reached up and snatched a piece of naan from his basket. The man leered, but Jake kept his cool. He pushed the envelope to go further inside.

Just past the tables, the hallway led to a dimly lit chamber with a low table and pillows all around. Two bare but surprisingly bright lightbulbs hung by their wires from the ceiling and illuminated the room. The bulbs fought back the darkness in each corner and cast long shadows in conflicting directions as Jake moved around the table and toward the back. A large Panasonic television held the place of honor at the head of the table, its huge electronic eye black with inactivity. Cigarette smoke struggled to mask the strong smells of human sweat, rotting fruit, and chopped onions.

This was the dining area.

The man spoke guttural Pashtun in harsh, choppy tones, ordering the "servant girl" to place the bread basket in the corner of the room furthest from the entrance. Jake obeyed, dropping the basket as told and making his way back. He glanced left, further down the hall. Two open doors with voices inside but no one could be seen. No confirmed target, anyway.

He moved back toward the entrance.

Two more trips should do it.

The men at the table stared hard at him. There were four in the hallway now, the two at the table, the door man, who was now behind him, and another at the opposite end. They talked in a low tone and cast glances in his direction. "… *kanjar*."

He hadn't heard everything they were saying. They were mainly speaking Pashto, but he recognized that word.

Kanjar is a bad word in Pakistan. It can mean several things. Technically, Kanjars are a social class, a gypsy ethnic group specializing in "entertainment." Kanjar means dancing girl, referring to a traditional, sensuous exotic kind of dancer who offers sexual favors on the side. Pakistan's most popular euphemism for a prostitute or a whore. If a man is called a kanjar he is being called either a pimp or "son of a whore".

Jake remembered his painted toenails. Now it all made sense.

Dang!

Jake was mad for not having considered it. This explained why the previous female food deliverers they'd seen during their surveillance had spent so much time inside. And why the men who delivered them to the Campus spent so much time haggling with Hostess. It was all about business. They weren't just delivering food. They were trafficking in delivery girls.

No wonder they took such an unhealthy, prurient interest in my size sevens!

One of the leering men at the table made the first move, reaching out and grabbing for Jake's loose-fitting outer garment. Jake sidestepped the groping hand.

Man!

Jake gripped the basket tight with one hand while reaching underneath his burqa for his silenced Ruger. *These guys are in for a big surprise.*

Jake never drew the pistol. Before he knew it, he was tripped up by one of the others in the hallway. He went down hard and the men were on him, pinning him down.

These jokers think they're gonna have their way with a woman! Guess they're gonna be disappointed.

The men held Jake by the limbs as he tried to squirm free. They rolled him onto his back, and one dropped both knees down on Jake's stomach nearly knocking the wind out of him. Jake stopped squirming. He felt them loosen their hold as he knew they would. They still thought he was a weak woman.

The man on his stomach pulled the burqa up from Jake's ankles. Jake had *shalvars* on underneath, the loose-fitting, pajama-like trousers worn by both men and women in Pakistan. His disguise would hold out for a little longer.

Jake felt the Ruger slip from its shoulder holster under his armpit and drop under him. He struggled to free a hand so he could get to the gun before his tormenters did.

His right arm came free, and Jake sent a terrific blow to the temple of the man on his stomach. The man went down stunned, falling to Jake's left. Jake rolled in the same direction, the men at his ankles losing their grip. He clawed for the pistol but the burqa had turned with Jake inside and he could no longer see through the eye grill. He jumped to his feet and jerked the burqa off his body and up over his head.

The men were shocked to discover what the burqa had hidden so well—a small, but lethal, male commando with close-cut blond hair and lean, muscular arms. All that remained of the disguise was the chest pad underneath the tee-shirt and mascara around each green-grey eye. The four began yelling alarms in Arabic and Pashto.

Jake scanned for the dropped Ruger. It lay where it had fallen, right on the floor between the legs of one of the jihadists.

Jake snapped open a small switchblade hidden in the palm of his left hand. He lunged and slashed toward the man straddling the gun. The man stepped back from the flashing blade, and Jake lunged again, this time downward with his right hand to grab back the pistol. But the man's left foot inadvertently kicked it out of Jake's reach.

Jake's fingers scraped concrete, and they were on him again.

More men entered the room. Jake was on his stomach as tremendous kicks were sent to his head and ribs.

A loud, authoritative voice shouted at his tormentors in Arabic.

They paused and raised Jake's head so the newcomer could see his battered face. A large Arab in a tan uniform, headscarf and black combat boots squatted in front of Jake and lifted his chin—the target, Abbas Bin Azzam, the man Jake had come to kill.

"So now we have two for the show," Azzam said in Arabic. "Secure him well and put him in the cell with the other one."

The squatting man acknowledged the order and dropped Jake's chin.

There were more kicks.

The last thing Jake remembered before everything went black was his chin hitting concrete as he was dropped down hard inside a holding cell.

CHAPTER 39

The Dream

The recurring childhood nightmare never changed.

Jake Drecker lying on a trail leading down a desolate hillside. Severely wounded, he can't move. He is naked and helpless.

Coming up the trail are men, fierce-looking soldiers, dark complexioned, like Somalis. Armed with machetes and guns, he knows they are coming for him.

A pack of hyenas is with them, snarling, vicious. He hears their guttural growls and sharp nails scratching on the stony ground. Jack can smell their foul breath before they get to him.

A comforting presence is behind him. Another soldier, powerful, somewhere up on the hill. He knows this ally is near, but he can't see him. Part of him doesn't want to see.

Then he hears words, comforting words, in a familiar voice. The voice of his father. The voice as he remembers it from long ago when he was a child.

"I'm here, Jake, I can help you, just call on me."

But Jake doesn't call. He won't. He insists on facing his enemies alone, like he always has. So, he lies still and waits.

With one word from the enemy, the hyenas are upon him. He can do nothing but roll once to his left onto his stomach. He can't see what is happening, but he feels his head, his back, his buttocks, his legs being beaten and torn by these hyenas and their evil masters. He cries out, but he still won't call for help.

The last thing he sees, as he lies on his stomach looking uphill, is the soldier coming down toward him, reaching out a hand to rescue him. It's his father.

"Take my hand, Jake, I can save you."

He screams, but he holds back his own hand, refuses the offer and does nothing. Yet, he cannot move or help himself. That's when the dream always ends.

CHAPTER 40

The Cell

Jake awoke on his stomach, his face pressed against the cool, grimy cement floor. The pain was everywhere. Shoulders, neck, face—he couldn't even raise his head.

Well, this changes everything.

His wrists and ankles were bound with his hands in the small of his back. His right shoulder and arm were numb from lack of circulation, his face felt puffy, and his eyes strangely out of alignment. He rolled over onto his back—easier. He stared up at the single white lightbulb hanging from a wire that illuminated the room. He was in a bad place, yet he felt calm, at peace. This was where he wanted to be, and if this was the end of his ride, so be it.

He took stock of his surroundings.

The room was small, dingy, no more than twelve feet by twelve feet. The lightbulb, far brighter than the usual underpowered Third World light source, hung stiffly in the center of the ceiling. A short metal chain ran down from its socket, just out of reach of any average man's grasp. Jake took a mental note. Anyone reaching for the chain would need to get up on the tips of their toes to reach it. Jake filed the thought away for future use. A narrow window, grilled with old fashioned iron bars, sat high up on the wall to his left. Too small to consider for an escape route. It cast a faint glow of natural light against a decrepit Arabic banner hanging on the opposite wall that read *Death to every unbeliever!*

The slogan made Jake smile.

Nice!

There was an odd symmetry in the room. He continued scanning until his eyes stopped at a new discovery. Another prisoner in the cell, the

American missionary. Jake rolled on his side and looked toward the cell's door. He couldn't face him just yet.

"Welcome to Pakistan, Chief Drecker, I wondered when you would arrive."

Jake rolled back over and stared at his cellmate.

Lean, gray haired and haggard, the missionary, Isidore Loewenthal, sat with his back against the far wall. If he were to stand, he would be considered above average in height but not tall. His complexion was pale, except for several red and purple facial welts inflicted by his hosts. His hands, like Jake's, were bound behind his back.

From his position, Jake could clearly make out the unusual color of the man's eyes. He had traveled half way around the world to see those eyes.

Jake stared at the man for several minutes. Then he glanced once more around the room. The missionary's words couldn't be ignored.

Jake opened his mouth. Dryness choked his words, and his eyes wanted to water. He needed to control himself. He cleared his throat so he could speak to the man he had risked everything to save.

"It's good to see you again, Dad."

CHAPTER 41

Pancho

At the sniper hole overlooking the target, Pancho's deep breathing threatened to alert the enemy and give away his position. He was distressed, to say the least, and needed to discuss the alternatives with the rest of the team.

'The plan,' as they say in the Army, 'had not survived contact with the enemy.'

He wondered if Jake had time now for ironic thoughts. Probably. Knowing Jake.

Something had happened inside the Cabin. Jake had disappeared. The only hint that something had gone wrong was that several jihadists, including Track Suit, were summoned to the Cabin about thirty minutes after Drecker had gone in. Within minutes, an armed group left the Cabin and proceeded down the road toward Kotkay, probably in search of Gino's truck. Another group, led by Track Suit, disappeared up the valley.

Guards had also fanned out around the Campus. Pancho watched a white-bearded, elderly mujahidin in camouflage jacket and black turban trudge up the hill to the mosque. The old man disappeared below him, and Pancho heard the man's footsteps around the base of the minaret.

Great! I've got my own personal 'minder' down there.

They must have discovered Jake's disguise and were looking for accomplices. The mission was compromised. Not good. Very bad, in fact. But how very bad, it was too soon to tell. At least it was getting dark. Darkness would cover them until they decided their next move.

Pancho squirmed. He hadn't planned on spending the night in the minaret. He had an encrypted PRC-148 radio with headset to call Ritter, but if he did, his buddy—the guard posted below in the mosque—might hear. There were physical considerations also. He would soon be out of water, and he really needed to climb down in the dark and relieve himself somewhere.

Pancho peered down the rough, log ladder into the mosque. He saw nothing.

He put on his night vision goggles. There was little to see, but he felt good knowing he could see in the dark and his opponent could not.

He considered using his pistol or his K-bar knife to dispatch the guard, but he'd have to take forty-five seconds to trundle down that ladder, creaking and rattling all the way, which would give his opponent too much warning. And if he killed the man, what would he do with the body? His buddies would be searching for him in the morning. There seemed to be no way out of this one.

He listened. The guard was not trying to hide himself as he smoked cigarettes, hummed a tune, and threw stones at the hillside.

Pancho thought about the man. He looked like a classic Pathan type, an elderly Taliban who had probably fought the Russians as a young man. Pancho felt no ill will toward him. This was no terrorist who hid behind women and children, a homicide bomber, or martyr wannabe. This was just a fiercely independent mountain man caught up on the wrong side of a huge, geo-political conflict he would never understand. One in which foreigners like Pancho invaded his homeland. Land and religion were all that mattered to these people, and Pancho didn't hate them. In fact, he admired the more noble ideals of Pathan and Arab culture and respected those who lived in accordance with them. But this one was on the wrong team, that's all.

Pancho kept listening for sounds from below. Finally, the guard seemed to have sat down to rest, because there was almost no sound at all but heavy breathing.

Then Pancho heard it, rhythmic and loud.

Snoring.

The man had fallen sound asleep.

Pancho could move now.

CHAPTER 42

The Prodigal

"How did you know I was coming?" Jake asked the man with whom he shared his gray-green eyes.

Jake and his father were alone. Their cell made for a secure, unlikely sanctuary for their reunion. Here they were, amid Al Qaeda terrorists, surrounded by hard walls and hard men who hated everything the two Americans represented. Yet, they were more together now than at any time before in their adult lives.

"Two reasons. First, I prayed. I prayed God would arrange this somehow, and when I arrived here, I felt His peace about it."

Jake squinted at his father. He tried to see the situation like his father did, but the religious reference touched a nerve. How did his father expect his new religion to erase the years of drunken neglect and self-centeredness that had destroyed their family? He'd abandoned his son at the very time in his life when Jake needed him most.

Jake's mind rolled back the years, and the memories flashed.

His father's middle-aged religious conversion, ten years after the divorce from his mother—an object of scorn and mockery for their broken family, the crowning act of the charade his father's life had become. Jake's sister broke the news.

"Dad's lost his marbles again" was how she'd said it. "He's found God up in San Francisco and wants us all to know how sorry he is for everything."

Jake laughed then. His dad, he figured, retired from the military, was probably off on another bender, living it up with some old hippie chick and attending occasional Alcoholics Anonymous meetings to keep from hitting rock bottom.

"No, this is serious," she insisted. "He calls himself a Messianic Jew for Jesus."

That was even more preposterous. Jake's self-reliance and secular Jewishness had served as a protective wall around himself, his marriage to Ruth, and the life he intended to live—utterly unlike his father's. He neither drank nor smoked, and he stubbornly refused to acknowledge even a whiff of a problem in his marriage. But even back then, Jake's chosen career was taking him down paths he never ever intended to go. Just as his father's marriage and family had been sacrificed on the altar of career and image, Jake's life was moving in the same merciless direction. Jake didn't realize he was building his own life on the same pile of shifting sand his father had for several more years.

His father's conversion seemed genuine. Out went the booze and the flaky girlfriends, and in came a fanatical obsession with telling everyone about God and Jesus. Jake remained out of his father's evangelical reach, but his sister stayed in touch with the old man. While Jake rebuffed his father's attempts at reconciliation, she maintained enough contact to keep him abreast of their father's new life. Their father's move to Phoenix, his street ministry working among alcoholics and Hispanics, his pilgrimages to the Holy Land. His move to Israel, where he applied for citizenship and became a dual citizen of the US and Israel. His later ministry back in Phoenix.

Then came his latest exploit—volunteering to go overseas as a missionary in Pakistan—to use his foreign area and linguistic expertise in a place where he'd spent much of his career as a US Air Force arms merchant and military attaché—a risky move on so many levels. In his previous life, he benefited from diplomatic protection and immunity. As a Christian missionary, he was alone, evangelizing in one of the stoniest harvest fields in the world, without US government cover and with an unpopular American war just across the border in neighboring Afghanistan.

Jake spent his life shielding himself from his father, hiding behind his stepfather's last name and disappearing in the special operations world. No one had suspected a relationship between kidnapped American missionary, Isidore Loewenthal, and Jake Drecker, Chief Warrant Officer, United States Army Special Operations Command.

Jake bit his lip. He couldn't mend the past now. He was losing the same family battles his father had once lost, ones he vowed he would somehow win on his own. Even Ruth was making a move he could not, or would not, understand or accept, unaware of the effect her decisions were having on her husband.

Like father, like son. The apple doesn't fall far from the tree. And now, this God of his father's was orchestrating the final act of a cosmic joke that drew Jake along against both his will and his better judgment.

Jake's mind wandered back to the cell and to the conversation with his father.

How can he be so full of pious platitudes after all he'd done?

Jake's eyes maintained their practiced, placid coolness. No losing his cool now. Not in front of his father.

"Okay, and the second reason?"

"Because I know you, Jake. You were always the rescuer of the family, always saving people, saving animals. Remember that summer when you were nine and you jumped into the lake to rescue your cousin, Elizabeth? You could barely swim!"

"Sure, Dad, I remember that. I also remember how you weren't there when it happened."

"I know. We were supposed to spend that summer together as a family. But I was in Africa on a contingency operation. I should have been there, but I had a job to do, the same kind of job you have now."

Jake changed the subject.

"So, you knew I would come and save you? Risk everything? Convince people in my unit you were worth possibly sacrificing their lives for?"

"I knew you would do your duty—no matter who you were rescuing."

"Okay, so here I am. I tried to save you, fine. But you don't understand the big picture. I've been compromised now, and we may not make it out of here alive, Dad. This is not a mission Uncle Sam is going to acknowledge if we botch it."

"You've got it wrong. I am already free." Isidore Loewenthal paused before continuing. "You may have come here to save me in the only way you know how, but God brought you here because God wants to save you."

Another pause.

"My prayer, son, was not that you would come and save me but that I would have one more chance to witness to you so you could get saved."

Jake looked hard at the man.

He studied the eyes. They were warm, greener than the gray he remembered so well, and clearer than he had ever seen them.

True, his father was different now. Had something Jake couldn't pin down. His father spoke again.

"Do you believe the prophets, Jake?"

"Dad, I don't believe—period. I'm Jewish, I'm secular, and I'm not interested."

"I mean our Jewish prophets, Jake," his father continued unfazed. "Moments like these are prophesied in the Jewish scriptures."

His father closed his eyes and began to quote.

"The last two verses in the Old Testament, Malachi chapter four. *'Behold, I will send you Elijah the prophet before the coming of the great and dreadful day of the LORD: And he shall turn the heart of the fathers to the children, and the heart of the children to their fathers, lest I come and smite the earth with a curse.'*

"That's the last thing God says in the Old Testament before sending his son, Jesus Christ, to die for our sins. Luke's gospel picks up exactly where Malachi leaves off. Luke describes John the Baptist as one who reconciled children with their fathers in preparation for receiving the Messiah. Jake, God wants to reconcile sons with their fathers. That is why my prayer was answered."

Jake nodded. For a moment he forgot the world around him, the mission, the circumstances of their captivity, and the physical pain wracking his body. He stared at his father's serene smile. The look of joy spoke of another time and place, an old memory trying to surface in Jake's mind. He couldn't hate this man, his own father. He had never hated him. Nor did he feel the condescending need to rescue his father anymore. Instead, he focused on the opportunity this moment gave him to finally know the man.

"*'Let not your heart be troubled: ye believe in God, believe also in me,'*" the older man added. "*'In my Father's house are many mansions: if it were not so, I would have told you. I go to prepare a place for you. And if I go and prepare a place for you, I will come again, and receive you unto myself; that where I am, there ye may be also.'*"

"That's Christian," Jake answered. He didn't mind Christians. Pancho was a Christian, there were plenty of Christians he knew and respected. People like Barnes. What he minded was his father's hypocrisy, that was all.

"Yes, Jake, Jesus was who the Jewish prophet was speaking about. Jesus came to reconcile us with his heavenly Father, and if we can accept God's forgiveness and forgive others, we will be reconciled to both God and man."

"Dad, we are going to get out of here, trust me."

"I know, son, I am going home."

"Right, like I said ..."

"... with Jesus."

Jake frowned. "What does that mean?"

"I am saying God is going to take me home, Jake. I'm not leaving alive. And I want to make sure you know the way so you can go also."

"'Not leaving alive?' Dad, where is your so-called faith? We're getting out of this!"

Jake had faith. A pragmatic faith to get himself out of any situation he got into. Faith one of his teammates would come crashing through the door at any moment and rescue them. He had faith. Just not the right kind for confronting the impossible. But there was something else inside now, something awful and alien to his self-reliant spirit. *Helplessness.*

There had to be a way out. He just hadn't found it yet.

"Jesus is the Way, son," his father said, as if in reply to Jake's thoughts. "Jesus is the way, the truth and the life, *trust God.*"

The door burst open, and three men in olive drab uniforms and headscarves shouted at them in Arabic. One kicked Jake's father in the ribs before the three turned their attention to the operator lying bound and helpless on the floor. Payback time.

CHAPTER 43

Pancho

Pancho climbed down the steep, hand-hewn ladder to the floor of the mosque. Through his night vision goggles, he saw what looked like a glowing pile of bright green nuclear waste leaning up against a pillar about thirty feet away—his minder, the guard, sound asleep. His snores were louder and more obnoxious down here than up in the minaret. He stepped closer to check the man.

Here was a truly ancient Pathan, in white beard, green camouflage jacket, and *chitrali* hat. Pancho recognized him as the muezzin, who called the faithful to prayer each day using a microphone at the base of the minaret. He was armed with an ancient AK-47, but there was only one clip visible, the one in the gun. Maybe there were more in his jacket pockets.

"Dream on, oh sleeping one," Pancho whispered as he passed. The man would be permitted to live through this night.

Pancho moved up the hill onto the south ridge. He found a clump of rocks near the top and hid among them. He didn't want to get too far from his sniper hole before calling Ritter. He fiddled with his radio and made the call.

"Condor, Condor, this is Papa Three, over."

He paused then repeated the call sign.

"Condor, Condor, Papa Three, over."

"Go ahead, Three." Pancho recognized Mitchell's voice. "Read you Lima Charlie, over."

"Roger, listen up, I need you to relay a situation report to Saber, over."

Team Condor had a communication base station in Mitchell's rucksack and could transmit back to Bagram.

"Wilco, standing by to copy, over."

Pancho gathered his thoughts. He didn't want to tell higher headquarters about Jake's compromise. Not yet. Not when there was still hope both Jake and the hostage could be rescued and Azzam taken out. Yet he had to report something. He would be held just as responsible for lying about their situation as he would be for getting them into it. And Saber-Six was not one to fall on his sword for the foolish decisions of a subordinate.

"Stand by for a situation update."

Gathering his thoughts, he continued.

"Team Condor in place. Link up with Team Owl completed. Target location confirmed and under observation."

He paused and took a deep breath.

"One Team Owl element unaccounted for at this time."

'Unaccounted for' was intentionally vague. Just short of 'compromised' and 'captured.' Until they could confirm either one, Jake was simply incommunicado. Pancho went on.

"Continuing with operation to neutralize target using Team Condor element. Will pursue contingency options for extraction, possibly under hostile pursuit conditions. End of report. How copy, over?"

That would suffice. For now.

"Roger, Papa Three, retransmitting to Papa Element. Over."

Papa Element was Bagram, Mike Moon's operations center. From there it would pass to Saber-Six in Qatar. Or Kabul, or wherever he was now.

Pancho slouched back and waited for the confirmation. He could hear Ritter's re-transmission but was deaf to Bagram's side of the call. Mike Moon would know what to do when he got the report.

He felt tired, thirsty, washed out, and alone. He stared at the minaret, black and exotic in the darkness. He was glad the moon chose to hide this night.

He put his night vision goggles back on and scanned the area. He needed water and looked for a well or pump to sneak up to in the dark.

The place was an anachronism. Despite Land Rovers in the Car Park and a satellite dish on the Cabin, Dir was stuck in the medieval past, complete with guard towers and religious warriors. Nothing moved, because nothing here ever really changed.

"We are just passing through," he whispered to the darkness. "Just let us finish our business, and we'll be on our way."

Mitchell's voice interrupted Pancho's meditation.

"Papa Three, retransmission complete. Papa element reads loud and clear. Over."

"Roger, Condor," Pancho replied. "I am returning to my observation point. Papa out."

Pancho headed back to his spot in the minaret.

CHAPTER 44

Retribution

The blows came fast and furious. Jake was sure they intended to kick him to death. He strained at the plastic cuffs binding his ankles and wrists. He knew tricks to break out of flexi-cuffs. And tricks to tear out of duct-tape. But they hadn't taken any chances with him. He was bound with both. Then he heard the gruff command in Arabic to cease and was rolled over onto his back like a captured animal put on display by a proud hunting party.

Abbas Bin Azzam again.

Azzam stood over him grinning like a maniac, and Jake had no idea why. He expected the leader of this group to be angry at his near successful infiltration of their lair. But instead, Azzam straddled Jake's hogtied body, smiling, and inspecting him like a prized pig at the state fair. Then, even more demeaning, he reached down and pinched his cheek.

"So," he began in Arabic. "This is the Mossad spy who dressed like a woman to sneak in our midst."

Jake chuckled. "Mossad?"

Did Azzam really believe he was a Mossad agent or was that just jihadist theatrics?

Azzam's face darkened, and he spit in Jake's eyes. Then he struck Jake with a vicious backhand.

"Dog! Infidel! Jew!" he shouted at the helpless form.

Jake remembered a childhood bully and felt brief shame. Then Jake's eyes turned to an icy gray. Show no fear, only defiance.

"You will die, tomorrow," Azzam continued shouting. "You will die like a Jew dog on camera, and everyone in your country, everyone you love, will see you die."

He struck Jake again, then stepped over him and went out the door. The guards glared at Jake but left him alone. The beating was over. The last one out slammed the door shut leaving Jake alone with his father again.

Jake's father got up and moved to Jake's side. Although his hands were bound, his ankles were free. Obviously, the Jihadists had taken greater precautions with Jake than with his father. Jake's father knelt by his son, who closed his eyes in a tight grimace of pain, but refused to make a sound.

Jake opened his eyes and spoke through gritted teeth.

"What were they talking about? What is happening tomorrow?"

"The great media event, son," his father replied. "The Arab news network is coming to film first thing in the morning for the TV and the internet."

"Film what?"

Jake's father paused before answering.

"Our beheading."

CHAPTER 45

Mike Moon

Mike Moon was catching a short nap in a lawn chair just outside the Bank when the call came in. The radioman, a veteran special operator who was used to handling such calls on his own, sent a runner for them but didn't wait for their arrival to start transcribing the message.

Moon, a light sleeping, catnap guy who rarely stayed horizontal for more than an hour at a time, jumped to his feet. Twister was by the door signing for a package from the agency guy at Task Force Dagger. *Wonder if Twister's signing for that intelligence stuff we've been waiting for. Why can't the CIA just send it over classified email like everyone else does? Gotta be hand-carried and signed for. Control freaks.*

He was a little annoyed when he walked inside the Bank and realized they began transmitting the report forward to Saber-Six before he'd seen it himself.

Must make a note of that. Gonna have to change some procedures around here.

But he heard enough to draw the main conclusions. He began to consider the information in his head and to war-game the possibilities.

Teams Owl and Condor are linked up and assessing the target together. No problem.

Team Condor is in position and could execute the hit. But if they do, they will need to disengage under less than favorable conditions and conduct a surreptitious escape to get to an extraction point.

That isn't good but it is still okay. I'll send a warning order to Randy Snow and his Quick Reaction Force guys to prep for a possible hot extraction of the team. And we have plenty of contingency pick up points near the border ... assuming Team Condor can make it there.

And they lost an element from Team Owl. What could that mean? Is Team Owl now compromised or just confused? That could be bad.

He gave instructions to his comms guy regarding the quick reaction force and looked at the handwritten note again. Twister interrupted his thoughts.

"Message from my agent in Dir, from Team Owl ..." he said, handing a printed message to Moon—a burst transmission from Gino Salvetti at the safe house.

Moon cursed. "So according to your guy, Team Owl has a guy trapped inside the target area. And he's one of ours, Jake Drecker, right?"

"Yep, he's either trapped or caught. You know the protocol, Mike, this jeopardizes the entire operation."

"Well, I got eyes on the target area, Twister. And what I'm getting from Pancho is that there is no change in the target area. No reason to panic—yet."

"Do we have SIGINT to confirm?" Twister asked, using the acronym for Signals Intelligence. "How do we know there isn't some alert being broadcast on the hookah telegraph?"

"We can find out. Let's send a request for information up the line. But we don't want to panic yet. I'm gonna patch through to Saber-Six and let him know what's going on."

Moon gave instructions to the intelligence analysts in the other room. The communication lines in and out of the Cabin were being closely monitored. The answer would come soon. He sent a runner to roust Pickett, their National Security Agency planner who was a master at exploiting SIGINT. Then he sat at the field table to think. A detailed, small-scale model of the enemy compound in Dir sat on the table.

"What options do we have if we pull the team?" he asked Twister, without looking up.

"Well, speaking for the agency, we do have that other preplanned option. It'll mean warning our agency guys in Pakistan to execute their plausible deniability protocols, monitor communications channels for battle damage assessments, and hope we hit our bad guy. If there is no collateral damage, we could even give credit to the Paks and have our man in Islamabad go in with their security forces to assess the hit."

"You are alluding to our Predator option, huh? Going right for the kill and eliminating our hostage, our compromised operator, and our targeted bad guy in one fell swoop, huh?"

"With the Predator, we hit them so hard we get our bad guy and eradicate all the evidence of our compromised element in one shot."

"And kill our captured hostage so he can't talk?" Moon concluded.

"It's called fortunes of war, Mike," Twister replied. "This is the best option now. It's not the agency's fault a hostage with a head full of secrets is in there. With plausible deniability we can eliminate a potential compromised agent problem *and* a brutal jihadist with a single hellfire missile. Sucks, but there are bigger stakes at risk here, Mike. Fortunes of war."

"What about our guy? Jake Drecker? I didn't sign up for this job to kill an American operator on my first mission in country."

"I think the military might have a few more options than we at the agency do."

"Right, like we could raid the target, snatch Jake, rescue the hostage, and kill all the bad guys. A platoon of Rangers or SEALs would do the trick."

His words came out harder and edgier than Moon intended. He scowled.

Twister raised a confused, skeptical eyebrow.

Moon felt unapologetic ... and a little hot. But he knew he had to stay professional. Jake Drecker took a risk. And overreached himself. They didn't have time for further options.

"Just kidding," Moon added.

Twister relaxed.

"Now you know why my agency hates working with you military guys so much," Twister said.

Moon closed his eyes for a moment. This mission was in trouble. Did they have time to organize a force to rescue Jake and the hostage? It was worth trying.

He thought about that iconic image from the war movies where the company commander calls down fire on his own position to prevent the enemy from overrunning them.

"God help us."

"If He can, I am open to suggestions." Twister stroked his beard and stepped closer to him. "But just so you know, Saber-Six already coordinated preplanned fires on that compound for our Predator. All we need to do is adjust the standoff orbit and establish your launch windows."

Moon stared at the tabletop model and thought hard. He hadn't heard about the Hellfire option from Pancho during their brief transition together. And, while he trusted Twister and accepted that Saber-Six may have coordinated the plan with the Agency, the thought of launching a deadly missile at one of his own men and an innocent American hostage filled him with revulsion.

No, we have time. We can organize a rescue operation. I'll lead it myself if I have to.

Moon decided then and there to make the rescue happen. They would need to burn the midnight oil, but they could do this. How long could Jake Drecker and Isidore Lowenthal hold out under interrogation? Forty-eight hours? Enough time to organize, coordinate, and execute a rescue? And what would happen if the bad guys discovered the relationship between Drecker and Lowenthal? They would exploit that. Use them against each other. And that might reduce the window of time.

"I've got another troubling report here," Twister said, interrupting Moon's thinking.

"Go on."

"It's about the hostage." Twister removed a sheet of paper from the bottom of his stack. "Looks like he is scheduled for an international news media event in the morning."

"What?"

Twister handed the sheet to Moon.

"Holy mother—" Moon exclaimed after a scanning the summary—a CIA intelligence report flash message, classified with special handling instruction meant to protect a CIA super-sensitive source. Moon, reading the report, now knew, without reservation, that the window of opportunity for action was going to be set by forces well beyond his control.

(S/PF) Source confirms the presence of an Al Haqiqa (AH) news team consisting of four AH technicians and/or journalists with attendant GOP [Government of Pakistan] escorts residing in the Dir Continental Hotel. Source further confirms that the purpose of this team is to record an MAK propaganda event.

(S/PF) Analysis: The MAK has determined that there is little political or monetary advantage to be gained by holding on to the US hostage, preferring instead to exploit such hostages for information operations purposes. For this reason, MAK invited journalists from AH to record a propaganda video for release to the international news media in an effort to influence decision-makers in the US.

(S/PF) Source confirms that the AH team will record the execution of the American hostage by ceremonial beheading at a location within the MAK's Dir compound.

Moon's heart dropped when he saw the date and time of the terrorist media event. A string of angry epithets poured from his lips as he slapped himself in the forehead.

"Shoot, this is going down tomorrow!"

"At or about eleven hundred hours," Twister added.

Moon slumped and looked at the model on the field table.

"So," Moon said, "What do you think? Can we put a couple Hellfires inside that Cabin first thing in the morning?"

"Why not sooner?"

"Why sooner?"

"Gives your Condor guys night cover to get outta there."

"No, can't do it, the hajis might think it was blown up by a team on the ground and start looking for them. If we hit them during the day, they'll know it was from an overhead. Plus, I want Condor to still be in place when the missiles hit so they can do their own battle damage assessment."

"Okay, then look," Twister said, squatting down to make eye contact with Moon. "My guy in Peshawar, he's itching to go in. I can arrange things so the Pakistani Army or Border Scouts arrive with my guy, coincidental with the hit. That way, they can mop up, stage all the Pakistani government official indignation stuff and make sure our side of the story gets told."

"Plus, your guy can verify my compromised operator is dead, right?"

Twister gave Moon a blank look and waited before answering.

"My guy can verify that the target is dead and ... and also secure any American covert operators who might still be alive in the target area for expeditious and surreptitious evacuation to the medical clinic at the US Embassy."

"Okay, Twister, yeah, yeah, I got it. I know what needs to be done. But I need to make a request first. Man-to-man. Right now. Between you and me."

"Okay."

"I still want to leave Team Condor in place until after the hit."

"What's the justification?"

"Because I want more time, even if it's just a couple hours more, to try to find out if our guy is actually still inside. Because I want eyes on that compound in case our target leaves the building before the missiles go in, so maybe we can get him ourselves. Because I want a little more time on site in case we can secure both Americans and still kill our bad guy. And because I think I owe Pancho a chance to exercise his prerogative, since he is the senior guy on the ground."

"I respect that, Mike. But everything is gonna go to pieces when the missiles hit, that's the object."

"I know, Twister. I know."

"Look, Mike, this is a joint operation, and you know what's best for your part of the team. But if they stay in place, they need to be on the move and out of sight before the smoke ever clears over that target."

"You got it, Twister."

"I mean, Mike, they have got to be out of there before my guy shows up with the Paks. Or we are dead, man, international incident dead."

"I know, Twister. I know."

"And I am going to pretend we never discussed this last thing—even if I need to pretend under oath, got it?"

Moon nodded, reaching for the secure phone to contact their higher command. He already knew what Saber-Six would say. He would agree, like Twister, with everything except for the last part about leaving Team Condor in place until after the missiles hit. So, Moon would just have to keep that last part out when he talked with Saber-Six.

"Yeah, Twister, I got it."

CHAPTER 46

Last Night

Late in the evening, Jake and his father sat in their cell in uncomfortable silence. Jake had a million things to ask but spoke little. He was troubled, and his mind raced. He was working all of the angles to get them out of the fix they were in and coming up empty. He agreed with his father about one thing, divine intervention would be needed to escape from this place.

"Jake?"

"Yes, Dad."

"I love you."

Jake responded the only way he could.

"I love you too, Dad."

With that, the old man smiled and drifted off.

Jake wondered how the old man could sleep on their last night together. Jake knew from his sister that his father wasn't well physically, had had some serious health issues during the last several years. Jake, on the other hand, fought in his mind and his body to find out an escape. His frustrated inner rage drained him as he spent a fruitless hour pulling on his arms. He only succeeded in driving the flex cuffs deeper into his wrists, bruising and cutting the skin. Finally, exhausted and empty, Jake drifted in-and-out of a fitful semi-consciousness, the sleep of the condemned.

Pancho didn't like the change in the plan, but he knew it was right. They had failed. Failed to fix their target, failed to find the hostage, and failed to prevent the loss of their own clandestine agent. It was a blown operation.

Saber-Six is probably tossing and turning in his bedsheets somewhere. Figures his career is done if the Hellfires miss their man tomorrow and this thing gets out into the press. I bet he'd like to see my head on a pointy stick right about now.

Where is Jake? Is he still alive? Is he going to lose his head in the morning also? Or will they save him for the next day? What are Azzam and his men thinking?

Moon's intelligence requests had come up dry. There had been no recorded spike in the number of cell phone, radio, or landline calls after the Team Owl element disappeared.

The only thing that kept the operation from going completely to pieces was the apparent obliviousness on the part of Azzam and the MAK. Their mujahidin security teams had failed to find Teams Condor and Owl. Their search parties had returned empty-handed. Even the guard in the mosque slept on, little dreaming that an infidel American had passed within inches of his snoring mouth to climb the tower just above his head. They seemed to not have made any connection between the cross-dresser with the painted toenails and a larger covert operation waiting just outside their doors.

Pride goes before the fall. These guys must think they are untouchable.

Odd.

Or maybe providential.

Master Sergeant Ritter had mixed feelings about the new plan.

Officially, they were to continue their surveillance of the target and report any changes back to Bagram. The Predator would be in standoff and available to launch its Hellfire missiles sometime between 0930 and 1130 in the morning. They were supposed to give their final report to their controllers back in Bagram, standby for them to assume the mission, and then exfiltrate out of the area.

Officially, he agreed to the modification authorized by his bosses, Moon and Pancho. Team Condor would stay until they could assess damages from the missile strike. Meanwhile, they would hope for a chance to possibly hit the target before the missiles went in.

On a personal level, Ritter felt tempted to just go in blazing himself, take out the guards, kill the bad guy, and rescue the two Americans. He knew they could do it. It was the kind of thing they trained for, to take on a group of this size and win. But their higher command overrode the idea. They were too far inside Pakistan for the clean, covert escape they needed to cover their tracks. And besides that, they were still blind to whatever hidden dangers lurked behind the Cabin door.

So, the modified plan of the colonel's was the only option. If Azzam left the building before the missiles flew, Pancho would take him out from his spot in the minaret. Pancho could do it. And if it went down that way, then all hell would break loose. They would all need to start shooting to cover Pancho's escape and prevent anyone on the site from giving chase. Either way, Ritter figured Azzam was a dead man. At least, if Pancho made the hit before the Hellfires, there still remained a possibility Jake Drecker and the American hostage might be able to escape. This was Team Condor's hope.

So, they waited. Ritter and Eason taking turns catching snatches of sleep while the other watched. In the morning, they would be ready.

CHAPTER 47

Last Rites

Somewhere deep in Isidore Loewenthal's left thigh, a rogue platelet, a painful thorn, and the object of countless prayers, broke away from its host and drifted along with the current. The clot visited several areas of the body, pausing now and again and then shooting through tight places like a canoe through rapids, journeying to the heart of its host where it entered the left ventricle and lodged in the aorta. The heart pumped against the blockage but could not remove the impediment. The faithful heart skipped a beat, then shook, sending spasms throughout the chest area and down into the right arm.

Isidore grimaced once in his sleep, and then relaxed. Breathing ceased, and color drained from his face. Isidore stepped into another room, and found himself in the presence of ministering angels. Jake's father had escaped.

Jake was in and out of consciousness all night. He couldn't think. And his father lay still, unresponsive to Jake's furtive efforts to wake him and talk. Just talk.

He didn't think he fell asleep until he awoke—awoke to the soothing but unfamiliar sound of birds singing outside the narrow, barred window of their cell. The air was cool, but the sky beyond the bars was clear and cloudless. The morning would be beautiful but bitter.

Jake looked around. His father lay upright and still against the wall. He appeared to be meditating, eyes closed, face still, legs casually stretched out and crossed comfortably at the ankle. Jake knew they would be coming for them soon, for the last time. He wanted to speak to his father once more, to exchange last goodbyes. He tipped forward and knelt facing his father.

"Dad. Dad, you awake?"

Jake crawled over and leaned close to his father's face.

"Dad …"

Something wasn't right. His father was too still. There was no breathing. He put his face up to his father's, cheek to cheek, so he could feel his skin—cold, too cold.

A memory began replaying from somewhere deep in his mind, Jake's earliest memory from childhood. He must have been around one or two years old, his photographic memory already beginning its amazing development. It was dark and he is in a bed, maybe a crib, crying, afraid. The room is shadowed by a light coming from the hallway, and he can see a man in a flight suit silhouetted in the doorway. "It's okay, son," he says, walking in and turning his face toward the light. "Everything will be okay."

The man in the flight suit reaches down, picks him up, and holds him. His father, a young man with trimmed, curly brown hair, green eyes, and warm smile. His father carries him toward the light, he sees the hallway, then outside, where he looks up and sees the stars for the first time. His father's face leans toward his in the moonlight, and he hears him whisper, "I love you, son."

Instantly, he is back in the cell with the man in the memory.

"Dad!" he rasped.

Jake broke into a sob, rolled over, and sat next to his father, weeping. It was too late. His father, like the memory, was gone.

"I failed. I didn't come back to you in time. God help me."

Jake had lost his father again.

CHAPTER 48

Confirmation

Outside the Cabin, in the pre-dawn grayness, a vibrating wrist-watch alarm stirred Pancho. He pressed the button to turn it off and listened until he heard the rhythmic snoring of the muezzin below. His minder was still asleep.

It won't be long until show time.

Pancho looked toward the east. There was an early morning fog in the Panjkora River Valley and the hint of a sunrise behind the eastern ridgeline.

Sun's getting ready to pop, he chuckled to himself. *These guys are slacking off with their pre-dawn prayers.*

He did not feel rested, despite having dozed for several hours. And he felt sore from lying on concrete.

Maybe I really am getting too old for this stuff.

The muezzin guarding the mosque had made things easier in one sense. As long as the old man snored, Pancho felt secure from prying eyes. And if the muezzin slept until it was time to perform the adhan, the call to early-morning prayer, then Pancho could catnap unmolested in the tower.

A golden shaft of early rising, late summer sun shot through a gap in the mountains and alighted on his position. The sunbeam's bright ferocity forced his eyes open. Sunrise in the minaret.

He lay still, praying his own silent prayers and adjusting his ears to the early morning sounds. The chirping birds sounded sweet. Not so the sinister clatter of men rustling about in the Parking Garage, donning combat garb while performing their ritual ablution. Track Suit had probably finished his pre-dawn run and would soon be leading the recruits in calisthenics, both religious and otherwise.

Pancho listened again for the snoring of the guard in the mosque but heard nothing.

Uh-oh, brace yourself. The muezzin is awake!

Then it began.

First came the electronic scratching and crackling of the loudspeaker emerging from its slumber. Then the adhan burst forth from the lips of the muezzin below, into the microphone and along copper wires to blare forth from the loudspeakers just above Pancho's head. He placed a fingertip in each ear and rolled onto his stomach to look out toward the compound.

The minaret cast a long needle-like shadow along the top half of the medieval watchtower on the opposite side of the little valley. But the Cabin and most of the compound remained shadowed by the ridges all around. Sunrise warmth hadn't reached the valley floor yet.

Two rows of men sat on prayer rugs in the Car Park. Inside the Cabin were others, no doubt, seated on their knees, ready to prostrate across their prayer rug to utter the approved repetitions of the daily ritual.

The worshippers were turned slightly away from the mosque so they could face toward Mecca. Pancho faced northwest, with the sunbeam dancing over the top of his head. He wondered if the layout had been planned this way so the Mosque would be the first place in the compound to experience the warmth of the morning sun.

Then prayer time was over, and the worshippers put away their prayer rugs.

Pancho had to be extra careful now. This was the big day. With the sun behind him, he might accidentally silhouette himself and give away his location. But the sun would also discourage those in the Car Park from staring too intently in his direction.

Someone started up a vehicle in the Car Park. Pancho looked for him through small, high-powered hunting binoculars. There were several there, supervised by the domineering one, Sergeant Major, rearranging the vehicles and probably making room for more. Seems they were expecting visitors.

Pancho got a kick out of watching the thin, bearded one nicknamed Hostess getting into a shouting match with the larger, more intimidating Sergeant Major. He could only hear shouting and wouldn't have understood their language anyway, but the face gestures and hand motions were comical. He assumed, for some reason, that they were Arabs, unlike the others who were mostly of Pakistani ethnicities. But he couldn't be sure.

The waiting was the worst part. Pancho's legs and back were stiff. He had to sit so the front of his rifle did not protrude out of the minaret's window and reveal his position. This meant lying with feet spread wide when he was in a shooting position. He sucked on dry, salty crackers and the final mouthfuls of water from his Camelbak. Patience, he reminded himself.

There were three windows in the minaret, each facing a different direction. One faced west toward the compound, one north toward the compound entrance, and the third east toward the Panjkora River. The south side of the tower had no window but it did have the small opening down into the mosque below. The crude end of the wooden ladder poked up into the minaret. Pancho's one security concern was he had to ignore the hole leading up from the mosque to focus on targets in the compound—his vulnerable point.

The minaret windows each had a ledge only six inches above the floor of the tower. This meant he couldn't sit or kneel without revealing himself. He had to shoot from the prone position with his left elbow elevating the front of the barrel above the ledge and his head and right arm propped up even higher to angle the shot downward into the compound. He figured he had one good shot from this uncomfortable position to take down the main target and then he'd adjust as needed to take down anyone else around the Campus.

The Campus soon filled with vehicles and people. It was a circus. When he saw equipment being unloaded from a truck, he knew what kind of a circus it was—a *media* circus.

The trio from *Al Haqiqa*, the Arab news network, arrived complete with camera and recording equipment. They had a fourth with them now, a technician carrying the heaviest of their gear.

Others arrived by vehicle, the Imam with his entourage in two Land Rovers. Oddly, they didn't park in the Car Park but by the storage sheds on the north side. One of the drivers reclined his seat and went right to sleep, but the other pulled out a cell phone, got out of his vehicle and walked slowly down toward the main road to Kotkay.

A pair of bearded men armed with AK-47s and leading a goat entered the Car Park on foot from the west, from the upper valley. They were not dressed like the fighters gathering on the sand for Track Suit to lead in exercise. They wore traditional Pathan garb and off-white turbans. The two were likely goatherds from the camp just over the ridge, delivering breakfast meat to the men of the MAK.

The trainees lined up for morning exercise wore head and face scarves today and carried Chinese-made SKS rifles. Pancho knew the change in routine was meant to impress the visitors. A man in a blue ski mask emerged from the Parking Garage wearing a matching Adidas warm-up suit. Sporty jihad style. He had to be Track Suit. Sure enough, he began barking orders to the men to tighten up their sloppy formation.

Pancho heard another sound, the bleating of sheep and goats. The noise was coming, he thought, from somewhere behind him, but he could see nothing,

There must be shepherds in the hills today. Great.

He looked at his watch. Oh-eight-thirty hours. At least an hour to go before the Predator would be in position. His stomach growled and dreamed of egg rancheros and steak. He hoped the compound wouldn't get too crowded. It could complicate things.

Wonder what kind of morning Jake Drecker is having ... if he's still alive.

Jake lay next to his father's lifeless body for God knew how long. He had no sense of time. He stayed until his eyes were dry, the hot tears ran out, replaced by the icy glare of his angry, defiant cunning. His father was gone. He had to plan his next move if he wanted to survive.

He could hear his tormentors outside the door of the holding cell as they prepared to make their unholy sacrifice. Something would happen soon. Showtime drew near.

The peephole kept opening and shutting, but he ignored their prying eyes. He could hear greetings in languages he understood and recognized the presence of guests at the Cabin. The news team from *Al Haqiqa* had arrived for the glorious event. He felt good knowing his father would not have to suffer that cruel humiliation.

But I'll be experiencing enough for both of us, Dad, if something doesn't change fast.

He rolled closer to the door, his hands and feet still bound. As helpless as ever.

The door burst open, and Azzam stepped through.

"Wake up, sleeping dogs! Wake up American spy. Zionist puppet!" Azzam shouted in nearly perfect American English.

Jake wondered where Azzam picked up the accent. Hollywood, probably. Azzam must watch American movies and TV in his spare time—when he wasn't plotting to destroy America.

Jake pretended to ignore him. Azzam's remark was aimed at the American missionary who stirred not a bit at the belligerent, berating tone of the terrorist.

Azzam leaned down toward his hostage's unmoving face.

"I said, wake up!"

Another man followed Azzam into the room, a young Arab mujahid. Jake recognized the younger man as the tormentor who had leered at him in the hallway. He looked stylish, dressed in full battle garb including an Arab fighter's head covering. He brandished a late model AKS-74U, the kind with the paratrooper stock, and he carried a sidearm in a polished black holster.

It sounded like there were others in the hall, but Jake couldn't see them and couldn't be sure.

He watched Azzam reach down to touch his father's face.

Pancho watched people exiting the Cabin for a reception party complete with refreshments and live entertainment outside in the compound. The *Al Haqiqa* news team, with their camera and equipment, mingled with a handful of local dignitaries including the Imam and his straphangers. A table along the Cabin wall was piled high with fruit, flat bread, and a samovar serving tea or coffee in small cups. Hostess was in his glory, ordering around three teenage boys with trays of cakes and soft drinks.

The woman reporter attracted a personal following, the Sergeant Major taking up a permanent position at her side. She wore the chador in the modern Pakistani style, her near perfect facial features uncovered and smiling as she laughed at a shared joke with those around her. She carried a notebook and pen but no microphone. She would not appear in the propaganda she was helping to film. She knew better than to violate her professional objectivity by appearing in front of the camera for this piece of questionable journalism. Pancho found not hating her hard.

Outside the compound, the trainees were going through their calisthenics—the cue for the camera crew to visit the Car Park and start filming.

A tall, intimidating character dressed in black jeans, black sweater, and black ski mask emerged from the Cabin. He carried a large, serrated hunting knife and seemed to distance himself from the others. He followed the crowd as it moved outside the compound, leaned against the compound wall, and watched.

Pancho focused his binoculars on the man and shivered. The black-masked man and his hunting knife had a special part to play in the upcoming drama. Pancho prayed Team Condor would end the drama before the man in black got on stage to perform.

Meanwhile, their main target, Azzam, was still nowhere in sight. *Patience, patience.*

Azzam touched the face of Jake's father and withdrew his hand quickly. "Dog, American …"

He kicked the man unceremoniously in the ribs. The lifeless body tipped over on its side and lay still.

"Curse you, Jew, curse you to hell!" he shouted.

He slapped the unfeeling face and unleashed a torrent of obscenities in mixed American English and Arabic.

"What is wrong?" the younger man asked in Arabic.

Azzam straightened up and turned. His face was red and twisted in rage.

"What is wrong?" Azzam sneered. "The American spy, he is dead, he is gone!"

He grabbed the younger Arab by his shirt, shook him, and screamed in English, "I have been cheated by the dirty, rotten Jews again. The American Jew is dead, can't you see? Dead!"

Azzam stormed out of the room, growling and cursing as he went. He was shouting something in Arabic to someone outside, but Jake couldn't hear what was said. The mujahid was left alone in the cell with Jake and his father's body.

The young Arab only stood still for a moment before stepping forward and bending down to check the dead man for himself. Satisfied, he stood and kicked the lifeless body in the stomach.

He turned slowly around. Tears of frustration and bitterness streamed down his cheeks. He looked out the door where Azzam had stormed out collecting his thoughts, seemingly oblivious to Jake's presence. He began to walk toward the door but paused. He looked down at Jake.

"Don't worry," he said in broken English. "We will be back for you."

He looked back toward the door, trying to regain his composure.

Jake looked up at the lightbulb hanging by the wire.

The young mujahid saw Jake staring at the ceiling. He followed Jake's eyes upwards to the hanging bulb and smiled, somehow concluding that the bound prisoner drew comfort from the shining orb. Knowing to remove any such comfort would be a cruel touch, the Arab reached for the chain to switch it off, making a weak attempt at western-style humor.

"Lights out, Jew-dog," he said in his lousy accent.

But the pull chain was too high. The Arab pulled his hand back down, looked at Jake, and smirked. Jake's face betrayed nothing. The man tried again, on his tiptoes, until he finally grasped the chain. He could not have drawn a more inaccurate conclusion about Jake's interest in that lightbulb.

As the Arab stretched upward on his toes, Jake swung his body in an arc, his bound ankles catching the Arab on the back of the Achilles tendon. The Arab fighter was swept off his feet and fell hard on his back, his head making a dull thump as it hit the cement floor.

The young mujahid was stunned for just a second, but a second was enough. Jake raised his bound ankles high and brought them down with a sickening crack on the front of the stunned man's throat, crushing his windpipe.

The man grabbed at his own throat for relief, and Jake rolled over on top of him, driving his right shoulder blade down on the man's throat, then gave the man a vicious head butt to the face.

The man grabbed Jake's throat and began choking him—a race against time.

Jake began to black out, gray fuzz moving across his vision as the other man tightened his grip. Then the hands began to slacken. They fell from Jake's neck. The mujahid was dead.

Jake lay still. He took a deep breath to regain his senses. He wasn't out of trouble yet.

The compound was empty, the crowd had moved out to the Car Park to watch the filming of the trainees. Then a man came storming out through the Cabin door, arms swinging, mouth roaring, out into the compound to vent his rage. Pancho found him funny in a way and chuckled.

Man! That guy is pitching a fit about something.

Pancho tried to identify the newcomer, but the man turned his face away as he moved around the left side of the Cabin in the direction of the guard tower. His arms swinging, his violent ranting shouts, incoherent to Pancho, now heard by the group in the Car Park.

Everyone stopped for a moment and turned toward the sound.

Then Hostess took off like a shot, slipping through the narrow opening in the gate to try and placate the raging man. Sergeant Major took control in the Car Park and redirected everyone's attention back on their film subjects. But even the recruits had paused at the commotion. Track Suit, on cue from Sergeant Major, got the training demonstration back on track, and the filming continued.

Hostess put a consoling hand on the angry man's shoulder, but the man savagely slapped the hand away. Hostess stood looking at the man with hands down and palms forward, a gesture of placating exasperation unheeded by the other man. Then Hunting Knife, the spooky man in the black ski mask, came into the compound and stood by Hostess. He was shaking his head in sympathy at something the angry man was saying, but Pancho couldn't hear.

Then the angry man turned.

Pancho focused his rifle's Bausch & Lomb tactical scope on the face. He had to be sure.

The face was still contorted with rage, the vicious mouth opened wide to pour forth angry, venomous bile over the two consoling listeners.

Pancho focused. For just a single moment the man paused, stood still and relaxed his facial features. The moment was enough.

Azzam.

Their quarry had finally emerged from its hiding place.

Pancho snapped in, stopped breathing and lowered his heart rate. He placed the cross hairs on the man's mouth and began a slow squeeze on the trigger. Time stood still.

CHAPTER 49

Consummation

Uphill at the hide site, Ritter was frustrated. Team Condor had seen little or nothing of the activity in front of the compound. Should have moved them in the night? Tried for a more commanding view?

Then he remembered the shepherds with their flock occupying the south ridge behind Pancho's minaret.

Yep, there they were. Bleating and eating in the only other site that could have sufficed.

Yeah, their options had been limited indeed. No sense second guessing yourself. Pancho would inform them of changes. If anything *had* changed.

As Team Condor watched and waited, Ritter grew more apprehensive about the demonstration in the Car Park. There were too many people down there, too many civilians, too much potential for unnecessary collateral damage if it turned into a firefight. Up until the visiting crowd appeared, Ritter still considered the possibility that Team Condor could take down the site and snatch the hostages. But now it was too late, too complicated for such an option.

The thought of letting the Predator's missiles finish the job filled him with dread.

There are two Americans down there, Jake and the missionary. God help them, they don't deserve to die by the hand of their own countrymen.

But circumstances were moving in that direction, to a point where the missiles would need to do their dirty work for them.

Ritter glanced down at his watch. 0930. The Predator was on station now.

Ritter knew the decision would be out of their hands the moment the guys in Bagram and Qatar saw the video feed. The number of bystanders in the Car Park, the compound with walls to shield them from the Hellfire missile's collateral damage, the compromised men with national security secrets in their heads trapped inside—it all added up to a no-brainer, as the boys back in Bagram would say. Plus, their own reconnaissance confirmed that Azzam was still inside the Cabin, like the proverbial sitting duck, waiting for Uncle Sam to drop twenty-two pounds of RDX high explosives into his foul lap. And then the mission would be declared over—mission accomplished. Azzam would be dead, Jake Drecker's existence would be eradicated from the record, and the hostage would be declared dead on arrival—killed accidentally during a botched Pakistani rescue effort. Plausibile deniability in full effect.

To a man like Ritter it would not make for a satisfactory conclusion. But a mission accomplished nonetheless.

Ritter was normally too much of a professional to let such things get to his head.

But this time it did.

In Qatar, a group of hard men, decision-making elder warriors, sat in a windowless, air-conditioned command center sipping hot coffee and watching the blurry video feed from an Unmanned Aerial Vehicle (UAV for short). It was the video from an MQ-1, better known as a Predator, a spy drone armed with all-weather, day and night electronic eyes and deadly Hellfire missiles. The video feed, projected onto giant wall mounted screens, provided the men and women of Central Command Forward with a larger than life "near real time" picture of events almost three thousand kilometers away. It also gave them an illusion of control, one that was often frustrated by a lapse in transmission or the inability to understand everything on the screen. The Predator sent back good pictures, but it still could not read minds. At least not yet.

This particular UAV was traveling in a surveillance circuit over northwest Pakistan, about ten kilometers from the Afghanistan border. To the uninitiated, this Predator, deployed to hunt jihadists in the austere Afghan hills, appeared to be intruding on sovereign Pakistan airspace, but nothing could be further from the truth. These birds of prey were homebased at Shamsi, a small airfield near the town of Washki, Pakistan, and they operated with the connivance of Pakistan officials, although no one in that government would ever acknowledge that this was so.

This Predator's electronic eyes were focused on a small compound just south of the city of Dir. The pictures displayed on the command center screen in Qatar disturbed these cold-eyed, gray-headed men. They were the pictures of a covert operation gone awry. Now was the time, they determined, to intervene at their level to take some definite action and bring the op to an acceptable conclusion.

At Bagram airbase, two youthful officers, one of Mike Moon's operations officers and an intelligence officer from Task Force Dagger, stood next to a flat-screen video monitor and took turns speaking into a camera. They were presenting their assessment of the situation portrayed by the Predator, transmitting their own words and images to the older, more experienced decision-makers sitting in air-conditioned comfort in Qatar. At both locations, liaison officers copied what was said and transmitted the assessment on classified work stations linked by satellite communications to their respective agency headquarters in the United States. At the Pentagon, a small, sleep-deprived, interagency Prodigal Avenger work group led by a tired-looking senior civilian from the office of the Undersecretary of Defense for Special Operations and Low-Intensity Conflict, watched the proceedings on their own wall-mounted video screen.

First, the two officers described what the decision-makers were watching.

The thermal blobs on the screen were people massed outside the compound walls on its south side. A wide-angle view displayed more thermal blobs—animals and other humans—clustered around the larger target area dubbed The Campus. These were confirmed as either part of the covert American team sent to kill Azzam or other unknowns, bad guys, approaching dangerously close to the American blobs.

Then the two briefers gave a "situational update" using the latest intelligence. They described the Cabin's details and the best means to neutralize the forces within.

"Inside the compound is a building called the Cabin. Multiple human intelligence reports confirm this as the residence of Abbas Bin Azzam. We have live human collectors monitoring the Cabin who confirm Azzam is inside. They believe an American missionary hostage, a former military attaché in Pakistan, who knows the existence and identity of a highly placed, sensitive intelligence source inside the Pakistani jihadist network, is probably collocated with Azzam. And we know without a doubt an American covert operator is also inside the Cabin, unaccounted for and likely compromised.

"The Cabin has only one entrance and several high windows just under the eaves. It would take a low angle approach to get a missile through a window. The door could be breached from a higher angle, especially if the gate were opened. However, it would only make a shallow penetration.

"The most vulnerable place to drop a missile is where a metal stove pipe or chimney protrudes from the roof's center. Although the unusually sloped roof could deflect a missile coming in at the wrong angle, if the missile struck the stovepipe, it would likely penetrate successfully. The stovepipe's central location, and the likelihood of a secondary explosion from propane tanks associated with the stove, make it the ideal strike point for a Hellfire missile."

"If the first missile in the stovepipe is successful," the operations briefer, a special forces major, added, "a second missile could be launched through the door entrance to assure complete neutralization and destruction of the target."

In Qatar, the gray-headed senior leaders asked questions, received tolerable answers, and expressed their frustration with the current state of affairs regarding Operation Screech Owl. "They should have been told earlier" became a common refrain among those who wore stars.

A certain Air Force colonel sitting among the gray heads in Qatar expressed surprise at how things turned out and denied any personal knowledge of the relationship between hostage and missing operator. He explained how his own decision to pre-plan Predator strikes to support the operation had opened up the best course of action for the decision makers to take, to neutralize the target and sanitize the area with Hellfire missiles. He recommended that the missile strikes be approved in accordance with the "exceptionally detailed recommendation" made by the briefers in Bagram.

The men with stars agreed. A thin-haired, pinch-faced State Department representative, in casual clothes and eye-glasses, nodded tacit support. The decision was made, the course of action approved, and Saber-Six passed the word back to Bagram to inform Team Condor, "Missile strike inbound. Initiate exfiltration plan immediately."

Ritter was watching a tedious show. A few odd developments but nothing which offered any help toward resolving their stalemated situation.

He looked over at Eason, and their eyes locked in a mutual, silent assent.

Their game was up. Operation Screech Owl was subject to circumstances beyond their control now. All they needed was the right something to happen to bring it to a close.

Through tired, blood-rimmed eyes, Ritter observed a herd of sheep and their shepherds massing on top of the south ridge. That was nothing new. The south ridge was a kind of thoroughfare for the hardy mountain people of the region, a short cut from the Panjkora Valley to hidden places in the mountains.

Then, a change. Three shepherds broke from among their flock, scampered down the ridge and disappeared behind the Parking Garage. Curious.

Ritter looked at Eason. Eason returned his stare. Yep, that was something they had not seen before. Perhaps these shepherds were trying to sell lamb to the insurgents as they'd seen before. But why behind the Parking Garage? No, these three were up to something.

"Keep an eye on those three," Ritter whispered. "I'll keep tabs on the Car Park crowd."

"Aye, aye, captain."

In the Car Park, the media circus with cameras rolling had lined up the recruits for a group run with their rifles. They shuffled in lopsided files around the compound perimeter, kicking up a thin, khaki-colored cloud whenever they crossed the dustier stretches. Track Suit and Sergeant Major contributed to the charade with guttural commands or blue-streaked curses of encouragement. The film crew loved it, manipulating the scene, making individual shufflers pause and pose as the camera zoomed in on their dramatic, perspiring scowls.

Mitchell crawled over to Ritter with a message.

"Got the call from Bagram. Hellfire inbound in one five mikes, execute exfil immediately."

"Roger," Ritter said. "Do me a favor and raise Pancho. Pass him the word and give him a full update. Tell him our mission is over, and he needs to move just as soon as the first missile hits home. The bad guys'll be distracted then. We'll cover his move out of the mosque and then link up at rally point Kathryn."

"Wilco, boss." Mitchell scampered back to his position in their rear.

At the Mosque, Yusuf Hāfiza, old, stiff, and cold from sleeping outdoors, fingered his ancient Kalashnikov and considered the ascent. His knees, which had carried him back and forth across the mountains thousands of times in the wars against Indian, Russian, and American infidels, were almost useless now. What remained were pain-filled, arthritic knobs that could no longer even carry him up into a minaret to sound the call for prayer. He was grateful for the wealthy Saudi Arabian visitor who had installed the public-address system in the Mosque. Not only did it save his knees the trouble of climbing the rickety ladder to the minaret but saved him from having to chant his prayers so loud with a throat gone weak with age.

He had volunteered to guard the Mosque after the spy was caught. As muezzin, this was his place of duty, the house of prayer. He was as a *manjawar*, a shrine keeper. The mosque was a refuge to escape the boastful, young Pathans. Why weren't they over the mountains fighting anyway? Then there were the debauched Arabs with their television and cigarettes and the many self-important visitors. Here he could be alone to pray, to think, and to remember.

Only a Jew from the west would dress as a woman to spy on the great Abbas Bin Azzam. And the hostage, he was a Jew also. To kill him for the reporters was wrong, but that was Azzam's affair. Better for men like Yusuf Hāfiza to focus on the work of the jihad—training, smuggling guns and fighting.

Yusuf Hāfiza, in keeping with ancient Pathan custom, considered himself a Bani Israel, a child of Israel, one descended from the lost tribes, from the tribe of *Yusuf* (Joseph). He was not a Jew, however, because Jews were descended from Judah. Pathans were from the missing tribes.

Yusuf Hāfiza knew little of the Israeli-Palestinian conflict but respected Arabs because of their support for their jihad war against the infidels who again occupied Afghanistan. Arabs were good Muslims, capable of great nobility. Westerners were cunning, smart, but hopeless atheists and idolaters, almost as bad as Indians, without souls. One day, he knew from his Koran, the sun would rise in the west and their unbelieving ways would cease forever.

It was quite some time since he had tried to climb the minaret. With Allah's help, he would climb it now. He had sent teenagers up from time to time to keep it clean, but it had been awhile. He felt there were birds up there. Black crows always gathered at mosques, even at Mecca.

It is sad. He began his ascent. *I never made the Haj, the pilgrimage to Mecca.*

A great sin. Instead he had spent his life laboring in jihad. In his youth against India, in middle age against Russia, and now, by the will of Allah, he was helping fight the Americans. He clung to the thought that if he died a martyr's death, then the Haj would be unnecessary. He would still be in Paradise. He was now old and alone. His wives were dead, his sons were with the Taliban, so he prayed he would not be cheated out of his last chance at martyrdom.

Despite his age, Yusuf's eyes were not dim. He had seen the shadow move in the minaret. Perhaps there was a crow nesting there. Or some other creature, he knew not what. There was still some time before the next prayer. He would now have a chance to look.

Yusuf could hear loud cursing down in the compound. Azzam was cursing in Arabic about the hostage. He didn't know what about. His rifle hung over his shoulder as he gripped the roughhewn ladder and climbed. The ladder creaked as he neared the top, then he heard a rattle in the Minaret, just inches above his head—a familiar sound to one raised around rifles. Was the noise a crow flapping its wings? He was breathing hard, and his knees were screaming when he reached the top.

Pancho had one cheek pressed up against his rifle and one eye opened half an inch from the rear lens on his scope when he heard the creaking of the ladder and an old man's labored breaths. For one brief second, he acquired his target. But the moment was lost when a weathered, claw-like hand gripped the back of his left knee. Pancho started in surprise.

"Akh! Akh!" the old man exclaimed. "Ay sarīya! Gora, gora!"

Pancho grabbed for his nine-millimeter pistol while the old Pathan tried to unsling his rifle.

PRODIGAL AVENGER

Booomphk! Booomphk!

Pancho fired two, deep-throated shots and saw the graybeard drop. The shots sounded like a bazooka in the close confines of the minaret, the crackling booms echoing around the mosque. He scrambled around and looked down the hole.

On the floor, the old Pathan lay hatless on his back, a puddle of blood running from the top of his head. From his perch, Pancho couldn't see where the bullets had struck. He needed to see what had become of his real target back in the compound.

He looked again through his scope.

Everyone in the compound was frozen, eyes on the mosque, mouths opened in curious surprise at the sounds from the minaret.

Azzam's mouth was wide open as he took a step toward the minaret. Pancho acquired the target and began the trigger squeeze.

As he did, Azzam's head suddenly exploded in a halo of pink and grey gore. A high-powered rifle shot echoed around the valley. Pancho had been *in the zone* and had not heard the shot when it was fired, only its echo—a perfect shot, the bullet entering via Azzam's gaping mouth and exploding out the back of his head. Pancho stared curiously at his right hand gripping the rifle.

He hadn't fired his weapon.

The shot had come from someone else, from somewhere else, from the ridgeline just behind him.

Up on the opposite hill, Ritter and Eason heard the shots. They recognized the first two as Pancho's nine-millimeter pistol in the minaret. Pancho was compromised. Their show was more than just over now. Then they heard the sniper shot from somewhere up on the ridgeline.

Eason, his SR-25 sniper rifle's scope trained on the compound, saw the briefest of black and red blossoms as an unidentified head exploded but he didn't know the direction of the shot.

Ritter, watching through the spotter scope, refocused to see the results of the drama in the minaret.

At the base of the minaret ladder, the old muezzin lay spread-eagled on his back.

In the minaret, a shadow moved.

Ritter scanned the area behind the minaret rapidly with his spotting scope. He thought he glimpsed the unknown sniper among the sheep, but then lost him.

In the compound, people were frozen, incapable of assimilating all that was happening around them. Then someone began shouting from the mosque and everything broke loose.

The muezzin, hatless, his white hair and beard covered in bright blood from a nine-millimeter gash along the top of his head, looking like an Old Testament prophet as he ran out of the mosque toward the Car Park shouting in Pashtun, "Gora! Jāsūs, jāsūs daz dūz!" *Look here! Spy, spy sniping!*

The people in the compound scattered while two men with rifles charged uphill toward the mosque.

Eason fired twice and both men went down.

The insurgent recruits were no longer running in formation but running for their lives. Some could be seen diving under vehicles. The news team, caught in the open, dropped their equipment and ran toward the Imam's vehicle on the north side of the campus. Track Suit disappeared, but the Sergeant Major, his arm protectively clutching the female reporter, took cover between two parked Land Rovers.

Ritter heard Mitchell sending an abbreviated message to Pancho that missiles were inbound. Pancho wasn't replying. Ritter pressed his transmit button and shouted, "C'mon, Pancho, get out of there, missiles inbound!"

Ritter looked toward the minaret. He could see Pancho's raised rifle but there was no acknowledgment on the radio.

Eason thought he saw a shadow move inside the castle-like watchtower on the northwest corner of the compound so he fired two rounds through the narrow slits to discourage whoever was there.

"Mitchell," Ritter yelled over the squad radio net. "Tell Bagram we need those missiles now, over."

"Wilco, over."

In the minaret, Pancho was still looking for targets. He heard the old man shouting but didn't realize who it was until the bloodied old muezzin came into full view after reaching the Car Park.

Tough old geezer. I'm kinda glad he's still alive.

Pancho heard his team leader over the radio, noted what was said about the missiles, but ignored the admonition to clear the minaret. He still needed to take care of something.

Pancho was looking for the tall, evil looking man in the black ski mask, the one he called Hunting Knife. He glimpsed the black-clad figure scampering through the gate to get back inside the protective walled enclosure of the compound. Hostess was in there, cowering under the eaves of the Cabin by the door. Azzam lay on his back, unattended and ignored. Hunting Knife paused for just a moment and said something to Hostess. Pancho lined up his shot.

Then Hunting Knife slipped inside the Cabin and disappeared.

"God help me," Pancho muttered to himself. "I missed my chance."

He sighed deeply and muttered again, "Vengeance is mine saith the Lord of Hosts."

He turned and sat up.

It was time. His contribution was over. He couldn't risk his men any longer by staying. They all needed to leave.

Pancho hurried. He crawled to the ladder and swung his legs through the opening. He slung his rifle over his shoulder and grasped his pistol. In his haste, he failed to see that the ladder had tilted out of position when the old man had fallen. He planted his weight on one of the cross pieces.

Outside, if one listened carefully, there was a faint monotonous buzz, like an airborne lawnmower, coming from somewhere in the distant sky.

On the hill behind Ritter and Eason, Mitchell glanced up and saw him—Track Suit, not more than forty meters away, walking toward him, stepping carefully over the large stones of the boulder field and brandishing a pistol.

Mitchell looked down at the radio and swore. Behind him the gunfire increased feverishly. He had no idea what was happening at the compound, he just knew he had a job to do. Track Suit was a distraction.

Then he heard what sounded like a belligerent, guttural command.

He looked up again.

Track Suit was thirty meters away now, walking toward him. His Slavic features and dark half-day growth of beard were twisted into angry contortions, the pistol shaking in his hand.

Mitchell couldn't remember the name of the language that people spoke in Chechnya, but he was sure he was hearing it now. He swore at himself again.

Mitchell, born and bred in Wyoming, was an award-winning western style shooter, a quick draw artist who spent a lot of time at the range. He was already in a foul mood. And he was left-handed, a fact Track Suit could not have known.

Eason and Ritter had their attention focused on the compound when they heard gunshots behind them.

"Mitchell in trouble?" Eason asked.

Ritter glanced back. He could only see the back of Mitchell's head as he worked the radio.

"Looks okay back there," Ritter reported as he resumed his own fevered shooting.

Ritter couldn't see that Mitchell was clutching a wounded right forearm to his side. And he couldn't see thirty feet beyond to where the lifeless form of the one they called Track Suit lay with two 9mm-sized holes between his eyes. But he could hear something in the sky, something droning in the distance high overhead.

In the Cabin, Jake lay on top of the dead mujahid waiting for his miracle.

A tall man dressed in black jeans, sweater and a black ski mask appeared in the holding cell doorway.

His name was Hassam Nidal Khalaf, and he was on a mission.

He felt cheated. Today was supposed to be his day, a glorious day for Islam and for his mentor, Abbas Bin Azzam—the day of vengeance when an American Jew dog spy would be sacrificed as an example to the world of their group's determination and power. But all had gone wrong, like everything else in Hassam's young, brutish life. Their American hostage had managed to die on his own of natural causes, and the great Azzam was dead, lying outside in the compound, his head split open like an overripe melon. How could Allah have allowed such to happen?

Hassam Nidal Khalaf, however, would not be cheated. There was still the mysterious second spy to dispatch—the one who disguised himself as a woman. True, there would be no news coverage now, no cameras to transmit his masked image back to the squalid little camp in Gaza where he was raised to be a *fedeyeen*. But at least there would be blood spilled. He would soon savor the sweet taste of personal revenge that went with it.

Hassam looked intently at the captured spy, his own cruel features still hidden behind the black material of the mask. He smiled. He didn't need the mask anymore. This Jew dog spy would see his face before feeling the blade on his throat. Hassam held up the knife and smiled at the terrified look on the face of the bound prisoner. The weapon wasn't a hunting knife at all but a large ceremonial blade with a serrated edge, the kind used to cut the throat of sacrificial lambs.

Hassam loved the theatrics of terror. He had been a drama student once, which was why he had volunteered to behead the spies for the video. Now he was performing for an audience of one, his victim. Hassam spoke both Palestinian Arabic and some broken English with an American television accent.

"Roll over on your stomach!" Hassam yelled. The trussed-up man on the ground didn't move right away. He no longer looked terrified, only resigned to his fate. Hassam decided now was a good dramatic moment to remove his mask.

As Hassam pulled his mask up over his eyes with his left hand, the hostage began to roll over, off the body of the lifeless mujahid underneath. If Hassam had been able to see, he would have realized the hostage was keeping his eyes on him as he rolled—only for a brief moment of time but enough.

When Hassam looked at the hostage again, the man wasn't on his stomach as ordered, but on his side. An ugly black barrel pointed awkwardly up at Hassam's face—an automatic pistol gripped between the wrist-bound hands behind the hostage's back. The shiny black holster of his dead mujahid companion was empty. It was the hostage's turn to speak.

"*As-Salaam-Alaikum, haji* nut job."

Those were the last words Hassam ever heard.

A fearsome, high-decibel screech ripped the air and drowned out the sound of the pistol going off in Jake Drecker's hands and the last, panicky shriek of Hassam Nidal Khalaf as a 40-caliber bullet tore through the top of his chest just above the heart. The sound was the aptly named Hellfire, inbound on final approach to its target, a small round shaft in the roof of the Cabin.

Before Hassam's body hit the floor, the Hellfire's warhead, twenty pounds of Composition-4 compound, better known as C4, detonated, shaking the compound, collapsing the walls inside the Cabin, and filling the room where Jake Drecker lay with thick dust and rubble. Almost immediately there was a secondary explosion as three propane gas tanks in the central dining room area exploded simultaneously, sending a fire cloud up through the roof and over the compound.

Outside in the mosque, Pancho came to his senses in time to see the ball of fire climbing into the clear, blue sky just as the shock wave passed over him.

Pancho took several minutes to realize what had happened. At first, he thought he'd tripped a mine or a booby-trap of some kind. He felt a knot on his head, and a searing pain in his left arm and shoulder. His head spun. There was the ladder lying on the floor alongside him. Then he realized. The ladder had slipped, sending him about twenty feet down onto the concrete floor. He had tried to break his fall but ended up breaking his arm and dislocating his shoulder instead. His head must have hit the ground momentarily knocking him out as well. He hurt, but he had no time to feel sorry for himself. He was in extreme danger.

He grabbed his rifle with his good arm and stood up to survey the scene.

The Cabin roof was split asunder, but its walls seemed intact, as were the compound walls and gate. The gate, in fact, was apparently still secured. Pancho wondered if there was anyone left inside to resist the Pakistani Army when they arrived. The scene was chaotic with shooting all over the Campus. Pancho did not recognize who was being shot at or who was doing the shooting.

There was an unusual looking group by the compound gate. Pancho thought they might be the shepherds he'd heard Ritter chattering about on the radio who had taken up positions near the Parking Garage before the shooting started. Now, remembering the phantom shot that had struck Azzam, Pancho began to think these shepherds were something else entirely. Could they be the Mista'arvim, the mysterious Israeli clandestine element they had long suspected was operating in their area?

There was an explosion, and the gate disappeared in a cloud of gray smoke as the mysterious team rushed in. Pancho could hear the shooting inside but saw no one emerge from the Cabin. He knew he couldn't hang around to find out. He needed to leave now.

Pancho stumbled toward the ridge behind the Parking Garage and began to climb in the direction of the southward trailhead. He was done fighting, intent only on steering toward the rally point where he was supposed to meet Team Condor. Everything hurt, even his tongue. He must have bitten it in the fall. He stumbled and hit the ground sending shooting pains from his left arm up into his neck.

I'm never going make that link-up with Team Condor like this.

He rolled over and laid on his back.

Too old for this stuff.

Suddenly hands grabbed at his web gear around his shoulders and pulled him to his feet. He panicked and swatted at their hands as he jumped to his feet.

Eason. "Time to move, boss. Break time is over."

Team Condor had been lying concealed exactly ten yards from where he'd taken his tumble. He stood still, the shock of his injuries robbing him of his bearings, and tried to figure out what he was supposed to do.

"C'mon, Pancho, we gotta move," Eason yelled, grabbing him by the collar and hauling him further up the ridge. "Time's running out, the Paks are on their way."

Pancho turned and made several more faltering steps up the ridgeline. He couldn't resist the urge to look back again.

There was more chaos on the ground. The strange men in the compound were exiting quickly through the gap where the steel gate once stood. They'd been alerted, no doubt, to the convoy of vehicles approaching the Car Park from Kotkay road. Several jeeps over-filled with armed men led a five-ton truck carrying more troops up into the Car Park. To one side, two Land Rovers pulled over. Men were standing by their opened doors radioing instructions to the men in the jeeps. One of them was the CIA agent known only as Bob, coordinating the last act of the theatrical cover-up to their botched covert operation.

Maybe there is hope if our CIA guy is here in time.

Reenergized by his men, Pancho scrambled, forgetting the pain and shortness of breath as he focused on reaching the top of the ridge. Ritter and Mitchell were already there, crouching and shooting down into the valley to cover him and Eason. No one seemed to shoot back; the mujahidin either dead or scattered, the mysterious shepherds escaping in another direction, up the valley, toward the west.

Pancho took stock of Mitchell as he passed him.

Michell's got a bandaged right forearm, hope it's not serious. Dang! I need to do something about my injury soon.

He scanned the hillside for cover and kept moving upward. At the top of the ridge, he took in the whole scene. There were more men about three hundred meters to his left. The rest of the shepherds. They were crouched or lying prone on the north side of the trail, the one that came up from the Panjkora. And they were ignoring the Americans, focusing on the final act being played out in the valley. A herd of sheep grazed in the scrub brush and clover behind their shepherds, just over the military crest of the ridge opposite the valley. The sheep were unusually still, oblivious to sights and sounds of human combat on the other side. Pancho remembered the sniper shot that had come from behind him, from somewhere on the ridge as he lay in the minaret.

Had these shepherds killed Azzam?

Pancho took one final look back toward the compound. As he did, the second Hellfire struck home. The deafening roar and shock wave pushed him back slightly before being absorbed by the hills. He shielded his eyes from the late morning sun and strained to see some sign of life from inside the Cabin. But there was only the smoke, a huge black plume gyrating upward, rolling and swirling its way into the bright, midday sky.

"Good-bye, Jake. Adios, mi hermano."

EPILOGUE

"That was the last time I saw him."

With that, Pancho stopped talking. He leaned back in his chair as was his custom and let his interlocutors absorb his story.

They were sitting in a cool, windowless vault deep in the double-walled bowels of Crypto City at Fort Meade, Maryland.

Pancho was clean shaven, a far cry from his operational appearance back at Bagram, and dressed in a short sleeved, US Army Class B uniform adorned with enough ribbons to make a Russian field marshal jealous. His left arm, wrapped in plaster cast and hanging in a sling, was another badge of sorts, reminding the others of his recent combat experience.

The circumstances of Task Force Pancho's final cross-border raid were a fading memory. To release the story felt good and right—for posterity's sake and for the men, for Jake Drecker, and the one named Isidore Loewenthal, whose real identity and relation to Chief Drecker was now a well-known secret. He knew by telling their story he would be keeping the memory of them alive a little longer. He glanced at the other faces in the room and relaxed.

He was among friends. Mostly, anyway. Pakistan was on the other side of the world. But there were landmines even here, among allies. At least there were no lawyers in the room. Still, he selected his words with care. Things had played out in an unexpected fashion. One that suspicious minds might not appreciate.

Two old friends, Fred Durst, National Security Agency, and Colonel Bill Melville, special operations liaison to the CIA, had set up the meeting as a kind of informal interagency after-action review. Both were here.

As were the Salvettis, Gino and Jannat. They were enjoying an extended stateside leave when Colonel Melville invited them. Their participation in the discussion was important, but they were also curious to know the rest of the story. A dozen others were present—special operators, intelligence personnel, and others associated with Prodigal Avenger. If they had the right clearance and a need to know, Colonel Melville let them in.

Two CIA interviewers, Nick Sanders and Landon Coyle, led the dialogue. They were typical, old school representatives of the Agency—blond-haired, smart, white Anglos, Ivy Leaguers, dressed in suits and ties. To Pancho they looked like, and probably once were, a couple of overgrown Mormon missionaries—very different from the Ginos, the Everett Scotts, and the Twisters Pancho knew from the field. But that was okay. They were pleasant, even laid back, which, for a couple of Beltway Bandits, was unexpected.

Everyone was relaxed, scribbling notes, sipping on cappuccinos from the food court café, and listening to him tell his story.

"And he was killed in the blast? You confirmed?" Coyle asked for clarification.

"I thought so," Pancho answered carefully. "I was convinced, but I couldn't confirm his death myself. Two Hellfire missiles in a confined space full of combustibles is pretty darn convincing."

Pancho watched their faces and swallowed. He had just laid out the entire mission for this audience from initial planning through to the final explosion that presumably killed both Azzam and Jake Drecker. To have a clandestine mission go awry was serious business—especially if the approval chain was a bit sketchy and an operator was unaccounted for. Plausible deniability was at risk if Pakistan or an Al Qaeda group got their hands on an unauthorized American body on the wrong side of the border. But that was okay. Pancho had an ace up his sleeve, one he was saving for the last dealt hand.

"There was no way you could have checked for yourself?"

Pancho shook his head.

"Look, everything was going to hell in a handbasket at that moment. The house gets blown, people are running all over the target, the Pakistani army is pulling up in a convoy of trucks, and my team is trying to drag me out of there. The sit-rep was a mess."

"Yeah," Colonel Melville chimed in, "and you just saw Jake Drecker, your friend and your teammate, disappear in an explosion."

A sobering moment in the interview. Tangible silence hung in the room.

"Note then, recovery of US service member remains wasn't possible," Sanders jotted as he spoke.

"And there were several others inside that cabin. They were probably unidentifiable …" Coyle stated before catching himself.

Poignant silence. Everyone was probably thinking it already, but it still sounded horrible. This was Jake Drecker they were discussing, not some nameless battlefield casualty.

Pancho swallowed and looked at the Salvettis. Jannat, in a black sweater, scarf, and blue jeans was beautiful as ever despite her watery eyes and pursed lips. Gino, in a beard and white oxford shirt opened at his bulging neck, cast his eyes down before glancing at his wife. He reached a comforting hand over to squeeze hers. She tilted her head to lean on one of his massive shoulders.

"Yep," Pancho went on. "I was having a hard time dealing with things at that moment. I didn't want to leave him behind, but I had to get out of there before the Pakistanis secured it and we were all trapped."

Everyone's head nodded. Then Coyle, sensing the mood, redirected the discussion.

"And you likewise assumed that the American hostage, Isidore Loewenthal, was dead also?"

"We assumed, but we didn't know for sure until we got back. The CIA's liaison guy, Twister, gave us that. I think it came through Islamabad Chief of Station."

Heads nodded again in recognition of this well-known fact. The US Embassy in Islamabad was first to announce the fate of the American missionary, Isidore Loewenthal. He had died, probably of natural causes, either during his captivity or during what was euphemistically described as "a hostage rescue operation by Pakistani security forces."

"And when we asked Twister about Chief Drecker," Pancho added. "All we got in reply was a negative head nod."

More knowing nods from around the room.

"Colonel Sanchez," interjected a major from the Defense Intelligence Agency, "Did you know that Chief Warrant Officer Drecker's father was, in fact, a US Air Force officer?"

"Yeah, was. He was retired, I knew that," Pancho replied. "He was one of yours at one time, wasn't he?"

"Yes, sir. He was the Air Force attaché in Islamabad before he retired. And a former security assistance officer there. He spent half his career in Pakistan."

"Yeah, it was like home to him, I guess. I knew, we knew, about the missionary, but Jake never talked about his real father. I mean ..." Pancho chose his words carefully. "He never, to my knowledge, ever told me or anybody else in the Task Force his real father's name."

He let that truth sink in. He continued.

"Now, Jake was practically native in some of the languages of Pakistan. We all thought it was just because of his gifted memory. We didn't make a connection with his past—where he had been raised. It never dawned on us to try. We knew Loewenthal was former Air Force, knew he was a real missionary, but we never knew he was Jake Drecker's father until later, until after we had Drecker's team down range."

"And you couldn't reel them back in by then," Sanders said, finishing the thought, "Because it would have jeopardized the operation?"

Pancho paused before answering. Everyone who was taking notes stopped to hear how he would answer.

It was so much more complicated than that, but what could he say? The man's father was an Al-Qaeda hostage. He just nodded and went on.

"Right, I made the decision to continue the mission as Jake planned it. We needed to develop the intelligence situation and to terminate Azzam."

Pancho took a deep breath.

He was exhausted from rehashing the operation ad nauseam. Inside he was reliving it, outside he was telling it, and the clarification questions were unnerving. He looked around the room and then back at Sanders and Coyle.

"Anyone up for a latrine break?" Pancho asked.

Coyle eyed him a moment longer than was warranted.

"Depends," Coyle answered. "Are we done or do we have more?"

"Oh," Pancho replied coyly. "I've got a couple more secrets to share."

Coyle smiled. "Okay, let's take five."

Pancho took a breath and leaned back in his chair. Coyle resumed the business at hand.

"Okay, Colonel. What else have you got?"

"Two quick things I haven't shared yet." Pancho continued. "First one happened on the second day of escape and evasion back toward PZ Clarissa.

"We were crossing this final valley here, near the border." He aimed a laser pointer at the wall screen where a Joint Operational graphic map of the Afghan-Pakistan border was displayed. "Our crossing site was at a place where the road narrows and the opposite ridges are at their closest. It's late summer, so the river was low, thank God. We expected to cross easily. Only problem was when we headed into the valley and because of the trees, we lost sight of the road, we couldn't see if anything was coming. We were vulnerable.

"Wouldn't you know, Eason and Mitchell get across the road, then me. I reach Eason, who then wades across the river while Mitchell and I cover Ritter. Then, about the time Eason reaches the opposite bank but before Ritter bolts across the road, we hear trucks coming from the south. Mitchell and I go flat, but I'm in a grassy field between the road and the river and Ritter's hiding in some bushes on the wrong side of the road. At least Eason has the river between him and the bad guys.

"It gets worse. A second convoy approaches from the north. This one has several fancy Toyota Land Rovers plus a flotilla of Subaru escorts.

"The group from the south stops, and a couple of guys jump out to stop this other convoy. Looks like they're trying to warn them, no doubt, about us being in the area.

"Anyway, the guys from the trucks all get out and begin to secure a perimeter. Lo and behold, Ritter stands up and pretends he is one of them. He's got the Chitrali hat, the scarf, and an AK-47, so he manages to mingle for a moment before anyone gets wise. They expand the perimeter with one haji walking right towards me and Mitchell. Meanwhile the lead guys from the two convoys are meeting in the middle of the road. Ritter is walking behind the haji who is heading toward me, and I figure we are all dead men. Then Ritter says something in Pashtu—Ritter, who's a French and Korean linguist by trade, talking to them in broken Pashtu—and this haji stops and turns around to face him.

"Well, I figure the game is up because, up close, Ritter won't pass for a haji. I spring up and take the guy down with my knife and me and Ritter—we're reading each other's minds by now—we both run full tilt into the river and start wading across."

Pancho's hands clenched and unclenched, heart racing with the memory.

"It must have taken a few minutes for the guys on the perimeter to realize what was happening," Pancho resumed. "I am waiting for a bullet in the back but keeping my eyes on Eason. Suddenly, he stands up and starts shooting—that's when I know the game is up.

"Run!" I yell at Ritter. Eason is firing his SR-25, and I hear nothing—not a round fired—from the other side. It's like I am having tunnel vision with my hearing.

"When we get to the other side of the river, there is plenty of cover, so Ritter and I go to ground and start returning fire ourselves. The bad guys are all hiding behind their trucks or on the ground. There is a draw leading up the ridge, running northwest. We can escape up there with natural cover and concealment between us and the guys on the road. We are shooting at guys two hundred or so meters away, and I've got my M25 with a scope, so I tell the team to move out while I cover them. I'm shooting like crazy and almost out of mags waiting for Ritter, Mitchell, and Eason to get up the ridge and cover me. Waiting for the distinctive sound of Ritter's or Mitchell's AK-74Ms or Eason's SR-25.

"Suddenly, it's quiet. I am scanning the row of vehicles and nobody is firing. Looks like they are all hiding, ducking for cover, being cautious—maybe they're not sure how many of us are in the area. I make my move and start following my guys. I get up the draw about a hundred and seventy-five meters, and we must be getting high enough to see because they engage again. The range is killing them, all they have are lousy AK-47s. So, I drop behind a rock and return more fire.

"From my higher elevation I can see down the whole row of convoy vehicles. The one from the north with the Land Cruisers and SUVs has about eleven vehicles. There are people toward the back middle, the nicer rides, who are getting out of their vehicles and watching the action. They must think they are safe because of the distance—they are about seven hundred meters away from me. But I can hit targets at nine hundred meters with my scoped M25. I scan the vehicles and see guys in white Bedouin garb. I realize these are VIPs. I start getting excited and looking for one to target. That's when I made the ID."

Pancho stopped and took a breath.

The room is still. Pancho's hypnotic, storytelling cadence has them locked in.

"ID?" Coyle asks, breaking the spell. "You mean you identified someone?"

"Bin Laden." Pancho answered. "It was him, the eyes, the nose, the beard. He was in the back seat and his tinted window was partway down. He was talking to one of his bodyguards, I am sure—a large bearded Taliban who was standing by the vehicle. I could see him so clearly in the scope."

"How can you be so sure?" Sanders asked, no doubt forgetting Pancho's convictions at the start of the telling.

"Look, I have been preparing myself for this moment for five years, from the days of the original Bin Laden Task Force, even before 9/11. It was him! I had him, cross hairs, range … everything I needed! But I hear Ritter yelling, and I realize there are a couple brave ones trying to cross the river in the open right near our position. I turn quickly, realign myself, and engage them. There's a familiar, subtle ping in my ears, but I am in denial. I turn back toward Bin Laden, he's there but the window is going up. I squeeze, but sub-conscious warning bells are already going off in my head."

Pancho dropped his head onto the table and shuddered.

Coyle, asked softly, "Then what?"

Pancho shook, clenched his fists and sat upright. His eyes were wet.

"I had him, I had him, dang it! I had Osama Bin Laden for keeps, right in my sights …"

"Okay, okay." Coyle stammered.

Pancho stopped shaking and regained his composure. He snapped up and looked at the ceiling.

"But," he finished, "I was out of ammo."

Pancho looked at the faces in the room.

Serious looking people. And some of them don't believe me.

"I kind of lost my mind at that point," Pancho said, resuming his story. "I started dumping my rucksack looking for loose rounds while the bad guys started moving toward us again. I'd lost blood and was operating on pure adrenaline with only my one good arm, but inside, I was utterly frustrated and desperate.

"Ritter and Eason had to come down and drag me up the ridge, tossing smoke and frag grenades back down toward the bad guys to slow them down. Meanwhile, up top, Mitchell's on the radio asking for the Quick Reaction Force to secure the pickup zone. We finally got so high they seemed to give up on us. We moved fast on top cause we thought we might be followed by a couple diehards. I think we reached PZ Clarissa about midnight, but I was in bad shape by then. There was some gunfire in the distance and Mitchell firing his GP-25 grenade launcher back along the trail.

"Last thing I remember is a Chinook opening up with Randy Snow and his Rangers securing a perimeter at the base of the ramp while somebody is pulling me inside. Then I hit the wall, crashed out until we get back to Bagram. That was the end of the operation, except for the debrief and all of that business."

Pancho took a breath and leaned back in his chair to signal the end of his story. The room was still.

"Well, Colonel Sanchez, that was one heck of a story," Coyle said. "Now we need to come to some conclusions about any possible loose ends."

A couple of people stood up and stretched.

"Colonel Melville?" Fred Durst, the room's senior civilian and de facto host, said. "I think we all need to come to an agreement about the last part of the operation."

"Yes, sir, I agree."

"Look, we have a perfectly good eyewitness account—a bit of raw human intelligence—of a possible, even probable sighting of Osama bin Laden," Durst continued, using the intelligence community's accepted acronym for Osama bin Laden. "But we have no other intelligence to confirm it, nothing, no intercepts, and no images. Just this anecdotal reference. Otherwise, an unconfirmed sighting."

Pancho furrowed his brow. *Anecdotal? What ...?*

"Agreed," Colonel Melville responded. Around the rooms, heads nodded in concurrence.

"We also have a sensitive situation involving our lack of capability to engage this possible Bin Laden sighting as a target for further exploitation during this operation."

"Uh, sure," Pancho interrupted. "But I reported what I saw during the debrief back in Bagram. It's part of the official record."

"Most of us have read that debrief, colonel," Coyle responded. "And it's not in there."

Expunged. Wow!

"Does this mean I can't tell my grandchildren someday that I was the guy who almost got Osama bin Laden?"

Melville smiled. "Sure, just as long as you wait until your non-disclosure agreement timeline has expired. Or we actually get him someday— whichever comes first."

Pancho forced his own smile. *Melville means well, but this is disappointing. They are gonna bury this little secret. Fine. But not my next one.*

Pancho leaned back and looked at the now familiar ceiling.

Fred Durst's bureaucratic tone communicated to everyone a subtle, unspoken message: *This thing needs to stay in this room ... and die.*

"I recommend," Durst continued, "that we strike this sighting from any record for this operation. And should this issue ever be raised again, I further recommend we all agree that, due to the lack of a secondary source, this is merely an unconfirmed sighting by an unnamed source."

Coyle and Sanders both smiled, "Agreed."

"Agreed," Pancho muttered under his breath.

"Any naysayers?" Colonel Melville asked. Nobody spoke.

"Okay," Durst said. "I appreciate everyone's participation in this meeting. Colonel Sanchez, my hat is off to you, an incredible operation and one heckuva story."

Everyone in the room nodded in polite agreement. Several stood up or shuffled papers. The meeting seemed to be concluding.

"Thanks, sir," Pancho said.

"Okay, any other strings left hanging?" Coyle asked, looking around.

"I have one more secret to share," Pancho said quietly.

Everyone froze and looked at him again.

"And what's that, Colonel?" Durst asked.

"It's about Chief Warrant Officer Jake Drecker," Pancho paused for effect.

"Go on," Durst prompted.

"He's not dead."

AFTERWORD

"Sorry, I left so abruptly. I didn't want to explain anything or lose my cool."

They were in the visitor parking area. Pancho, Gino, and Jannat on a warm, sunny Indian summer day, the leaves ablaze in color, moving along the sidewalk toward their parked cars.

Jannat touched his arm. "We understand, Pancho. Tell us more, please."

Pancho hoped they understood. The system had been quick to use plausible deniability and protection of sources to justify killing his friend when the mission went awry. In total contrast with Jake's *never shall I fail my comrades* and *no man left behind* way of thinking.

The system irked Pancho.

Deciding not to lose his cool in the meeting, he just dropped his bombshell, got up, and walked out. And thankfully, no one chased him down to try and pry out more.

Yet despite the CIA's complicity, Pancho owed Jannat and Gino an explanation. They were Jake's most trusted clandestine teammates. Genuine friends to the end. The Agency's murderous backup plan was no reflection on them.

"He's alive and well. He was brought to the Provisional Reconstruction Team at Asadabad seven days ago, barely conscious, but patched up and alive."

"How?" Jannat asked. "Brought? Who brought him?"

"Don't know. Some shepherds. They showed up at the PRT and demanded to speak to a medic. When the medic came, they turned over a stretcher with what the medic assumed was some unconscious Afghan needing medical attention. They brought him into the clinic, and the shepherds disappeared. By the time our guys realized who the patient was, the shepherds were back up into the mountains."

"So, he is okay?" Jannat asked.

"Yeah, I've talked to him. About everything. He's holed up someplace overseas. JSOC has his back. He's fine, but he won't be returning to work for a while."

"Do you have any leads on those shepherds?" Gino asked.

Pancho smiled. "Yeah, I think so, but nothing I can confirm."

"Bani Israel?" Gino grinned at the memory of Everett Scott's conspiracy theories.

"Mista'arvim, or whatever Scott called them," Pancho suggested. "Who knows?"

"A miracle," Jannat said, awe in her voice.

"Yeah," Pancho said. "I think it was."

"What an ordeal." Jannat said. "I can't imagine what it must have been like for Jake. I mean, he must have known his role was a near suicide mission. What would have motivated him to go through with it like he did?"

Pancho paused before answering.

"I don't know if he knows the answer to that himself."

"And what do you know?" Gino asked.

He paused again.

"For his father, obviously. But not for the obvious reason."

"Jake did it for his father, of course," Jannat added. "And that sounds like something he told me once."

"Yeah," Gino added. "Twister told me he thought Jake would be driven to rescue his father no matter what the cost. The Agency was banking on it, in fact. To recover their former asset. But I didn't agree. I thought they were too estranged."

Pancho stopped.

"I was thinking about his heavenly Father, actually," Pancho explained. "You know the story of the prodigal son in the New Testament?"

Gino smirked. "Of course, I've got twelve years of Catholic school under my belt."

"I'm a Christian," Pancho went on. "I believe in miracles. I think God made Jake want to go and rescue his father, Isidore, so they could be reconciled in the only way that would work for someone like Jake."

They all made awkward eye contact with each other. It didn't matter what anyone else thought. Pancho believed. That was enough. Then they turned toward the parking lot and resumed walking. They were near their cars.

"Yeah," Pancho added. "It was that Father."

CONCLUSION

Jake Drecker swam up from a deep slumber to bright sunshine and soft German voices. An angelic pair of civilian nurses in pink scrubs were fluffing pillows and shaking out fresh linens for his bed. Golden shafts of the sun, animated despite the cleanliness of the room by a light storm of dust, slanted between the curtains to illuminate and warm his fresh sheets. A guardian angel in woodland camouflage stood at the foot of the bed admiring the angels in pink. Sergeant Gary Gavin's job was to protect the identity of the room's special guest and to bar any unauthorized visitors. Jake smiled at the visual.

This place is a kind of heaven.

He was at Landstuhl Regional Medical Center, the US Army's sprawling medical complex near Ramstein Air Force Base in Germany. LRMC was the place where soldiers came to recover, a haven of soft beds, female nurse angels, and puffy, anesthesia clouds. The combat nightmares of Afghanistan and Iraq were just that—bad dreams and distant memories. Surreal and unreal. Or was this hospital the unreal part? Hard to tell, especially under the painkilling spell of pharmaceutical grade narcotics. Jake was just glad to be there.

The nurses tidied up the room, checked his vitals, adjusted the devices hooked up to his body, and narrowed the curtains to prevent the sunlight from burning holes in his eyeballs while he slept. They both smiled at him without speaking then left the room.

Maybe they think I don't understand German.

Jake smiled as the door closed behind them. Gavin sat down in a chair and resumed reading a novel.

Jake's body was totally relaxed, which was a good thing since he had multiple breaks and bruises that would scream if he moved. His mind, however, was wide awake. He had learned to sleep this way, with his body off but his brain on. Mental alertness while physically resting. The pleasant sensation in his head was not just due to a disciplined relaxation technique, he reminded himself, but good drugs. He surveyed the room.

Something new was here. A glass vase with a dozen roses sat on the tray table parked alongside his bed. Something sent by a well-wisher, maybe his sister or the guys at Tampa.

But my sister doesn't know where I am. And the guys in Tampa don't send flowers.

A package was also on the tray table. He reached for it, wincing from the effort, and tilted it to read the return address.

It was from Ruth, his wife, addressed to him care of their headquarters.

He brought it to his chest and fumbled with the wrapping. His bandaged hands, with the fingers bound together and splinted, were almost useless.

"Hey, Gary," he spoke hoarsely through cracked lips. "Can you help me with this?"

The soldier jumped to his feet and put his novel down.

"Hey, sir, I didn't know you were awake."

Gavin came over to the bed and took the package from Jake. He pulled a folding knife from his pocket, snapped it open with a flick of his wrist and cut through the wrapping tape to open the package.

A black book with gold embossed pages slipped from the wrapping paper. Jake caught it as it came out.

"Thanks, Gary."

"No problem, sir," he replied as he wadded the packaging material and returned to his chair with it. "Anytime."

Jake's studied the book. A Bible, a Christian one with both Old and New Testaments.

A Bible from Ruth. Odd. Does this mean what I think it means?

He fumbled it open, and a letter slipped out. He grasped the paper with some difficulty and began to read.

My Wounded Warrior Jake,

My precious and incredible husband, I miss you so! I hope it's okay now to send this to you, and I hope you will understand. I have been praying for you. You mean more to me than anything on earth, and I want you to be with me in heaven someday. After what happened to your dad, I thought you might be willing to give this a try. Plus, you once said you would "figure this religion stuff out one day if I ever got the time." Well, I think you have a little extra time on your hands now.

It's a Bible. Sandy Sanchez, Mike's wonderful wife, helped me pick it out. All I am asking you to do is be openminded. Read the New Testament, and remember that I love you and I am praying for you. I am not supposed to know where you are recovering until you get back stateside, but I hear that the weather in Germany is nice this time of year. Let me know and I will sneak over. It's all set. Sandy and Mike will watch the kids.

I love you so much. Get better so we can make more babies!

Aloha, Love and Kisses, and Shalom from your devoted wife,

Ruth

Jake blinked as tears welled up and stung his eyes. He smiled, leaned back, and waited for the emotion to pass.

Yes, Ruth, I need you now. Come over, I will wait for you here.

"Hey, Gary, are you sure no one knows I am here?"

The sergeant looked up from his book. Then he got to his feet.

"Yes, sir. Even your wife's package had to come through official channels. My job is to make sure you don't have any unauthorized visitors."

"Okay, but what if my wife should mysteriously appear?"

Gavin smiled.

"Well, sir, some rules *are* made to be broken."

They both chuckled. Jake closed his eyes freeing Gavin to return to his book.

Jake opened his eyes and placed the Bible aside.

Maybe I'll read it—someday soon. When I'm ready.

Jake looked at the flowers. A strange thought occurred to him.

"Hey, Gary."

The soldier looked up.

"Yes, chief."

"If no one is supposed to know where I am, how did these flowers find me?"

"Um, I have no idea. They were delivered about two hours ago while you were sleeping."

Jake looked at the arrangement—a standard set—one dozen red roses with a card attached.

"Who delivered them?"

"A young woman, sir, in a business suit. I never let her in the room, just took them from her at the door."

Gavin paused, awaiting more questions. Then he added, "Now that I think of it, she never even said a word. I figured she was just the delivery person, even if she did seem a little overdressed."

Jake examined the flowers carefully. So, nobody knew who they were from.

He opened the envelope and slipped the card out. On one side, something was printed in Hebrew script. Jake had never learned more than a few phrases of spoken Hebrew. He assumed the words said 'Get Well' and thought to save it for his wife to translate later.

He turned the card over in his hand. On the opposite side were two more printed phrases, one in English and the other Hebrew, written in italicized English script:

> *A mitzvah is written in Heaven and Hashem never forgets. Kol Yisrael Arevim Zeh Lazeh*

Jake closed his eyes. *A mitzvah in Hebrew, that's a good deed. And Hashem— the Jewish title used in place of God's name. The rest of it is phonetic Hebrew. A phrase about Jewish solidarity or something. But who would send this? And why? Whoever it was, they must know I can't read Hebrew text, but I can understand phonetic Hebrew. How would they know that? Another mystery, like the Mista'arvim and unexpected miracles.*

He lay still for a moment longer before reaching over to the nightstand and grabbing the Bible. Clumsily he rifled through the pages until he found what he was looking for—the very last line in the very last book of the Old Testament.

> And he shall turn the heart of the fathers to the children, and the heart of the children to their fathers, lest I come and smite the earth with a curse.

He leaned back, closed his eyes and placed one bandaged forearm over his face. The room was quiet. He drifted back to the final memory of his father, the last triumphant smile on his father's face—the triumphant smile of an overcoming faith and an unearthly joy.

He opened his eyes and glanced at the late afternoon sun blazing through the space in the curtains. Then he grasped the book again, one bare thumb sliding the page over to the next page, to the very next verse.

A cell phone buzzed on Gavin's belt. Gavin stood, unclipping and opening the phone.

"Gavin, sir," he answered in proper military fashion. Recognizing the voice, he turned toward Jake and their eyes met. Gavin winked.

"Yes, Colonel Biggs, I know. I've informed Chief Drecker that you needed to talk to him about his next assignment. He's still out, sir, heavily sedated, but I can relay the message to him when he comes to. Yes, sir, roger that, Gavin out."

Jake mouthed a silent thank you, and the sergeant smiled as he closed the phone, hooked it back on his belt, and sat down again.

Jake returned to his own book. And he began to read again, the very next line, the first verse in the New Testament.

> The book of the generation of Jesus Christ, the son of David, the son of Abraham.

And because of his father, he kept reading.

THE END